THE LONG, LONG TRAIL

THE LONG,
LONG TRAIL

MAX BRAND

DODD, MEAD & COMPANY · New York

ISBN: 0–396–06984–3
Library of Congress Catalog Card Number: 74–6805
Printed in the United States of America
by The Haddon Craftsmen, Bloomsburg, Penna.

CHAPTER 1

He was popularly nicknamed Morg, and it may be understood that strangers were apt to spell the name Morgue; yet his full name, as he signed it on the day of his wedding and never again, before or after, was Morgan Algernon Valentine. Someone discovered that hidden and forbidden signature and once addressed the rancher as Algie, and the result was a violent accident.

Yet Morgan Valentine was a peaceful man. He was one of those who accomplish romantic results in an everyday manner. Banish his mountains from his horizon, and he would have been a wretched man, and yet when he thought about the mountains at all, it was only to remember the trails that netted them and the sweat of the hard climbs. His labor in life had been noble and was apt to prove enduring. Thirty years before—he and his brother, John, followed the Crane River, where it splits through the higher mountains and comes out upon the lower, rolling hills on the farther side—it occurred to John Valentine, who was the dreamer of the family, that the slopes might not be too steep to preclude cultivation with the plow! and though the regions of the hill crests were a jagged soil, much broken by rocks, there might be enough grass to graze cattle on. Five minutes later he was painting a picture of the house which might be built there—one for Morgan and one for John, on opposite sides of the Crane River. There they could live in eyeshot, each with a broad domain separated by the arrowy, yellow waters of the Crane. There was ample room for both—a hundred thousand acres of hill and valley land.

And still another five minutes found John Valentine already tired of his dream and ready to spur on. But Morgan would not stir. There he resolved to pitch his tent. And though John tried valiantly to dissuade him, the tent was pitched and the two brothers remained. Forthwith, the empire which John had seen, the younger brother proceeded to build. Who are the greater men—the empire seers or the empire makers? At any rate the thing was done; front to front, a couple of miles apart, and with the noisy river splitting the landscape in the middle, rose the two houses. The house of John Valentine was planned as a nobly proportioned structure, and though it had never progressed beyond the columns of the entrance and the first story of the original, it was nevertheless beautiful even in the piece. On the other hand, practical Morgan Valentine built himself a plain shack and gradually extended it. Now it stumbled up the hills on either side, big enough to shelter a whole clan of Valentines and their supporters.

From which it may be gathered that John Valentine lived his life as Byron wrote his poems—he leaped once, tigerlike, and if he failed in the first attempt, or grew weary of labor, he was off to fresh fields and pastures new. He was the sort of man of whom people can easily expect great things; he could have sat on a throne; he could have painted pictures or written verse or made shoes for his own horses; but in accomplishment he was continually falling short. But Morgan Valentine seemed to have reached above his height; people wondered at what he had done. Yet perhaps his neighbors overlooked this fact: that simplicity may be profound; and though few thoughts came to him, those he had worked deep into the roots of his being.

For instance, there was only one human being whom he had ever truly loved, and that was his brother. And when John died, Morgan transferred a portion of that love to the orphan daughter of the dead man.

But Morgan's own wife and children were merely incidents in his life.

It is necessary to be so explicit about this Morgan Valentine, because, in spite of his simplicity, this narrative could never have been written were it not that he did some astonishing things. Indeed, so unusual were some of the things that he did, that one is tempted to add fact to fact so that there will be no misapprehension—no tendency to call him a dream figure. On this night he was exactly fifty-one years and three months old. He stood five feet nine and three-quarter inches and weighed one hundred and eighty pounds; he had a gray head and a young, stern face; he was slow in speech and agile in movement; and at this particular moment he was smoking a stubby corncob pipe on the front porch of his house, with his heels cocked upon the top of the railing.

His wife was in bed; the servants dared not make a sound in the house even if they were awake; the songs and the laughter of the men in the bunkhouse had long since died out; but Morgan Valentine, who slept never more than five hours a night, was still wakeful at twelve.

But if his body waked, his mind slept indeed, and only his eye roved lazily through the valley. A broad moon, nearing the full, had rolled like a wheel up the side of Grizzly Peak, and it cast enough light for him to make out the details of his possessions. In the heart of each valley there was the black-plowed land in narrow strips—incredibly rich loam; and over the rest of the unfenced ground where the cattle ranged, the moon flashed here and there on a bit of outcropping quartz, or twinkled along a line of new-strung barbed wire. But far and wide, over the neighboring hollows, all to his right was his, over range after range of hills, rocking away toward a dim horizon. And looking straight ahead all was his to the silver streak of the river. Indeed, this was little more than an imaginary boundary, for though the great district beyond belonged to his niece, it would be, by all prospects, many and many a year before Mary Valentine was married, and until such a time, he was the executor, his will was law through all the rich region of that valley.

No wonder that the bowl of the pipe tilted up as he set his teeth, and he was filled with the solid sense of possession.

Into his quiet thought beat the swift tattoo of a horse coming across the valley road; it rounded the hill, and at once the hoofbeats rang loudly through the night with the speed of the fugitive—the speed of the pursuer—the speed of anger, perhaps. Now the horseman lurched into view, a black form, with a black shadow trailing beside it over the white road. Straight up to the front of Morgan Valentine's house; then out of the saddle with a leap; then heavy heels and ringing spurs on the high flight of steps. He caught sight of the figure of Morgan.

"Morgan Valentine?" he called.

Now, midnight hushes voices and makes men walk lightly, but the ring in this question was uncontrolled, as if the fellow had a right to waken the entire house if he felt so inclined.

"Gus Norman?" queried the rancher, rising.

"That's me!"

He came along the porch more slowly now, with the slowness of one who deliberates and prepares words. But when he came close, the calmness of Morgan Valentine snapped his self-control, and he burst out: "Valentine, it's got to stop!"

"What's got to stop?"

"That—that girl!"

He turned his head as he spoke mechanically and looked across the shining strip of the Crane River toward the unfinished house of John Valentine which stood on the crest of a hill, white under the moon, and with a solemn, Doric beauty.

"What girl?" persisted Valentine obtusely.

"What girl? Mary Valentine; your niece! That's what!"

"Stop? How stop?"

"Stop her from going about—man-killing—"

"What!"

"That's what it amounts to. It's murder, Valentine!"

The ugly word came out with an ugly oath behind it, and the change in Valentine was instant.

"Seems to me," he observed in his unhurried manner, "that you're talking kind of foolish, Norman. Suppose I give you a minute to think that over and then say it again!"

The other shifted his position a little, but he rushed on with his speech of accusation.

"I don't need no minute, nor nothing like it. My boy is lying home, bleeding; that's why I'm here talking to you now. What I got to say won't keep. He's shot down, and it's her that has it done!"

For a time the glance of Valentine traveled gravely up and down the form of the other.

At length he said quietly: "I'd sort of hate to have Mother woke up with news like this; mind talking sort of soft?"

"There's no use talking soft," said the other, but nevertheless he lowered his voice. "The whole world is finding out things about Mary Valentine, my friend, and the whole world won't be talking in a soft voice about what it knows."

"Ah?" murmured Valentine. Suddenly his tone changed, as though the idea had just filtered completely home in his brain.

"Now, what the devil d'you mean by that, Norman?"

"I ain't here to argue with you. I'm here to point out facts. My boy is shot down; your son Charlie is the one that done it. How d'you explain it?"

"By the fact that your boy Joe ain't as handy with his gun as my boy Charlie. That's a tolerably clear explanation, I figure."

"Tolerable clear for some, maybe, but it ain't the fact. The hand that held the gun was Charlie's, but the mind that directed it was Mary Valentine's."

"All these here remarks," declared Valentine, "is considerable compromising, which maybe I'll be asking for more talk later on. But now, keep right on. Charlie shot Joe, but you say that Mary had a hand in it? Where's Mary now?"

"She's taking care of Joe; your boys, Charlie and Louis, is both there, too; up at my house."

"She's taking care of Joe?" echoed Valentine.

"Listen, Morg, while I go back a ways in this story. You remember that there was a dance last Saturday night at Dinneyville?"

"I don't."

"Anyway, there was. Well, did Mary say anything to you the day after that dance about her and my boy Joe?"

"She didn't."

"Then, sir, she knows how to keep a lot to herself. But Joe had something to say to me on Sunday. He says: 'Dad, I'm the luckiest gent on the ranges. I'm going to marry

6

Mary Valentine.' I was struck all of a heap by hearing that. But Joe tells me that they can't be no mistake. She'd as good as promised to be his wife. He'd never knowed her much before the night at that dance. But he took a liking to her right off; and it seemed she done the same by him. He smiled at her; she smiled right back. It kind of went to his head. He started talking to her real serious; and she seemed just a wee bit more serious than him. Well, she scarce danced with anybody but him the rest of the night, and when he come home the next morning after the dance, he was like drunk. Couldn't think, couldn't talk of nothing but how beautiful Mary Valentine was and how quick he was going to marry her, couldn't hardly wait to get started with an outfit of his own.

"I spoke to my wife about it. The old woman didn't say nothing. She just grinned at me. Pretty soon she allows that it's all right. But maybe Joe had better make sure of the girl before he got out any wedding license. That sounded like funny talk to me, but I didn't pay no attention.

"Well, along comes the dance at Salt Springs school-house tonight. My boy goes over. He don't see nothing nor speak to nobody until he sees Mary Valentine come in. Then he goes straight for her.

"Then something mighty queer happened. They was another man with her. His name was Henry Sitterley; Hank Sitterley's boy. And when Joe goes up to her and starts talking sort of foolish, the way a boy will when he's in love, she looks right through him. Acts the way she'd hardly ever met him before. And pretty soon she goes dancing off with young Sitterley, and Joe can see her talking to him and knows that she's making a mock out of him—my son!

"Well, it gets into Joe's head and starts him seeing red, and it gets into his heart and starts his heart aching. He don't think it's really no ways possible. He waits till the dance is over. He tries to see her ag'in. But she sees him coming and slips away into the crowd and laughs back at him.

"Then it comes into Joe's head that she's jilting him, and—"

"Wait a minute," broke out Valentine. "Did she promise to marry him that other Saturday night?"

"They's other ways of promising things than with words, friend Valentine. She sure promised Joe with her eyes and her smiles and her sighs. So when she give him the go-by like that tonight, he mighty near went crazy. He goes out into the hall where they was some of the other boys standing smoking, and there he busts out with something about Mary being a flirt.

"Quick as a wink, your boy Charlie takes him up—like a bulldog, he was, Joe says. Besides, Joe was too mad and sad not to fight it out. First thing you know, guns is pulled —"

"Who pulled his gun first?" cut in Valentine, snapping his words.

"Joe."

Valentine sighed.

"Joe pulled his first, and Charlie beat him to the draw. But here's the point. Your girl starts flirting with my boy; she gets him so he can't sleep for a week, thinking about her—and then when she meets him ag'in she don't know him, or lets on that she don't.

"Then my boy says something he shouldn't of said; they's a fight; he gets shot through the arm—thank Heaven it wasn't no worse!—and I tell you that it was Mary that had him shot, and not Charlie Valentine! Because why? Because when Mary and Charlie drive my boy back home in their buckboard and while they're fussing over him, and after Joe has told me what happened, I go to my wife and tell her I think Joe was crazy the first time he seen Mary. He was crazy with love—calf love. But she just grins at me. 'Why,' she says, 'don't you know she's the worst flirt in the country?'

"And that's why I'm here, Valentine. Two inches more to one side and that bullet would of gone through my boy's heart. And the murderer would of been your girl Mary. Valentine, I'm new to the country; I don't know your folks nor your ways, but I know that in the part of the country that I come from a girl like that ain't allowed to run around loose. She's kept up close, and if her dad can't look after the way she handles her eyes and her smiles, then her ma goes along to watch out for her; and if her ma can't do it, then she ain't allowed to go out where they's young men to be made fools of and their hearts broke, if it don't come to no other thing. I'm a tolerable reasonable man, Valentine, and that bullet wound don't amount to nothing.

"Two weeks, and it'll be all healed up; but what if it had struck two inches away? So I come here straight to you and say, 'Something has got to be done!' I leave it to you, what."

During the latter part of this talk Morgan Valentine had abased his head and stared at the floor of the veranda, but now he raised his head, and even through the shadow the other could see the black frown on the forehead of the rich rancher.

"You got a reason for your talk, Norman," he admitted. "Now step inside and I'll tell you just how this matter stands. You ain't the first that's had cause to complain. I wish you could be the last; but come on inside and we'll talk."

CHAPTER 2

But Gus Norman shook his head.

"In my part of the country," he said stubbornly, "we like to talk in the open air; it keeps us cool."

"Not a half-bad idea. But before we start talking serious, maybe you'll tell me just what you're aiming to do?"

"I'm aiming to keep out of bad trouble, Valentine. I don't like trouble; I'm a peaceable man; but I ain't the only Norman around here. They's a lot of us and some of 'em take this shooting sort of to heart. They want blood for blood. My brother and my nephew are at my house, and they want action. But I talked to 'em and told 'em to keep quiet till I come back."

The other considered his visitor gravely in the dim light. Short time though this clan of Normans had been in the mountains, they had established a name for bulldog ferocity in fighting.

"Look over yonder," he said at length. "You see that house?"

"Yep. What has that to do with it?"

"A whole pile. That's the house my brother built. He started building it and stopped halfway. All through his life he was starting things and stopping halfway. Well, Norman, his girl Mary is the same way. She's always starting things and stopping when they're halfway done. When she was a youngster, she was a regular tomboy. Doing everything that my kids did. When Charlie first got interested in guns, she started practicing, too; and she got so she could beat Charlie with a light rifle or a light revolver. She's still almost as good as Louis, but she got tired of fooling with guns in a couple of months. Same way with hosses. Long as a colt was a wild one, she'd go riding every day and fight it. But as soon as the hoss got tame, she was done with it. And it's the same way with men. She's interested in every strange man that she meets. Shows 'em that she's interested, and thinks they're the finest in the world until they begin to think she's in love with 'em. But after a while she gets tired of 'em. Now d'you understand about her, Norman?"

The other shook his head and growled: "Guns is one thing and hosses is another; but my boy is something more'n either; and he's got to be treated human."

"D'you aim to make me force Mary to marry him?" asked the other calmly.

"I ain't forcing my boy on no girl. Speaking without no offense, Valentine, I wouldn't have your girl in my family. But I think you ought to keep her in hand. They's other young men in my family. Maybe another'll fall in love with that girl when she makes eyes at 'em. And then there may be another fight. And the next time it may be your boy that gets drilled. Luck is always changing. But if she was my girl, I'd use the whip, Valentine."

For some reason Valentine smiled at this, but the darkness covered the expression.

"They's another side to her," he said gently. "She's a true-blue girl, Norman. No malice in her. Keeps to her friends. Plays square—every way except where some strange young gent is concerned, and then she runs amuck with her eyes and her smiles, just as you say. What can I do? Whip? Why, she'd murder me and then kill herself out of shame and spite if I so much as touched her. Don't you suppose I've thought of this before? Haven't I got most of the people around here down on me because of the way Mary has treated the boys, one time or another? Ain't she always making trouble for me? And ain't my boys in peril of their lives because she keeps making places where they got to fight for her sake and their own.?"

"Then send her away."

"Ah, man, blood has got a feeling for blood! Can I turn out my brother's daughter?"

The other was silent for a moment, breathing hard. He was a wild-looking man, with unshaven face and a beard that began at his eyes and ran ragged until it terminated in a shaggy point beneath his chin. He was a lean, hard man, and he had reddish eyes as bright as the eyes of a ferret and as restless.

"The day'll come when you'll have sorrow in your home for keeping this girl here," he announced gloomily. "The day'll come when you'll wish you'd sent her off."

"She's been away to school, man, but nothing changed her."

"Sometime, Valentine, she'll find a man that'll be her master. Mark me when I say it. And when that man comes, she'll go to him and foller him whether he be good or bad. If she could find a hoss that would never be safe under the saddle, she'd never want to ride nothing but that hoss, I figure; and when she finds a man that won't pay no attention to her, she'll be following that man, Valentine, you mark my word. She'll love the man that laughs at her; she'll follow the man that runs from her; she'll kneel to the man that beats her." He paused again.

For Morgan Valentine had shifted so that the moonlight struck abruptly across his face, painting the wrinkles and his frown black and making the rest deadly white. He stood with his jaw set, and through the shadow of his brows the eyes glittered. He spoke nothing, but Gus Norman saw enough to make him wince back a step. He put out his hand in a conciliatory gesture.

"I don't wish her no unhappiness and I don't speak out of no malice. I ain't come to talk hard, neither, nor to make no threats. But I'm here to put my case in front of you. You got a big reputation around these parts, Valentine, for being a square shooter. Put yourself in my boots and figure out what you'd do. My folks are a tolerable tempery lot, and they're a pile cut up about this fracas; but I'm holding 'em back. I don't want 'em to run foul of Charlie; most of all I don't want 'em to run foul of you. Think over what I've said. Good night."

He turned on his heel, strode across the veranda, went down the steps, and once more sent his horse up the road.

Before he disappeared into the moon haze, Valentine was walking up and down the veranda with a short, quick step. And of all the people in the world only his wife, no doubt, could have read the meaning behind his manner. Only his wife did know it; for the loud voice of Norman had wakened her in her room just over the veranda, and she had gone to her window. From it she had overheard the conversation, and now she knew the meaning of that pacing, that short, quick, decisive step. She gathered her dressing gown about her, put her feet in slippers, and hurried downstairs. Her husband was coming in just as she reached the lowest range of the stairs, and she paused with her hand on the rail. It was a lovely hand in spite of her forty-five years and the hard labor which had been hers during the early part of her married life. Her slippered foot, too, would have been the pride of a debutante; and the dressing robe fluttered about her in graceful lines. She was still beautifully formed; her skin retained its glow and purity of texture. But cover her hands with winter gloves, her feet with boots, her body with a heavy coat, and Maude Valentine became a homely farmer's wife. There had been a fine spirit in her face, but never beauty; and now that the grace and hope of youth was gone there remained only the lines of the unloved wife and the un-heeded mother of two wild sons and one headstrong daughter.

"Are you up, Mother?" he asked from the hall beneath.

"I couldn't sleep, Morgan."

"Read a bit; then you'll sleep."

"I wish to talk to you just a little minute, Morgan," she replied. Her voice had the gentleness of long sorrow.

"Come on into the library, then."

They went into the big room ranged high with books, for John's library had been brought here after his death, and it was a rare collection. How few had been opened since his hand last touched them!

"Are you warm, Mother?"

She looked up at him quickly as she slipped into the big chair, a furtive glance. For one brief moment at the time of their marriage—whether it were a matter of days or weeks did not count—she had felt that he loved her truly, with a fire concealed by his customary self-restraint. And ever since those passionate days of happiness she had been probing him with these half-frightened glances in search of the vanished tenderness. And though she lived with him a hundred years there would still be a hope in her heart. But he was hardly glancing at her now as he asked the question, and settling back into the chair, she smiled at him a still and quiet smile, for pain may take on the gentlest seeming.

"Now, Mother, what is it?"

"I guess maybe I shouldn't have said that I couldn't sleep. It was Gus Norman's voice that waked me up."

"He talks like a roaring bull. Some of these days maybe a ring'll be put through Norman's nose and he'll be led about!"

"I heard all he said."

"Well?"

At his carelessness she fired a trifle.

"And I heard that Charlie shot a man!"

"His third man. He's starting well."

"Morgan Valentine, do you know what lies ahead of

your son one of these days? Murder! I've seen him getting angry in the house and reach natural for his hip. And someday he'll get in trouble—and shoot—and kill!"

Her voice had raised very little, but her changing expression answered a similar purpose. Indeed, Morgan Valentine looked sharply at her, so astonished was he by any variation in her monotone.

"He's sowing his wild oats, that's all. No cause for worry."

"He's never worried *you*, Morgan." There was a bitter emphasis on the pronoun. "None of your children have. Seems like you don't care, sometimes."

The remarkable fact that his wife was actually complaining finally reached the understanding of Valentine, and now he watched her calmly, waiting. His quiet made her flush.

"Charlie, nor Liz, nor Louis—they none of them worry you, Morgan. You act—you act—as if Mary was your daughter, and my children didn't have your blood in 'em!"

"Mother!" murmured her husband.

"I ain't going to make a scene, Morgan," she assured him, and she gathered her robe a little closer to her as if to cover her trembling. "I'm just going to tell you a few facts. This ain't the first time that Mary has made trouble for me and mine. She—"

"You don't like her, Mother. You get a bad light in your eyes every time you think of her. I've seen that for a long while."

"I've done what's right for her," said Mrs. Valentine stubbornly. "They ain't nobody can say I haven't mothered her as much as the wild thing would let me—after her father died."

Again he was silent, and again the silence spurred her on more than words.

"And here she is paying me back. She's putting my boys

15

in peril of their lives. That's what she's doing. And who but her has made my girl Liz unhappy?"

"Why, Mother, Mary is always kind to Liz—always doing little things for her—taught her to ride, taught her to shoot, taught her to dance, even!"

"That's it. She's always led the way. Now Liz can't do anything out of her own mind. When she's in trouble, she don't come to her own mother. She goes to Mary. If she wants advice, she goes to Mary. And half the time—half the time—her and Mary has secrets that they're keeping from me. I come on 'em whispering together, and they break off as soon as I come. Mary makes a mock of me in my own house—with my own boys—my own girl!"

He had taken his pipe from between his teeth. He held it now in his stubby fingers until the wisp of smoke that curled out of the bowl dwindled.

"Besides, what is they ahead for Liz? Who'll she ever have a chance to marry so long as Mary is around? Nobody looks at her except because they think it might make Mary smile at 'em. At parties, they only dance with Liz because maybe then Mary'll dance with 'em. They wouldn't ask Liz except to get Mary. And—and I can't stand it no longer. Ain't Liz pretty? Ain't she gentle and kind? Ain't she got winning ways? But as long as Mary is here, she'll have a secondhand life. That's what she'll have. I've watched and watched and watched, and my heart was—breaking all the time. But I wouldn't talk until tonight—but now I see where things is leading. I see what Mary is doing—she's bringing into my house—murder!"

Morgan Valentine stirred in his chair.

"She's got the whole Norman clan worked up now. They'll all be laying for Charlie. That's the kind they are. Hunt like wolves in a pack. And they'll pull down Charlie —and maybe Louis. And you'll stand by and see it all— and do nothing!"

He expected her to break into tears at this point. But when her eyes remained dry, he moistened his lips and spoke.

"What d'you want me to do, Mother?"

"Send her away!"

"Send Mary away? Mother, she's the last living thing that can remind me of John. I can't turn her out. She ain't fit to be sent away. She's got to have them near her that love her, Mother."

"Men? She'll always have them."

"Now you ain't playing fair and square. You know what I mean."

"You don't have to send her away alone. Send her to her sister in Chicago. Lord knows she's asked to have Mary often enough. She'll let her study music, or something."

She left her chair and slipped to her knees before Morgan Valentine.

"Don't do that, Mother. Get up, won't you?"

"Don't you see what I want, Morgan? I want back all the things that Mary has stole from me—Charlie and Louis and Liz and—you!"

"Get up, Mother. It ain't right you should kneel to me!"

"But here's where I stay because I'm begging you for my happiness and for my boys and my girl, Morgan. Will you answer me?"

He looked down at her with a gray face, and she saw for the first time how deeply this cold man loved the girl. The pain of it made her cry out.

"In all the time we been married, it's the first thing I've asked you, Morgan!"

"Stand up," said Morgan Valentine. "I'll send Mary away!"

CHAPTER 3

The law of compensation works in this manner: those who give their hearts to few things give in those cases wholly and without reserve. The life of Morgan Valentine had been a smooth-flowing river until the death of his brother; that blow aged him ten years. From that day until this it seemed to him that his life had been a blank, and now another blow was to fall. For if the girl left him, she left him forever. The city would swallow her—the city and her new life. He might see her again once or twice, but after the parting he would be dead to her and she would be dead to him. He set his teeth over the pain and smiled into the face of his wife. He raised her gently to her feet, and she put her hands timidly imploring upon his shoulders.

"Will you take it to heart a whole pile, Morgan?'

"It's for the good of all of us, Mother. I've seen that for some time. You see, I been looking on Mary as a girl all these days, and here all at once she turns the corner on me, and I see that she's a full-grown woman. It kind of beats me. But—I guess she's got to go. This ain't no sort of a country for her. Back where men don't wear guns and where they don't do more'n raise their eyebrows when they get real mad—that's the place for Mary to do her campaigning. But she'll be turning these parts around here into a regular battlefield if she stays."

Mrs. Valentine caught her breath with joy.

"I hoped you'd be reasonable like this, Morg," she murmured. "But then ag'in I was afraid you'd get all gray in the face, maybe, the way you did when—"

"Well?"

"When John died."

"Mary ain't dying."

"Of course not. And it's for the best. It ain't the first time she's started trouble, and you know it. There was the boys of old Jack White; they got into a fight because Mary smiled at Billy one week and at young Jack the next. Might have been a death if their father hadn't found them, it's said. Then there was 'Bud' Akin who—"

"Hush, Mother. You're getting all excited. Besides, you ought to be asleep. Now you go back to bed and stop worrying." He stopped. The rattle of galloping horses had topped the hill and was rushing down toward the house. The cavalcade swept near.

"Maybe more trouble!" cried the poor woman, clasping her hands.

But as the riders poured past the house, a chorus of voices and laughter rose.

"That's Charlie and Louis and Liz," cried the mother, recognizing all three voices in the chorus.

"And Mary," said Valentine.

"Her, too," she added shortly, and sent a glance at her husband.

The horses were put up; the voices grew out again; they were racing for the house; a shrill peal of laughter; a clatter on the steps—the door flew open and a girl sprang in. A flash of black hair and eyes and the flushed face, and then laughter.

"You tripped me, Mary!"

"But I got here first," she was crying in triumph as a burly youth crowded through the doorway; and behind him his brother and sister were coming.

"Why, Mother—you up so late?" asked Charlie.

And the wonder of this strange event made the four faces of the young people grow sober.

"Now, Mother—" cautioned Morgan Valentine.

"Charlie!" she broke out. "What you been doing? What you been doing?"

He went to her and tried to take her in his big arms, but she fended him off and kept her head back to search his face.

"Some hound has been here talking," he muttered.

"It was no worse'n he said?" she queried. "You only shot him in the arm?"

"It was only a scratch," said Charlie. "He won't know he was touched in a couple of days."

"And, oh, Uncle Morgan!" cried Mary Valentine, taking his hand in one of hers and waving to big Charlie. "You'd have been proud if you'd seen him! I'm so proud of him. Joe Norman insulted me and Charlie—oh, Charlie, you're a man!"

She turned full upon Charlie as she spoke, with such joy shining from her face that the boy crimsoned with happiness.

"It wasn't nothing, Mary. Don't make me feel foolish," he stammered; and it was plain to be seen that he would venture a thousand times more for her sake. And in the background was his brother Louis, with a shadow on his face. As if he, too, would have been gladly a part of this ceremony of rejoicing and was determining to seize the first opportunity that came his way to strike a blow for the sake of Mary. But the voice of the mother cut in, cold and small, and withered all the happiness at the root.

"Mary Valentine," she said, "it's you that's been drawing my boy into peril. It's you!"

"Aunt Maude!" cried the girl, and ran to her; but she stopped in the act of taking her hands.

"Have I deserved it of you, Mary?" whispered the older woman. "Ain't I tried to be kind to you and is this the way you pay me back—making murderers out of my sons?"

"Mother!" cried Charlie. "I won't stand you talking like that! She didn't."

"You see?" said Mrs. Valentine sadly, turning to her husband.

"Charlie, you shut your mouth and keep still," said Morgan Valentine sternly. "Ain't you got manners with your own mother? Liz, take your mother up to bed."

The girl was taller than Mary by an inch or more and strongly built—as blonde a beauty as Mary was dark—yet when she went to her mother, she turned a glance of appeal upon her cousin, as though asking for direction. Mary slipped between her aunt and the door to which Elizabeth was leading her.

"If ever you think hard of me, Aunt Maude," she said, "I want you to tell me what it's about. And if ever I've hurt you or done you wrong, I'll go down on my knees and beg you to forgive me! Tell me now, while your heart's hot with it!"

For a moment words trembled on the lips of Mrs. Valentine, but, looking past Mary, she saw the face of her husband, bowed her head, and hurried from the room.

"Go to bed," said Morgan to his two sons. And they trooped out in silence, casting back frightened glances, not at their father, but at Mary.

She waved a smiling, careless good night to them, but the moment they were gone, her bravado vanished. She ran to her uncle and caught one of his burly hands in both of hers.

"What have I done?" she whispered. "Oh, what have I done?"

"Speaking personal," he answered, "I'm hanged if I know. Sit down, and we'll talk about it."

They sat down; she was still holding his hand, and though he made a faint effort to draw it away, she kept it strongly in her own.

"Aunt Maude—looked—as though—she hated me!"

"Stuff!"

"But she looked straight into my eyes; and women have a way of understanding other women, Uncle Morgan!"

"Ah, girl, there's the trouble; you're a woman now."

"Do you mean that I've changed?"

"I dunno how to put it, Mary."

She cried out softly: "Do *you* think that I've changed?"

"I knew your father before you."

A little silence fell between them in which both of them asked many questions and were answered. At length the rancher began speaking again, slowly.

"If you was a man, Mary, you'd be a fine man. But you ain't a man."

She waited.

"You're about nine tenths woman, I guess, with just enough man in you for spice."

"Is that a compliment?"

"Instead of spice I might say deviltry."

"Oh!"

"I've got worse things than this to say to you. When you were a girl, Mary, I took all your mischief for granted."

"Yes, I've been very bad."

"Not bad. But you were always hunting for action. Same's a boy does. You got into lots of scrapes, but you come out ag'in just the way a boy does. But all at once you changed. You come pop out of a door one day, and you weren't a girl any more; you were a woman. That was when things started to pop. You see, nobody understands a woman."

"Except you, Uncle Morgan."

"Kindly leave me out. I don't know a thing about 'em."

"But you know everything about me."

"Not a thing, hardly. For instance, I don't know

whether you just can't help making eyes at young gents, or whether you do it on purpose."

"Is that the cause of all the trouble?"

She dropped his hand.

"You see it's the way I told you. I don't know a thing about you."

"Do *you* believe what people say?"

"But tell me, aren't they right?"

She gasped.

"I thought so. You're turned into a man-eater, Mary."

"I think you're making fun of me."

"Me? Never!"

"It's this way: I don't mean any harm. But when I see some boy I've never known very well, I just can't help beginning to wonder about him. What is he inside? Maybe he has a touch of the fire; I always keep hoping that!"

"What fire?"

"I—I don't know."

"Well, go on."

"Maybe I've met him at a dance. The music is in my head. He dances well. He doesn't talk much. My imagination begins to work on him. All at once he dawns on me —a new picture—he's strong, brave, gentle, clever—and has the spark of fire. I begin to burn with it. I'm happy." She dropped her chin upon her knuckles and stared gloomily into the distance. "And that's all I can say about it."

"But mostly you tell him that he's making you happy?"

"Mostly."

"And then what does the man do?"

"Mostly he says that I've made him happy, too. Sometimes they start being foolish. They want to sit in a corner and hold my hand. I don't like that. Or if we walk out of the hall they—" She shuddered. "Why do men want to put their arms around a girl when they're happy?"

"What do you expect them to do?"

"Why—talk—or be silent—and—"

"Well?"

"I don't know. But mostly they do something that makes me despise them before the evening's over. Or if they don't, then I think about them until the next time we meet. And then—everything pops into thin air. They always seem different. You understand?"

"Maybe. It's just what I thought."

"Am I bad, Uncle Morgan?"

"No, but you need room, honey. I'm going to send you away to a big city."

"You—send—I won't go. It's Aunt Maude! She's never liked me!"

"Hush, girl!"

She saw suddenly that his hand was trembling, and the sight of his grief struck her cold with awe.

"In some city," he went on slowly, "you'll see crowds of clean young fellows. Maybe you'll get over this; or maybe you'll find a man that's worthy of you. But there ain't any round here. And I know them all. Why, rather than have you marry one of these unshaven, thickheaded fellows, I'd shoot the man, first! I want you—to marry— a gentleman."

He spoke this last slowly, hunting for the words. She sat with her head bowed. Then she looked up to him.

"You'll do what I want you to do, Mary?"

She made a little gesture. He could not tell whether it meant yes or no, and all the while there was a glimmer in her eyes like the changing colors of watered silk.

CHAPTER 4

But two days later Morgan Valentine bought a ticket to Chicago and made his reservations; Mary had made up her mind apparently, though not half a dozen words had been spoken on the subject of her departure since that first night. But the next day she was talking of Chicago as though all her life had been spent there, and this experience in the mountain desert was only an excursion off her beaten trails.

"Between you and me, Uncle Morgan," she said, "why not New York?"

This, for some reason, had rather staggered him. But now that the ticket was bought—dated ahead several days—and the step irremediably taken, he was easier. He made a short stay in Salt Springs that day. After he had the ticket in his wallet, he went to the bank and drew out the cash for his monthly payroll. His cowpunchers were numerous as befitted the keeping of his big range, but moreover there were the hired men who worked the cultivable ground, and in the northern part of his domain—the territory of his dead brother—there was a small logging outfit. Altogether, he had some thirty men to pay off each month, and the payroll ran around sixteen hundred dollars. He got it all in gold coin, and it made a heavy little canvas sack—fifteen pounds, or so. It was three in the afternoon before his buckskins jogged out of Salt Springs on the back trail of the twenty-five-mile trip, and though the going was fairly smooth most of the way, it would be dark before he arrived.

That, however, was a small worry to him. The two geldings were sure-footed as goats; and, given their own sweet way and a shambling trot, they could take the buckboard home in rain or shine, through the night and the rocks. They had done it before, so now Morgan Valentine bunched his duster around his shoulders with a shrug, settled back into the right-hand corner of the big seat, and let the reins hang idly.

An hour and seven miles dropped behind him, and still the buckskins were jolting steadily on. The suddenness of their stopping jerked him through a thousand miles of dreams back to the cold facts of earth. The buckskins had their heads high. And just before them was a horseman with a revolver pointing between the geldings and straight at the head of Valentine.

He put up his hands with the utmost unconcern.

"Thanks," said the stranger. "If you've got any coin handy about you, you might throw it this way."

There was deprecatory gentleness in this—the same tone of embarrassment which one uses when one asks a stranger for a match, and it made the rancher regard the holdup artist with more attention. The man sat a down-headed roan, an ugly brute which looked undersized in comparison with the bandit's length of limb; for he was a tall man, with formidable shoulders. He had long arms, also, which appeared extremely capable; and the heavy Colt was poised lightly as a feather and firmly as a rock.

He seemed indiscriminately somewhere between thirty and forty and might have been at either end of this limit. What little hair appeared beneath his sombrero was sunburned and dusted to a pale-gray brown. He had one of those lean, long faces which are thin through the cheeks and wide through the cheekbones and the jaw. He was far from good-looking; and a very wide mouth and a highly arched nose which showed that he clearly belonged in the predatory type of mankind, made up a further debit on the side of beauty. To complete the impression, his eyes were an uninteresting but very intelligent gray. In fact, one might say that the color of this man was gray; for the rest, he keenly impressed Morgan Valentine as being about equal portions of sinew and sinew-hard muscle.

"I suppose," said Morgan, "that you want my gun first?"

"I'm getting old, pardner," admitted the other. "I'm forgetting my A B C's. But—"

The last word was so explosive that Valentine paused with his hand on the way down to his weapon.

"But," continued the stranger, "guns are things that I most generally like to take for myself. Thank you just the same."

"As you please."

He stood up and turned, his hands well above his shoulders, while the revolver was removed from his holster.

"Which I'm acting like a fool amachoor," the bandit was saying apologetically, "and pretty soon you'll begin to be ashamed of being robbed."

He skidded the weapon into the back part of the buckboard.

"Now you can sit down ag'in, pardner."

Valentine accepted the invitation. At close hand, he found that the stranger lived fully up to his first impression. He was, indeed, a grim-faced fellow. Only his voice, which was of the most exquisite and tender softness, counteracted the general effect.

"Now, if you'll gimme your kind attention just a minute, sir," went on the tall man, "I want to explain that holding a gun is plumb tiring to a gent of my nature that hates work. So I'm going to put it back in the leather. But here and there I've met curious gents that wanted to see just how quick that gun could come out of its house ag'in and say how'd you do. So they've let me take a gun off their hip, and then they've sprung a surprise by fetching out some little token of affection from under a coat or a shirt—say a knife, or a derringer. And them that have tried my gun have most generally found it right there on the job talking business."

So saying, he slipped his weapon into its holster.

"I think I follow your meaning," said Valentine. "Which I'm tolerable quick to do when men talk sense."

He added: "Here's the coin." And he kicked the canvas sack so that it jingled at the touch. "I have some in my wallet if that ain't enough to satisfy you."

At this the stranger smiled gently upon him.

"They's one part of my heart that's an aching void sure enough," he declared, "and that's the part where a plumb reasonable man fits in. Pardner, you seem to be it. Nope, I don't want your wallet, I guess. That is"—and here he lifted the canvas sack and weighted it in his hand—"that is, if this here talk is gold talk."

Now, when he lifted the sack and held it lightly at arm's length, Valentine had seen a rippling of muscle under the shirt sleeve that fascinated him. So he murmured absently:

"Yes, it's all gold."

"Maybe it's the price of a few hosses you've just took into town, now?" went on the other thoughtfully.

"Maybe it ain't," replied Valentine.

"Yes, and maybe it ain't. Maybe it's the cash from some little claim you been working for some time?"

"Maybe."

"To cut it short," said the bandit a little sharply, "is this going to bust you or not?"

"Fifteen hundred dollars is quite a bit," observed Morgan Valentine. "Took me three years to make that much."

"Three years' work in this bag?"

"Yes."

The gray eyes puckered and gathered, and a gleam went out of them, but Valentine withstood the stare. At this, the outlaw stepped back and glanced over the equipage swiftly.

"Judging by that harness and the way them hosses is set up, I reckon I can put that down safe as the granddaddy of all the lies I've heard lately."

"You forget," said Valentine, "that I didn't say what three years they were—recent ones or a long time back."

The other grinned. There was something remarkably contagious in his smile; in spite of himself Morgan Valentine found his face wrinkling.

"I dunno why it is," declared the bandit, "but I take to you uncommon strong."

"And I think I can begin to say the same about you, my friend."

"Dear me," said the outlaw, and the feminine expression did not seem at all out of place for some reason, "we're getting real friendly, ain't we?"

"Seems that way. You're the first holdup gent that's ever troubled to ask whether or not what he took would bust me."

"Judging by that maybe I could say that sticking you up is one of the favorite sports around these parts?"

"Maybe you could; it used to be."

"How many times have you been entertained?"

"Eight times," said the rancher.

"Dear, dear! Who'd of thought you was that rich?"

"The other eight," said the rancher, "lived in these parts and knew the size of my bank account."

"Eight times you've left your roll behind you?"

"Two of them," replied Valentine, with a glittering eye, "I shot and buried. Two more I carried back to town after I'd bandaged them. Two more were killed by the posses, and the other two gave up before they were salted away."

"You don't tell me!" exclaimed the other, with all the

happiness of one who hears the ending of a pleasant tale. "And maybe this little job will gimme more fun than I was looking for."

The rancher examined him for a time.

"No," he said, "I guess the ninth man will be the lucky one."

"How comes that guess?"

"As I said, the others lived in these parts, but you've come a long way, and you'll probably go on a long ways still."

"You talk better'n a riddle," declared the bandit with open admiration. "How d'you know I've come a long ways?"

"By the way your hoss is gaunted up; by the knot in your handkerchief; and by the look of your eyes."

"Eyes?"

"As if you'd been riding into the sun for a good many days."

"Them are all good signs. But I never heard of that last one before now."

"Besides," said the rancher, "you've got a professional air; I wouldn't even waste time sending the posse after you."

"Now, that's what I call real friendly. You wouldn't even put the sheriff out about me?"

"Certainly not. Suppose he caught you? He'd probably get two or three men knocked in the head doing it; and fifteen hundred ain't worth all that bloodshed."

"I see you got a kind heart," said the other carelessly.

"Also, I've noticed that every real professional along your line has a pile of pals. Suppose I get you; the word is passed along. One of your friends comes and tries his hand with me just to get even. You see I ain't bluffing?"

"I see you ain't bluffing," said the other. He flushed and straightened a little. "But if you come from my part of the country, you wouldn't say that I hunted with any gang. I play a lone hand, pardner. I've never seen the crook yet that you could trust as a friend."

There was in this speech such naive and direct comment upon the bandit himself that the rancher could not forbear a smile. The other replied with instant good nature.

"Which you've already said I'm a professional."

He dropped the money bag into the saddle pouch.

"You really work alone?"

"Why, you can call it that. But I got my gang. I got a hoss and a gun, which makes three of us. And they's both been well tried out and not found wanting."

"No? But that hoss of yours don't look particular like a prize, Mr.—"

"Dreer," replied the other quietly, "Jess Dreer."

Valentine looked back into his memory. It presented a blank to him.

"It's the right name," said the other, "but you won't remember it. I'm a quiet man, sir, and I got quiet ways."

CHAPTER 5

At this Valentine looked him in the eye; after a moment a faint smile came in the eyes of the rancher, and the same smile was reflected in the eye of the bandit. It was an expression of infinite understanding.

"I am Morgan Valentine," said the older man at length.

"Mr. Valentine, it's a pleasure to know you."

The rancher extended his hand but the other, appearing to be in the act of bowing very lightly in a most courtly manner, was apparently unaware of the proffered hand, which Valentine presently dropped back upon his knee. This time his smile broadened, deepened, and struck the corners of his mouth full of wrinkles.

"My hoss, as you say," went on the bandit, "ain't a blue-ribbon winner in a beauty show. But she has her points. Step up, Angelina!"

At this, the mustang lifted a weary head, flattened both ears against her neck, and came at once to her master.

"Why, she comes to you like a dog," said the rancher in admiring surprise.

"Sure, and she'd sink her teeth in me like a dog, if she got a chance. Get back, you she-devil! The outsneakingest hoss I ever see, Angelina is, Mr. Valentine."

The mustang had, indeed, slipped around to the back of Jess Dreer, and her great yellow teeth were bared as her upper lip twitched up. And at the same time her eyes gleamed with a malevolence that made the rancher shiver. He even started up a little, but at the threat of Jess Dreer the roan shrank away.

In the meantime her master stood back; always keeping an eye upon his holdup victim, he expatiated upon the fine points of his mount.

"She's got a lumpish head," he admitted. "And her neck ain't particular full. But look at those quarters. And look at those well-set down hocks and the way her high withers turns; and see how deep-girted she is, though she's a bit tucked up now, as you say. Give me a hoss with plenty of bone, and she's sure got it. Yes, sir, eight years Angelina and me has been pals."

"Eight years with a man-killer," said the rancher, his interest still growing. "You ought to do very well as a lion tamer, Mr. Dreer."

"Lions," declared the outlaw genially, "has nothing on Angelina. She's ripped up my forearm with her teeth"—

he pointed to part of a white scar which ran down beneath the cuff of his shirt almost to the palm of his hand—"and she's nicked me with her heels." He indicated a white scar which began at the top of his forehead and furrowed its way into his hair. "If she can't kick she'll strike, and if she can't strike she'll bite; and if she's fooled one day she'll be a lamb for a month and then try to murder you in ten ways in ten seconds."

He paused and smiled upon the mare with an open-hearted affection.

"Why the devil do you keep her, then?"

"Partly because, though they's plenty that can out-sprint her, I ain't ever seen anything that can keep up with her after the first ten miles. And, my work is chiefly long-distance stuff."

He confided the last remark to the rancher with perfect calm.

"Personally," said Valentine, shuddering, "I've never seen a hoss with so much devil in its face. I'd rather have three men with guns behind me than that hoss under me."

"The chances is about even for me to kill her or for her to kill me. Either way, it's been a good fight, and I've had a ringside seat."

"You're a queer creature," the rancher smiled, clasping his hands about one knee and rocking back in his seat as though he wished to get a more distant and complete perspective of his new acquaintance. "If I had that mare, the first thing I'd do would be to fill her full of lead. I wouldn't sell her any more than I'd sell a man his own death warrant."

"Sir, she's a genius; she got her brains from the devil. For eight years we've been studying each other, and we've both still got a lot to learn."

As he said this, his lower jaw jutted out a little and the muscles stood out in hard knots below the ears. Morgan

33

Valentine blinked. He had had a glimpse of a face of such demoniac cruelty, such murderous hatred, that he was shaken to the core.

When he looked again, he saw that the bandit had smoothed his expression again. It was the former calm, sad face.

"I begin to see," the rancher nodded. "Even a nightmare may be interesting. Has no one else ever ridden her?"

A shade crossed the face of the outlaw.

"If anyone else ever did," he said, "I'd give her away— or shoot her and leave her for the buzzards. A thing that's mine has got to belong to me. Got to be all mine. The reason I can ride Angelina and nobody else can, is because I go at her in the right way. I get her scared; she don't never know what's coming next—what I've got up my sleeve—and so we get along tolerable well. But if she ever finds out that I've been bluffing her, they won't be enough of me left to put in a box."

And so saying, he smiled again genially upon the roan; and her ears flattened against her neck. "Well, much obliged for the coin and the friendly chat," the outlaw remarked in tones of finality.

"Wait a minute."

Morgan Valentine was rubbing his chin with his knuckles.

"Well?" said the bandit a trifle impatiently.

"Which way might you be going?"

The other looked sharply at Valentine and then shrugged his shoulders.

"Over yonder," he said.

"That's the way I'm going, Dreer. Suppose you rest your hoss for a spell and come along with me."

A gleam of suspicion flashed into the face of the bandit, and once again Valentine glimpsed that fathomless, cruel strength of will and insight. Then he thought of a way to tempt the big man.

"They ain't much to be afraid of," he said. "My gun is in the back of the wagon."

"Why," and Jess Dreer grinned, "this sounds to me like a real party."

And he sprang instantly into the wagon and sat down beside the rancher.

CHAPTER 6

Morgan Valentine concealed his triumph, or sought to do so, by busying himself with taking up the reins and fastening them between his fingers.

"But will your horse follow?"

"It took me two years off and on to teach Angelina to follow. And I figure that if she lives to be two hundred, she won't forget what she's learned," the outlaw replied.

Valentine spoke to the two geldings, and they struck their collars at the same instant in answer to his voice; but at once they settled down to their time-honored pace. In the meantime he was adjusting himself to his companion. It was plain to see that the other had accepted the invitation to ride with his victim simply in the light of a dare. Morgan had put himself side by side with a man who had already admitted to several killings, and he had allowed that man to choose his time and place for an attack. Yet the bandit, scorning to sit far to one side or to keep his head turned toward Valentine, sat perfectly erect in the seat with his eyes fixed far down the road. It was not until Valentine, jerking his hand up swiftly to his cigarette, had made a definite move that could be construed as hostile that his companion showed the slightest sign of being on the alert. Even then he did not turn his head, but Valentine was aware of a flash of those gray eyes to the side and a tint of yellow in them. And all at once he knew that Jess Dreer was fairly a-tremble with an electric watchfulness; that he was concentrating a tremendous energy in keeping aware of his companion, and that in the space of a split second he could have whirled in his seat and got at the throat of the rancher.

It was not altogether a comfortable feeling for Valentine, but in his day he had had to do with many a hard man and had even possessed a certain name for hardness himself. There were few men in that part of the mountain desert who would have cared to risk their lives on the speed and certainty of their gun play as opposed to the speed and certainty of Morgan Valentine. For he was a cold-headed man, a cold-blooded man, and he fought with the same nerveless accuracy with which he lived, with which he had married, with which he had raised his children. The death of his brother—the coming departure of his brother's child—these were the emotional landmarks of his life.

Indeed, it was a sense of loneliness, of lack of food to fill his mind and his heart that had made him ask the bandit to ride with him. There was also a lingering hope that he might be able to turn the tables upon his antagonist. For there was never a man born—at least none worthy of the name of man—who did not have somewhere in the bottom of his heart love for an honest fight. Yet he had sense enough to guess that whatever his prowess might be with weapons, it would be as nothing compared to the man in the seat beside him. For Jess Dreer was his antithesis. If he was without nerves, Jess Dreer was full of little else.

And the calm exterior of Dreer was a disguise maintained by an almost muscular effort; beneath the disguise there was a mind of wolfish alertness. It suddenly occurred to Valentine that this man might be many years younger than he seemed, for he was of the kind who age rapidly.

And the interest of Valentine was by no means entirely malicious, as has been hinted. In Jess Dreer he crossed a new type of man, and he was curious to read beneath the surface.

"You've had your horse for eight years," said the rancher, and he looked down to the holster at the hip of his companion, "but I'll chance a guess that you've had the gun a good deal longer."

"This gun?"

With a gesture so smooth that the eye failed to appreciate its speed, the bandit reached back, and with the tips of his fingers—so it seemed—flicked the revolver out. It lay in the palm of his hand under the eye of Morgan Valentine.

Suppose he were to strike up, would he knock that weapon out of the open hand and send it spinning? Something told him that swift as his blow might be, the long brown fingers would move with vastly more speed to curl around the gun. The very thought of what might happen perceptibly lowered the temperature of the rancher's blood.

He saw that it was, as he had guessed, a very old weapon. It bore evidence of the most meticulous care, but in spite of that an expert could see at a glance that it had passed its palmy days as an engine of destruction.

"Now, there's a gun that ain't much to look at," said the bandit, and his singularly winning smile softened his face for a moment. "And between you and me, it ain't much better'n it looks. It bucks like a wild colt. It's got funny ways. It shoots the way a one-eyed hoss runs. It keeps veerin' off to one side. Well, it's a hard shooter—if you know its ways."

He paused, then added: "I seen it thrown out of the door into the ash can one day, and I picked it up."

"Just like this?"

"All the parts was there, but it was considerable chewed up with rust. You can see where it's eat away in places. It was on a Friday that I seen that gun throwed away."

"Unlucky day?"

"Unlucky for most, but I run by opposites. And when I seen it fall, I says: 'There goes somebody's bad luck. Maybe it'll be my good luck.' So I took out the gun and spent the off time for the next couple of days oiling it up. Then I went out and tried her. Lordy, lordy! I shot a circle around a knot. She had twenty queer tricks, that gun had. But after a while I got to know the tricks. And now she does pretty smooth, neat work. You see?"

The gun flipped up in the long fingers, and without raising his hand off his knees, the bandit fired. Twenty yards away a squirrel, standing up like a peg beside its hole, was blown to bits.

The geldings plunged at the explosion of the gun, and the bandit burst at once into a stream of excuses.

"Now ain't that a fool kid thing to do?" he cried. "Shooting a gun without asking you if your hosses was gun-broke? Well, sir, call me a blockhead, because I am one. Mr. Valentine, I sure am sorry!"

Indeed, his words did not seem overdone, for his earnest gray eyes were upon the rancher in a species of entreaty.

"Dreer," said the cattleman earnestly, as soon as he had quieted the horses, "you don't have to apologize. It was worth it—to see that gun act all by itself."

38

But the other shook his head and returned the weapon to its leather.

"You see," he explained, "that gun is almost human to me. Suppose you had a friend with you when you got into a fight, and it was a dead-sure cinch that you'd get plugged if your friend didn't stand up and play the man by you. And suppose you never knowed whether that friend would fight like a devil or else lie down and quit—like a greaser? Well, sir, that's the way it is with that gun. If I shoot with it, I have to look twice to see if I've hit a thing."

"And yet you still carry it? You still let your safety depend on that old rattletrap?"

The crimson departed suddenly from the face of the stranger. And the muscle at the angle of his jaw leaped out into prominence.

"Sir," he said quietly, "they's one thing that I appreciate, and that's a gent that chooses his words. Rattletrap ain't particular accurate, speaking about my gun!"

"Why, Dreer, you've as good as said as much as that yourself."

The other turned his face, and there was the old unpleasant glint in his eyes.

"I'm a peaceable man, Mr. Valentine," he said. "Matter of fact, I'm a quiet kind of a gent and I mostly hate trouble, but I don't think you and me are going to agree."

Morgan Valentine was too dumfounded to reply.

"In the first place, sir," went on the stranger, "you say you don't think nothing particular fine about my hoss. Then I let that pass, and I just throw in a few qualifying remarks about the roan. And pretty soon you up and say my gun—*my* gun is a rattletrap!"

He was unable to continue for a moment.

"But after you'd just said practically the same thing yourself, man."

"Sir, whatever else may be wrong with that gun, it's mine, and, being mine, they ain't any man in the world that I'm going to hear say things about it that they won't stand up and prove. And, speaking man to man, I can sure digest a pile of that sort of proof before I admit that I'm wrong."

A veritable devil was in his face as he spoke. And the long brown fingers were becoming restless upon his knee.

Then, very suddenly, and most welcome sight to Valentine, the blood rushed into the face of the tall man again.

"Hanged if I didn't forget for a minute," he said, "that I was your guest, riding in your wagon. Mr. Valentine, I got to ask your pardon again. Just stop the buckboard and I'll get out and climb on the roan. They ain't any man living whose pardon I've asked three times hand-running. And I've done it twice by you already!"

"Sit still," replied Morgan Valentine. "I figure to keep you right here and take you home with me."

CHAPTER 7

It should not be thought that Valentine was that cheap type of fellow who attempts to carry his points by surprise, but as the stranger talked with him, the gradual conviction grew in him that he must see more of Jess Dreer. In the meantime Jess stared at his host as though the latter had gone mad.

"Mr. Valentine," he said, "I ain't prying into what's behind your mind. I'll just say one little thing: I ain't been under the roof of another man for eight years—as a friend."

"Why, then, if you object to coming as a friend, come as an enemy."

"With the bars down and you free to call in the sheriff when you please?"

"Dreer, do you think I'm the sort who'd call in a sheriff while you're under my roof?"

"I didn't mean no insult," replied the bandit more gently. "But I ain't a mind reader, Mr. Valentine. Why the devil should you want me to come home with you?"

"Because," said the rancher, "although I've lived some fifty years and a bit more, I don't think I've met more'n two men that particularly interested me. And you're one of 'em. As a matter of fact, there's nothing so strange. You've taken some of my money. Well, what you've taken won't break me. I'm what you might call a pretty well-to-do man, Dreer. Now, I'd spend fifteen hundred on a fine hoss and never think twice about it. Why shouldn't I spend fifteen hundred for a man and enjoy talking to him? Think it over."

"I stick you up and lift fifteen hundred iron men. Then you step out and ask me home. I go to your home. I put my legs under your table. I eat your chuck—" He made a face of disgust. "I couldn't do it, pardner, even though you don't mean nothing but kindness."

"Think it over," echoed the rancher.

A silence fell. The geldings jogged relentlessly, tirelessly forward; the roan cantered softly behind the buckboard.

"If I could figure how you'd gain anything," the bandit murmured finally, "I might chance it, but—"

"Take your time and think it over," insisted Morgan Valentine.

"Well, sir," said the bandit suddenly, "I call your bluff. If it's a trap—well, a nerve like yours ought to catch something. I'll go home with you."

Valentine stretched out his hand. But the tall man glanced down at the stubby, proffered fist, and then back to the rancher.

"Some ways," he said, "you might put me down as queer. But I ain't any too fond of shaking hands. You see, a handshake means a pile to me. I shook hands with a man that sold me to a sheriff once."

"And the sheriff got you?"

"No, the other way round. But I couldn't touch the gent that had double-crossed me—the skunk!—because I'd shaken hands with him. Now, remembering that, I guess you'll change your mind about this handshaking?"

"It goes with me as far as it goes with you."

Suddenly they shook hands.

Then they said in one voice, like a trained chorus: "That takes a load off my mind!"

In the meantime the evening was approaching. The early night had patched the mountains with purple and filled every ravine with tides of incredible blue. Before them the hills began to divide.

"D'you know something?" said the bandit.

Valentine saw that his companion was leaning far forward, his elbows on his knees and his face wistful. It meant a great deal more than words, that unguarded attitude. It meant that Morgan Valentine had been judged by this man and had been accepted according to his standards.

"What's that?"

"Yonder—behind them hills—well, I'll be stepping out into a new part of my life."

"I wouldn't wonder much if you were."

Still the geldings jogged on, and the hills moved by them slowly, awkwardly, growing each moment more dusky. They turned a sharp bend, and below them lay the valley of the Crane River; above it the red of the sunset filled the sky, and the river itself was a streak of dark crimson.

"Gimme the reins," said the bandit.

Silently the rancher passed them to his companion, who now gathered them in closer. He did not speak a word, but perhaps the tenseness of the reins, the new weight vibrating against their bits, carried a message to the geldings. Of one accord, they stepped out into a freer gait, their heads raised, their ears pricked. Life came into their step. If two whips had touched them at the same instant the effect could not have been more noticeable. And it seemed to Morgan Valentine that a current of strength and knowledge was passing down the reins and into the minds of the dumb brutes. To him it was more than a miracle.

"Do you know," he said, as the buckboard was whipped forward with redoubled speed and jolted noisily over the bumps in the road, "that's the first time I've seen those nags change that old dogtrot of theirs?"

The bandit made no reply for some time. He was changing the pressure on the reins. First the off horse came up on the bit and strained against the collar; then the near horse, who had been pulled back, was released and quickened his pace until he was snorting beside his companion and even ahead of him. And then both increased their pace, and the jolting was redoubled.

"Look at that!" murmured the bandit. "As long as they agreed, they wasn't worth a nickel. As long as they went ahead at that same old sleepy trot, they wasn't worth powder and lead enough to blow their heads off. But now they're beginning to try each other out. They're beginning to race. I tell you what, Valentine, the way to get the most out of men—or hosses—is to play 'em one agin' the other."

Indeed, the two geldings now had their heads as high as if they were just beginning a journey—higher than they had ever held them for Morgan Valentine.

And the latter was naturally full of thought as the buckboard careened down the hillside and dropped into the valley floor. Now and again, as the dusk thickened, he looked behind him and saw the roan mare following patiently, always with her ears flat against her neck. It was almost as if the fear of the master she hated were still in the saddle, spurring her on, curbing her free spirit, and breaking it to do his will.

Something in this thought made him look up at the face of the bandit, and he saw him sitting with his face tense and a light of cruel enjoyment in his eyes. It was as if he drew a deep delight out of the rivalry which he had put in the hearts of the two geldings.

It was, of course, night when they reached the stables behind the ranch house, although the moon, which hung over Grizzly Peak, was sending a faint, slant light down the valley. One of the hands came out to unhitch the horses, but the outlaw insisted upon handling his own mount. He led it into one of the individual corrals.

"A roof over her head always sort of bothers Angelina," he explained, while the rancher looked on in curiosity.

He watered her carefully, fed her grain and hay in cautious portions, and rubbed away the sweat under the saddle blanket. Yet the instant he turned to answer a word from the rancher, she whirled on her master. He did not turn his head to make sure that she was coming; though she veered noiselessly, her master did not pause, but leaped straight for the bars and vaulted over them. The teeth of the mare clicked with the noise of a steel trap shutting, just at the place where his hand had rested on the top bar.

"Ah, beauty! Ah, Angelina!" cried Jess Dreer, and came

back to the bars. "Eyes in the back of my head, girl, and tomorrow you'll pay for this. Remember? Tomorrow? Or the next day; it's added to the score."

There was, at this point, a sudden outbreak of snorting and a rattle of harness from the big watering trough.

"What the dickens! Jud! Harry!" a man was crying. "What the devil has got into you? Quiet there!"

"By Heaven," murmured the rancher, "the geldings are fighting!"

"Is that strange?" asked Jess Dreer.

"They've lived like two brothers—which they are—ever since they were foaled."

"All the better," said Jess Dreer gaily. "A hoss is like a man. Needs a good fight now and then to keep 'em on edge."

And Morgan Valentine shivered. He did not say another word on the way to the house. He was beginning to think of many things.

CHAPTER 8

It was not until they had reached the very shadow of the sprawling old house that the rancher recovered from his absent-mindedness.

"How am I to introduce you?" he asked.

"As Jess Dreer," said the bandit. "I guess I've outrode my reputation."

"I think so. But where have I met you?"

"Somewhere south."

"I haven't traveled about much in the south. Let me see. Five years ago I was in Ireton; have you ever been there?"

"Nope. What's it like?"

"Common cow town."

"All right. I know it then. You met me there."

"That's all I'll have to say unless Mary starts asking questions. She's the outbeatingest girl for talking when she gets started on a thing."

At this the bandit sidestepped and scowled at his companion.

"You hitched up to a pile of womenfolks?" he muttered.

"My wife and my daughter won't bother you none, and my two boys knows what's manners between men, but Mary—she's my niece—can make a murderer talk if she sets her mind right on it."

At this the bandit chuckled. It was always a surprise to hear the soft, musical voice of this man.

"Leave her to me, pardner. It's been a good many years since I got my imagination all going at once, but when I get oiled up, I can spin the yarns out all night. What was the name of that town—Ireton? Nothing queer about it? Well, leave the rest to me, Valentine. If she wants talk, I'll let her have it."

"Aye, but one thing more, while we're on the subject of Mary. She's a fine girl, Dreer, but she has her ways. And one of them is to get all excited about any stranger man that comes around. She starts in by being foolish about 'em and most generally they wind up by being foolish about her. Now, I don't mean that you're the kind to get foolish about any girl, but I'm just telling you beforehand that if Mary begins to smile at you and act like you was a gold mine that she'd discovered all by herself, don't let it bother you."

"Don't bother none about me, Valentine. I'm well broke, pardner. I ain't gun-shy and I ain't girl-shy. Lead on!"

Since the night had turned crisp, Valentine found his

46

entire family grouped near the big fireplace in the living room. They were in characteristic attitudes. Maude Valentine sat with her feet tucked well back under her chair and her knitting needles flew with soft precision. Elizabeth, her daughter, lay in a big chair with her hands locked behind her head, looking dreamily out the black window. In another corner Mary was plotting with Charlie Valentine, and Louis, disconsolately out of the picture, attempted to bury himself in a book, out of which he lifted envious glances at Charlie from time to time. When the door opened, there was a general shifting of eyes and attitudes; the tall and deceptively graceful form of Jess Dreer became the center of attention.

"Mother, I've brought home an old friend. Jess Dreer. Dreer, this is my girl Elizabeth. Mary Valentine, my niece, and my boys, Charlie and Louis."

They shook hands.

How much did the bandit learn from the touch of their fingers—from the cold, faint pressure of Mrs. Valentine; from the grip of Charlie, boyishly eager to test the comparative strength of this tall stranger; from the nervous touch of Louis's hand, for Louis was always ill at ease and apt to be embarrassed before newcomers. "Lizbeth" greeted him at the full distance of her rather thin arm. She was one of those who come late to womanhood. Her eyes still held that infinite quiet of childhood; her throat was small, but her mouth had a kindly softness. She would never have Mary Valentine's gemlike beauty of detail, but in time she would ripen to a rare womanhood. And as for Mary, her hand and her glance both lingered on him. It was as if she had seen him before and was now trying to resurrect the complete memory.

Mrs. Valentine took them into the dining room, and there she busied herself all the time they were eating by popping up out of her chair and running to get something

47

as soon as she was once fairly seated. She discovered that Morgan's napkin was spotted, that his favorite chow-chow had been left off the table, that the baked potatoes were underdone, for which the cook received a brief, stern sentence, that the window was too widely open; in short, she spent the entire space of the meal asking Jess Dreer how long he had been in that part of the country, and interrupting herself every time before she got through with the interrogation. Finally she forgot all about her question, and sat as usual, with a smile of attention on her lips, listening to the men talk, while her eyes roved wistfully about the table hunting for the missing things. Yet never once did she win a glance from Morgan Valentine. She filled the time of the meal with an atmosphere of flurry and uncertainty, quite unheeded by her husband. But once, twice the gray eye of Jess Dreer fixed her through and through and tumbled her sad, small soul into full view. Not that she understood it; she only felt a vague fear of the stranger, his silences, his alert calm.

When they went back into the living room, two big chairs were drawn comfortably near to the fire, and the other chairs arranged in a loose semicircle on both sides of the fireplace so that the travelers could rest in ease.

"And how's young Norman?" asked Morgan Valentine.

He had turned to Charlie, but the latter indicated Louis with a jerk of his thumb.

"I dunno. Lou went over to see how Joe was coming on."

"I rode over," said Louis, embarrassed by the sudden focusing of all eyes upon him, "but I might as well have stayed away. They was about a thousand Normans hanging around the house. When I come up the path from the hitching rack, they was about a dozen of 'em on the front veranda. I hear 'em say: 'It's him.' 'No,' says someone, 'it ain't him, but it's his brother.' Then I come up and says howdy to 'em, but all they do is grunt like pigs—"

"Which they are!" cried Charlie.

The chair of Morgan Valentine creaked as he turned, and under his glance his eldest son lowered his gaze. All of this byplay was noted by the shrewd eye of the bandit. And the fact that he had been observed by a stranger to endure a reprimand made Charlie jerk up his head again and glare defiantly at Jess Dreer. The latter did not turn his head politely as another man might have done. He met the challenging glance of the younger man with a calm indifference so that it could be felt he was coolly measuring the other and filing an estimate of him away.

"Anyway," went on Louis, "I went up to the door and knocked. Mrs. Norman came, and I took off my hat and says: 'I've come to ask after Joe. How is he?'

"She didn't say nothing for a minute. She just stood there drying the dishwater off her hands and looking me up and down.

" 'Oh,' she says after a while, 'it's you, is it? And why didn't your brother come and ask about his murdered man?'

"And when she said that, all the men on the veranda growled. I turned away and didn't say any more—"

"Oh," cried Mary Valentine, "I wish that I'd been in your boots! I'd have found something to say!"

"Mary," said Mrs. Valentine, "it looks to me like you'd found too much to say other times."

Her husband checked her with a swiftly raised hand, but Mary continued to stare defiantly at her aunt. Since the episode of Joe Norman they had been almost openly at war, and now Mrs. Valentine compressed her lips and knitted with a venomous speed.

"You needn't think that I wouldn't have talked back fast

enough if one of the men had talked up," said Louis, turning red. "I wasn't afraid of any of 'em, Mary, if that's what you mean."

"You know it isn't what I mean, Lou," she said with a diplomatic change of voice. "Nobody is fool enough to doubt your courage; you're a Valentine, I guess! But it makes me mad to think of you turning away without giving that mob a few hot shots between wind and water."

"I wish I'd had the chance at 'em," said Charlie ferociously, and he flashed Mary a glance that sought approval.

"Good thing you hadn't," replied the girl instantly. "You'd probably have had ten men on your hands in no time. Better to say nothing at all, like Lou, than say the wrong thing."

It made Charlie glower at her, but Louis smiled in triumph. Plainly Jess Dreer saw how the clever girl balanced one of them against the other.

"But here we are talking family shop before a stranger!" continued Mary Valentine, and she smiled an apology at Jess Dreer.

He shifted his regard from Louis to his cousin, and, if ever a smile failed to strike its target, certainly Mary's smile glanced harmlessly away from the impersonal eyes of Dreer. She found herself suddenly sobered.

"Don't mind me," he was saying in that surprisingly gentle voice.

"A little fracas," explained his host swiftly. "Charlie had a mix-up with Joe Norman and dropped him—through the arm—nothing to talk of."

Here Mrs. Valentine raised her eyes, let her glance fall pointedly upon Mary, sighed, and shook her head. It was impossible to miss her meaning. Mary had been the cause of the quarrel. But Jess Dreer was looking toward the ceiling and had apparently seen nothing. Mary did not know whether to be relieved or piqued. But now that the stranger's attention was diverted to other things she took the occasion to examine him more minutely. Ordinarily she was not in the least interested in the few acquaintances whom her uncle brought home, but now she discovered that this stranger was probably not quite so old as his weather-beaten appearance had at first led her to imagine.

Then she found that the conversation had taken a new turn. Mrs. Valentine apparently felt that it was the part of a perfect hostess to draw the stranger into the center of attention.

"How long have you and Mr. Dreer known each other, Morgan?" she asked.

CHAPTER 9

At this Morgan Valentine flashed a glance at his companion, indicating that the danger line was being approached.

"Oh—about five years," he said carelessly. He should have said more. His very carelessness made Mrs. Valentine continue her inquiry as though she feared that Dreer would consider himself slighted by so summary a dismissal from conversation.

"Five years? Well, you're a secretive man, Morgan. Would you believe, Mr. Dreer, that he's never mentioned you in all that time? I've known him to do the same with some of his oldest and best friends. That's Morgan's way! Where was it you first met Mr. Dreer, Morgan?"

"Down in Ireton."

"Well, well! As long ago as that?" And the subject was closed for Mrs. Valentine. Then Mary entered the lists.

"Why, that was the time you bought the timber, Uncle Morgan?"

"I guess it was. I disremember."

"Were you one of the men Uncle Morgan bought it from?"

"I never been interested in timber," said Jess Dreer. "Horses is more my line. But speaking about timber—"

Who knows how far he might have rambled afield on the subject of timber and all its possibilities had not chance interrupted him. There was a snap, and a bright coal leaped out of the fireplace and onto the rug. In the flurry of putting it out Dreer's promised anecdote was forgotten, and before he could resume it, Mary was back on the subject.

"Oh, did you buy that string of grays from Mr. Dreer, Uncle Morgan?"

"I disremember how it was that I met Dreer," said Valentine, with a mild voice like that of one who labors in vain to find a suitable lie.

Dreer came to his rescue.

"It was in Tolliver's saloon. We were drinking—"

"Why, Uncle Morgan! I thought it was ten years since you'd had a drink!"

"Not drinking whisky," put in Jess Dreer calmly. "Leastways, he was taking lemonade, and I was tossing off my redeye. That was how we come to talk."

As plain as day the steady eye of the girl said to him: "You are lying, Mr. Jess Dreer, and I know it."

But he went on: "And I'll tell you why Mr. Valentine ain't ever mentioned me. It's because he's a modest man. But here's the facts. I was saying that I had been drinking whisky. Well, when I went out into the sun, it got into my head and made it spin. When I climbed onto my hoss, I raked his side with a spur, and the next thing I knew my pinto was ten feet in the air. When he landed, I kept right

52

on traveling. And when pinto seen me on the ground, he allowed I was his meat and started for me. He was a maneater, was pinto.

"There I lay stretched out with eight hundred and fifty pounds of red-eyed hossflesh tearing for me and about twenty fools laughing their heads off in front of the saloon. But they was one man cool enough to see what was coming off: a man-killing. He had a split part of a second to keep that hoss from reaching me, and he done it. He outs with his guns and drills pinto clean through the temples. As pretty a snapshot as ever I seen. And that man was Morgan Valentine!"

He dropped his hand lightly on the shoulder of Valentine.

"But he's so modest that it ain't no wonder he's never talked about me."

Now Mary Valentine sat next to the tall stranger, and she was leaning forward to catch every syllable and read every detail of his expression, but for some reason he did not seem to see her. His target lay beyond. It was Elizabeth who had pushed her chair a little out of line with the rest of the circle, quite content to let Mary take the lion's share of the attention of the evening. On her Jess Dreer bent his steady eye, and every inflection of his voice was aimed at the girl, so that she, too, leaned forward, and before the end was smiling in breathless interest.

While the general exclamation went the rounds at the end of the tale, Mary snapped a glance over her shoulder at her cousin. Then she turned her attention back upon the tall man.

"I guess you've made that a bit strong," Valentine was saying.

"Facts are facts," said the bandit, and rolled a cigarette.

He had adroitly pushed his host out of the embarrassing center of the stage and stepped into the spotlight himself.

"Pinto reared when the lead hit him; coming down, one of his forefeet clipped me here."

And the bandit touched the scar upon his forehead. There was a general leaning forward and an intaken breath; Mrs. Valentine fixed her starry eyes upon her husband. In the clamor Mary could say to the stranger without fear of being overheard:

"Mr. Dreer, how much of that is made up?"

He neither smiled nor flushed.

"Guess," he said.

"The whole thing."

"Lady," he answered calmly, "you sure got faith in my imagination!"

At this point the fire blazed up so hot that Mrs. Valentine had to move her chair. It was Jess Dreer who read her wish and pulled the chair back, and when he sat down again, it was in a place beside Lizbeth.

It would not be fair to Mary to say that she was piqued by this occurrence. She was not angered; she was merely gathered up in the silence of a vast astonishment. For the first time in her life she had been overlooked, it seemed, and her cousin was preferred. And yet she had given Jess Dreer his full share of intriguing glances and bright smiles.

Indeed, the interest of the stranger in Lizbeth was so pointed that the whole family began to notice. He gave his host and hostess a phrase or a word now and then, but he contrived to make his talk go constantly toward the girl. And it was plain that Mrs. Valentine was not altogether displeased. As for Elizabeth, Mary saw her at first embarrassed, and then flushed, and then lost in a great interest. She was beginning to dwell on the face of Dreer while he spoke. Mary drew her uncle to one side.

"Your friend likes Lizbeth," she said pointedly.

"And Lizbeth seems to like him."

"Now, Mary, what are you aiming to come at?"

"I aim to know who Jess Dreer is."

"Ain't you been told tolerable in detail?"

"Too much detail, dear Uncle Morgan. Do you think I was taken in by that cock-and-bull story about the mad horse?"

"Hush, Mary!" and his glance sought his wife guiltily.

"I knew it!"

"Mary, you're a nuisance."

"But just tell me who he is, and I won't bother you a word more."

"He's a man. Two legs, tolerable long; two arms, tolerable strong, and, speaking in general, he's like any other man."

"He's as much like any other man," said the girl, watching him earnestly, "as a wolf is like a dog. Look at his hands, Uncle Morgan. They're brown. He hasn't worn gloves much, the way honest cowpunchers do. Look at the inside of his palms. No calluses. I noticed when I shook hands with him. Look at the way he moves! Like a cat moves, Uncle. Don't tell me he's an ordinary man!"

"They's all kinds of men, and when you're older, you'll know it. Wolf? That's foolishness, honey."

"A wolf, Uncle."

"You think he's talking too much to Lizbeth?"

"Oh, no. Lizbeth is too much of a baby to be harmed."

"She's grown up, Mary."

"On the outside; inside she's about ten years old. But I'm right about this stranger. Even Charlie and Louis see that he's different. Usually Charlie starts edging up to new men, but he keeps clear of Dreer. See how he eyes him!"

"There you go again."

"Then tell me the truth about him."

"I'll tell you this much, honey. He's not the kind for you to set your cap at."

"You mean that you think I'll flirt with him?"

"Maybe."

"Uncle! With a man fifteen years older than I am?"

"Maybe not so old as that. But he's old enough. You've played around with boys, Mary, and they was no particular harm in it, excepting for getting Charlie into scrapes now and then. But when you start making eyes at a grown man, trouble will hit you and not them."

"You admit that it isn't very safe to be friendly with him. And yet you've known him five years?"

"No matter how long. I know him. And you keep away from him, honey."

"How long does he stay?"

"Till after you go."

"Somewhere there's a mystery," said Mary Valentine, and she added suddenly: "There he is laughing at us now. Why, he knows we're talking about him, and he's mocking me."

"Honey, he ain't laughing."

"With his eyes, Uncle Morgan. Oh, he's a deep one!"

CHAPTER 10

If Valentine had sought to create a diversion and start new interests by bringing his bandit home, he had indubitably succeeded. The advent of the stranger had the effect of a bomb which is about to explode. No one could really have said why Dreer was exciting, but before he had been in the room for ten minutes, each member of Valentine's family had felt the same influence of excitement which had affected Morgan Valentine and induced him to bring the stranger to his home. Perhaps it was that in spite of the grave decorum of Dreer's manner one felt about him a native wildness. In a way, it might be said that he carried a gust of fresh air into the room. And he was constantly alert and active after the manner of wild things. His hands were rarely still, and though he seldom turned his head, his eyes went everywhere.

When he smiled at a remark of Elizabeth's, Mary felt that he was laughing at her, and Charlie felt that he was being mocked. Not that the stranger pointedly ignored the rest of the room, but it seemed that he had happened to sit down by Elizabeth, and he found her sufficiently entertaining. But the great point of wonder was that Elizabeth was actually talking. At first haltingly, confused because the eyes of the others in the room were occasionally turning upon her with wonder, but by degrees warming into complete forgetfulness of the rest. She lowered her voice. She was talking to the tall man alone. About what? The others caught fragments of phrases about her horses, about her last hunting trip, about the lobo she shot last spring. She had begun by asking timidly polite questions. She ended by chattering gaily about herself.

It was a pretty thing to see her grow excited. What Mary Valentine could not decide was whether her cousin was excited by Jess Dreer the man, or Jess Dreer the audience.

She was similarly puzzled by Dreer. In another she would have thought his attitude one of polite indifference. But she could not be sure of him and his mental status.

She had known many a boy and many a boy's mind. They always showed their entire hand at once. One read the cards, was fascinated for a moment perhaps, and the next moment became bored because the antagonist was a known quantity. But Jess Dreer was not known. He lurked behind a screen. He revealed not half, not a tithe of his strength—or of his weakness, for that matter. As far as Mary could make out, this fellow had brought Lizbeth out of her shell as another woman might have done. It was odd. Mary would have given a great deal to know why he winced when a door was opened behind him, why his eyes were apt to flash suddenly up, glitter, and droop. She felt that he would be more content if his chair were back against the wall.

It was at this point in her train of thought that the doorbell rang, and Mary sprang up to answer it. She was glad to get away from the room. She wanted to have the chill air of the night against her face—to breathe of it in the hope that it would clear a mist from her mind and enable her to think logically and brush away her rising excitement. For the question was beating into her consciousness always: What is Jess Dreer? Her uncle had put her off. Why? Or did he know? And was Jess Dreer there because he had some claim and power over Morgan Valentine?

She threw open the front door after she had gone thoughtfully down the hall, and she saw—dim figures in the moonlight, and with the reek of a long horseback ride about them—Sheriff Claney of Salt Springs, and another man. Now Sheriff Claney's boy had been one of Mary's victims in the near past, and that was the reason that she threw a conciliatory warmth into her greeting:

"Why, Sheriff Claney! Come in. Dad will be happy to see you."

The sheriff smiled at her, and in smiling the ends of his drooping mustaches bristled out to the sides like tusks.

"Mostly folks feel another way when I come along to

say how d'you do. But wait a minute, Mary. I ain't here on a pleasure call."

"You have business—here?"

She thought of Charlie's affair with Joe Norman.

"That miserable Norman family—have they sent you after Charlie?"

The sheriff smiled, disagreeably.

"I dunno anything about Charlie and the Norman boy," he said. "I don't go prying after trouble. Mostly, enough of it comes my way without hunting. All I want to do is to ask you a few questions, Mary."

"And you won't come in?"

"Nope. Is there a man in your house called Jess Dreer?"

The floodgates opened, the water burst through the dam, and Mary Valentine was picked up in a torrent of sudden knowledge. Jess Dreer! The question flashed a lantern light on the man.

"Jess Dreer?" she repeated.

"That's the name. Is he inside?"

She fought for time. As a matter of fact she was balancing between two impulses. The first was to hand this fellow over to the law at once. The second impulse was— she did not know what—but certainly it was to keep him safe.

"What does he look like?"

"About as tall as my friend here. Mr. John Caswell— Miss Mary Valentine. About as tall as Caswell, maybe a mite smaller. Big shoulders, I understand, and the sort of a face that's easy to remember. Quiet. Soft-spoken. Active with his hands."

She still paused. How fast her mind was working! And therefore her speech was slow.

"Oh, yes, I remember now. Yes, there was a man like

that here, and, now that I remember, I think he said that his name was Jess Dreer."

"But he ain't here now?"

"No. He rode away—quite a while ago."

"I told you so," said the big man who had been called Caswell. "That gent is a fox. He's got these people on his side."

But Sheriff Claney hushed the other with a raised hand.

"I think maybe you're mistaken, miss. We've got an idea that Dreer is in the house right now. Maybe he's hiding, and you don't know it. But we got his hoss and his saddle. In fact, we've found his hoss in the corral and saddled her, and now we got that hoss waiting for Mr. Dreer!"

"Of course you have his horse." Mary Valentine nodded. "He left the mare and took one of Dad's horses. I think he paid Dad something into the bargain for the exchange."

"How long ago?" Sheriff Claney asked.

"An hour; but, Sheriff, come on inside and search the house if you want."

"Not if he's gone. Which way?"

"He took that road. You ought to catch him in the mountains."

"How's your hoss, Caswell?"

"Played out."

"So's mine, pretty nigh."

"Well, then, come in, Sheriff."

For she knew perfectly that this bulldog would not leave the trail. She leaned against the side of the door and laughed at him.

"I think that for a moment you suspected that we were sheltering him. But what's he done?"

"What's he done?" Caswell said explosively. "What ain't he done? He's done enough to bring me a thousand

60

miles on the trail. What's he done? Why, that's Jess Dreer; they scare their kids with that name down south!"

One might have thought that Mary Valentine would shrink in horror at this news. She did not. No, a fire came in her eyes.

"Is he as bad as all that? Oh, I hope you get him, Mr. Caswell!"

"Right down that road!" She ran to the front of the veranda. "Hurry! I'll go back and tell Dad about it. He'll be after you in five minutes with fresh horses. He'll take along a couple of fresh mounts for you."

"Come on, Caswell!"

But Caswell, with his foot on the verge of taking the first step down, paused.

"What I don't figure," he said, "is why Dreer left his own saddle behind? It's hard enough to figure why he left the hoss."

"Because he knew you were on his heels, Caswell," cried Claney. "Hurry up, man. He's gaining miles on us."

"How'd he know I was on his heels? Nobody else has give him a run—not for five years. He's always give the others too hot a reception at the end of the trail—them that ever come up with him.'"

"Facts is facts. Come on."

"I'm thinkin'."

And he rubbed his chin and stared hard at Mary Valentine.

"Don't you see that he's getting away?" she cried in an apparent frenzy.

"Seems to me, ma'am, that you're in a considerable trouble to have him caught. Most of the womenfolk I know most generally hopes he gets away."

"Caswell, I'm going on without you."

"Wait a minute. Claney, it won't do."

61

The latter turned and hurried back up the steps.

"I'll tell you why," explained the man from the south. "That hoss has been with Dreer for eight years. Ten times he could of changed her for a fresh hoss when he was being trailed, but he never wouldn't do it. And why does he do it now? Even if he knowed I was after him, that mare could of kept on going and run down a fresh hoss. She ain't common hossflesh. She's all leather inside and out. I know her."

"Well, where are you aiming?"

Claney turned on Mary.

"I'm aiming to search this house, and I don't think I'll have far to go."

She stared at him an instant.

"You're a little insulting," said Mary, drawing herself up. And then, seeing that he would persist in his purpose, she slipped before him and opened the door.

"Come in, then," said Mary.

But when he made a step forward, she slammed the door in his face, and the astonished sheriffs heard the heavy bolt click home.

CHAPTER II

In the living room there had grown up a slight suspense.

"What keeps Mary so long?" asked her uncle at length.

"I'll go to find out," suggested Elizabeth.

And then, to the astonishment of the others, big Jess Dreer was seen to slip from his chair. The fire cast a gigantic shadow behind him against the wall.

"If you don't mind," he said gently, "I think I'll step out and see."

But at that moment the front door crashed; there was the metallic ring of the bolt driven home, and then Mary whipped into the room. A beautiful picture. A wisp of hair had blown down across her cheek. Her eyes were alight with excitement. And yet there was something akin to a laugh on her lips.

"Jess Dreer," she cried, "follow me!"

And before one of the others could so much as rise from a chair, she had raced across the room and out through the farther door with Dreer gliding at her heels; even then he appeared unhurried.

"This way!" commanded the girl, and ran up the brief flight of steps that joined one stretch of the back hall with another at a higher level. They went down the passage at full speed, and then, at the foot of it, she cast open another door and beckoned him into the room. Once inside, she bolted the door behind her.

From the front of the house there was a thunder against the door, and the voice of Morgan Valentine was calling: "Mary, what's this all about?"

Jess Dreer took quick stock of the room. The moonlight struck in a broad shaft through one of the windows, and the rest of the apartment was filled with a dim, dim light. It was a girl's room. That indescribable fragrance lived in it, like a spirit. And there were splashes of bright color made faint by the night.

"They're after you," cried the girl softly. "Sheriff Claney and a man named Caswell, who has followed you from the south."

She was shocked to see him leaning idly against the wall.

"Now, think of that," murmured Jess Dreer. "I figured

63

that Caswell was a sensible sort of gent, and here he is trying to make a reputation by catching me. Well, well, they ain't any way of judging a man when he starts out to try to get famous."

She gasped away her surprise.

"No matter what he is. He may be a fool, but Sheriff Claney is a dangerous man. He's well known. Too well known."

"Mighty good of you to let me know about him."

"Come here. Quick! It isn't far to drop to the ground from this window. You see how the hill slopes away up just underneath?"

"Dear me, now! But they's one great trouble. I have to get out to my hoss and saddle her before I can start on."

"You'll never ride that horse again. They found her in the corral, and they've saddled her to take you away on her."

"I knowed Caswell was a terrible considerate man."

She paid no attention.

"You see that hill? Strike for that. Just beyond there's broken country. No horse can follow you over it. You have a gun?"

"A sort of a one."

"Then go!"

"Lady," said Jess Dreer, "I'd a pile rather go on Angelina as a prisoner than go on foot a free man."

She stared at him.

There was the unmistakable sound of the splintering of wood.

"Quick!" she pleaded, almost sobbing in her frenzy of excitement.

"They's one or two things that sort of holds me back," murmured the bandit.

"What? What?"

"Look out yonder!"

She saw to one side—fifty yards away—two men sitting motionless on their horses.

"Then you're lost!"

"I'm squeezed, anyways. And yonder is Angelina, I see."

And following the direction in which he pointed, she saw another pair of men on their horses, with a spare horse held between them.

"There's no hope? Tell me how to help you!"

"Lady, I sure appreciate all the interest you're showing."

And with this, he sank down upon a chair and crossed his legs.

She stood back from him at that.

"Are you going to give up without a struggle?"

"I'm going to have a little think," said the outlaw. "I'd rather start a fight after I've thought it out than I would to have a pardner to help me. Two minutes of getting ready is worth an hour of hard riding sometimes."

"I see. You don't really care if they *do* catch you? You haven't done anything very wrong? It doesn't mean that—"

"A busted neck. That's all it means."

"Then what he said is true?"

"Most probable it is. Lady, I ain't one of them parlor bad men that wears a bad look and a nervous hand. You got a lot of questions to ask me. Am I a downtrodden man that's tried to right my wrongs and got tangled with the law? No, I ain't. Am I a wild but nacherally noble heart that's persecuted by the miserable world that don't understand me? No, I ain't. I'm plain Jess Dreer. Too lazy to work with my hands and just able to get a good living with my gun. That's all. Now take my advice. Get out of this room and wash your hands of me."

"I don't care what you are," cried the girl. "I believe in

you. There never was a scoundrel yet that was a truly brave man. Jess Dreer, I believe in you. But quick, quick, quick. Do something! There's no time. They've broken in the door."

"That's what I been waiting for," said the bandit, and he raised his great length from the chair and stretched himself. "Now that I got part of 'em inside the house, they're divided. That's the way old Napoleon did, I guess."

"But they're coming. I can do something. Raise a false alarm on the other side—"

He broke out with a strange heartiness: "You're the salt of the earth. No, don't raise your hand. The fools have give me a chance, and I'll take it."

A heavy rush of feet in the hall. A body smashed against the door and the room quivered.

"Open, Mary!"

The surprise had brought a revolver in the hand of Jess Dreer, and even in that dim light the girl saw his face change. But he instantly put up the gun when he saw the door would hold.

"Now wouldn't you think that wise gents like them would look before they leap? However, I won't wait for 'em."

The door groaned under a new shock, and then Jess Dreer slipped his long body feet-first through the window and dropped to the ground. She looked out. He had sunk into the shadow at the base of the wall and had not yet been seen, and now she heard a brief, shrill whistle, twice repeated.

It was answered by a snort of a horse, and instantly Angelina burst from the men who held her and plunged toward the house with flying bridle reins. Out from the shadow leaped Jess Dreer to meet her. He had covered half the distance before he was seen and before the others could start their horses toward him, he was in the saddle with a catlike bound. The four men converged on him, and straight toward the middle of the gap he sent the flying Angelina.

He lay flat on the back of the mustang; he had not even drawn his revolver, so far as she could see. But the others galloped with naked weapons. One of these flashed, and on the heels of the report there was a shriek from one of the posse who had been closing in on the other side. The bullet had missed the enemy and struck a friend.

It gave Jess Dreer a winking moment of a chance. For the shout of the hurt man and the plunge of his body to the ground threw the rest of the posse into confusion. Three horses were reined in three directions; Angelina rushed through the narrow gap between, and then Mary Valentine saw the fugitive strike out toward the nearest hill with three pursuers laboring behind him.

Each of them had a gun unlimbered; each of them was pumping a hail of bullets after Jess Dreer; but they doubly defeated themselves by that very eagerness. For the racking gallop ruined their chances to shoot true, and, sitting straight to fire, they could not get the best speed out of their horses. And in the meantime Jess Dreer was jockeying the cat-footed Angelina through the rough ground at the base of the hill. She veered and dodged like a dancing will-o'-the-wisp and presently darted around the hill into oblivion.

The fusillade of shots had drawn the two sheriffs from the door of Mary Valentine's room. She heard them plunging through the house, leaving a trail of crackling oaths behind them in lieu of musketry.

Afterward she waited in her room, terrified by what she had done, and, though her aunt and then Elizabeth came and called her, she would not come out.

She was spending that hour in profound thoughtful-

67

ness, and her thoughts were turning on that thing she had cried to Jess Dreer in her excitement: "There never was a scoundrel yet that was a truly brave man!"

Had she not spoken the truth by inspiration?

She heard the wounded man groaning as he was carried past her door. That was one result of her work, no doubt. Then she heard the posse returning from a fruitless chase. At this, Mary breathed freely for the first time.

CHAPTER 12

When she went out at last, she carried her head with a high stubbornness and walked bravely into the living room. Elizabeth was not there; she was tending the wounded man. And the rest of the posse was either gone home or had found quarters in the house. But the two sheriffs sat opposite each other. They scowled at Mary when she came in; only from Morgan Valentine did she receive the faint glimmer of a smile. As for Mrs. Valentine, she turned upon her niece a somber glance that betided no good.

"A pretty night's work for you, Mary Valentine," she said. "Turning your uncle's house into a refuge for outlaws—and getting a man shot. All your work, too, Mary. And I'd like to know what you got to say to Sheriff Claney —and Sheriff Caswell, that's come so far all to be fooled by your doings."

"Hush, Mother," said Morgan Valentine. "That's a little too much."

"Don't bother about me," said Sheriff Caswell

gloomily. "I don't hold no spite agin' the young lady—which I never knew womenfolk yet that didn't take the side of the underdog."

"More power to the women!" muttered Morgan Valentine.

"Right!" observed Sheriff Caswell with surprising clamness. "I wouldn't wish my own girl to help corner a man. No, sir. And I don't hold no grudge, young lady, though you did lie most amazing for that fox Dreer."

Mary Valentine stood where the firelight could play full on her face—and there is nothing like firelight to bring out the luminous tenderness of a woman's eyes. She cast out her hands toward the two men she had disappointed.

"How could I help it?" she said. "There were so many of you. And he was alone!"

They would have been more than men if they had not melted to some degree. Indeed, Mary would have done well on the stage.

"And yet I suppose," she said, slipping into a chair, "that he's a scoundrel; a worthless rascal!"

Mary was not very old, and, I suppose, she was not very wise; but she understood that the way to guide a man is to oppose him.

"Really," she said, "the moment I looked at Jess Dreer I knew that he was worthless."

It caused Sheriff Caswell to take fire immediately, and inwardly she rejoiced.

"Then you know more'n I do," he muttered.

"But haven't you chased him a thousand miles?"

"I had to. I dunno just how many thousand they is on his head. It ain't the money I want, but if I can get rid of Jess Dreer—why, they ain't much chance of another bad one ever crossing my trail. They'd keep clear of my country if they knowed that I'd run Jess Dreer to the ground."

Mary Valentine shivered. She gazed with open admiration on the sheriff.

"It must take courage," she murmured, "to follow a cold-blooded murderer!"

The sheriff looked at her. He was not displeased by her admiration, but he felt that he must put this very absolute young woman in her place.

"If you call him cool," he said, "why, I call him that, too. But murder is a pretty strong word. Man-killer he is. They ain't any doubt about that. But murder, I ain't ever heard of his doing."

"Isn't that a close distinction?" she said. "Is there much difference between a murderer and a man-killer?"

"To you, maybe not," said the sheriff deliberately. "To me, they're just about the world apart. A murderer is a snake that strikes for the sake of striking. A man-killer is one that fights when he has to. But Jess Dreer—why, he'll almost take water before he'll fight. That's how mild he is."

She had to lower her eyes, such a warm happiness had come in her blood that she feared it would shine out in her glance.

"For my part," she said, "I think his mildness is just a sham. It looked snaky enough to me."

"Then," said the sheriff, "you and me see with different eyes. What chance did Jess Dreer have, I ask you? Jud Linsey's hoss is stole. It looks bad for Pete Dreer. Jud gets a crowd together. They put on masks and go to Dreer's house. They take Pete out, and when he says he's innocent, they laugh at him, the case was so black agin' him. They take him out, string him up, and let him swing. Along comes Jess Dreer and sees his father dead before the door of the house. He busts around town and finds out that Linsey done it.

70

"Along about that time the real hoss thief is found with the goods. They bring him in. They ain't any doubt that old Pete Dreer was innocent when he was lynched, but he was such a queer, silent old cuss that nobody would of believed it—considering how black the case was agin' him.

"Well, Jess Dreer buries his father and then he goes to the sheriff and asks for justice on Jud Linsey. Did he get it? No! Partly because they wasn't anybody that seen the lynching except them that was in the mob, and everybody in the mob was just as guilty as Jud Linsey in the eyes of the law. So would they talk? Would they accuse Jud and accuse themselves at the same time? No, they wasn't any chance of that.

"Besides, the sheriff was pretty thick with Jud Linsey, Jud having married his daughter. So he tells Jess Dreer to get out of his office and stop talking like a fool.

"You see, he didn't suspect that they was anything very hard about Jess. Nobody did. He'd been quiet as a lamb all his life.

"So Jess Dreer leaves the sheriff and goes out to the saloon where Jud Linsey was. I was there at the bar, and I seen everything that happened. Jess walks in and stands there with his hands on his hips.

" 'Jud Linsey,' he sings out, 'I've been to the sheriff and asked for the law on you. But the sheriff has cussed me out and told me I couldn't come at you through the law. So I'm going to use my own hands. Linsey, I'm going to kill you.'

"Well, Linsey turns on his heel and has two guns out before you could wink, and he hits the floor without shooting either of them guns off. The reason why was because a slug out of Dreer's gun had gone through his heart.

"Now, that was what opened our eyes to Jess. Jud Linsey was called a quick man with his shooting irons, but beside Jess that day he looked as if he was standing still to have his picture taken. After Jud drops, Jess sings out in his quiet way: 'Well, boys, you see what I've done. And I ask you: What other way out was there for me?'

"They wasn't any other way, and we all knowed it. So we didn't say nothing. And Jess turns his back and walks out without nobody lifting his hand. But old 'Pike' Malone says to me, he says: 'Caswell, they's a good man gone wrong today.'

"And Pike told the truth. The sheriff went near crazy when he heard about the killing of his son-in-law. He rides up to the house of Jess Dreer and calls him out and cusses him up and down and tells him to come with him. The sheriff was aching for a gun play, but Jess didn't come halfway. He goes right along to the jail.

"Then comes the trial. They was twelve fair men on the jury, but what could they do? It was a plain case of manslaughter, the easiest they could let Jess off. And after he heard the decision, he busted jail.

"The sheriff followed hotfoot; some said that he left the way open for Jess so that he could have the pleasure of dropping him with his own guns instead of waiting for Jess to serve his sentence. The sheriff runs Jess down easy —because the first place Jess went was home. The sheriff goes in for him, and the sheriff never comes out again. But Jess Dreer comes out and rides off on the sheriff's hoss.

"They wasn't anything for it except to start after him with a posse, not that any of us really wanted to tackle the job. But we couldn't have our town put on the map as an easy place for a getaway. That wouldn't do. We got our guns and climbed on our hosses and followed Jess Dreer for blood.

"He'd have got away, because he has the real eye for a trail, and he knows how to shake any crowd that ever got together. But his hoss went lame, and we caught up with him."

At this point the sheriff paused, sighed, and looked for a long moment at the fire.

"That was the time," he said at length, "that Jess Dreer cut his name into the memory of the Southwest—and he cut it deep. Afterward Jess Dreer went on, and we went back. I got this that day."

He touched a scar where a bullet had furrowed the base of his broad, tanned neck.

"And now here I am on his trail," said the sheriff. He shook his head gloomily. "I may get Jess. Chances are that Jess'll get me. I ain't got no grudge agin' him. But I got to make a place for myself. It's a gamble how the trail will turn out, but it's a sure thing that they don't want a sheriff long down my way until they find the man that can get Jess Dreer. What've I got on my side? Numbers. They don't count. You've just seen how he slides through them. What else have I got? The fact that Jess has got away so often that maybe his luck is just about played out.

"Eight years of luck. Pretty soon he'll tumble. And—maybe—I'll be there with a gun to catch him when he drops!"

At the conclusion of this tale there was a silence; even Mrs. Valentine was motionless and her knitting needles were crossed idly for the first time in many an hour. But Mary, without a word, got up and left the room. She walked with her head fallen. There seemed to be a haze across her eyes, for when she reached the door, she fumbled blindly for it a moment.

All of this Morgan Valentine saw. What passed through his mind it would be impossible to say, but when the door had closed upon his niece, he said softly to Caswell: "Sheriff, between you and me, I think it'd be a pretty good idea if you didn't talk no more to Mary about this Jess Dreer."

"Why not?"

"If you had a house built of dead leaves," said Morgan Valentine, "would you encourage folks to come and light matches in it?"

CHAPTER 13

There was no sleep for Mary Valentine when she reached her room after Jess Dreer had escaped. She had drawn a picture by guesswork, and the picture had become a living thing.

She lighted the lamp to undress. At once the thought of going to bed became detestable, for she foresaw long hours of sleeplessness, twisting and turning from side to side. She tried to read, but the print tangled on the page, became a blur out of which grew a face and a form and a voice.

Throwing the magazine away, she tried to daydream, but the living reality cut into the midst of her dream. She blew out the lamp, but the moment it was extinguished, the pale moonlight cut into the room and brought back with breathtaking vividness the picture of Jess Dreer as he had got up from the chair and stretched himself before the window.

At length she slipped into a deep chair beside the bed and dropped her face in her hands. Time cannot be measured in some moods. She could not tell whether it was hours or moments before there was a faint scratching sound outside her window, but when she looked up, there sat the long body of Jess Dreer in the window, jet-black in the moonlight, in the very attitude he had been in when he dropped for the ground. She hardly dared to look again, and then she heard the ghost murmur: "Whist! Mary Valentine!"

At that, she started up, half fearful and tingling with a singularly happy excitement.

But when she ran to him, his greeting was characteristic.

"Well, well! Not in bed yet? Is that the way to treat yourself, Mary Valentine? I wouldn't treat my old hoss like that!"

"Do you know that the sheriffs are still in the house? That they haven't gone to bed? That their men are here? Do you know that, Jess Dreer?"

"I scouted around a bit first and seen their hosses saddled like they was hesitating about giving me another run."

"And yet you came back?"

"Not for fun," said Dreer.

"Come inside. They'll see you sitting there!"

"This is good enough for me."

"But if it wasn't out of madness, what was it that brought you back?"

"Common sense. They'll hunt for me tomorrow over the hills. I'll be riding off the other way."

"You're doubling on them. But Salt Springs lies the other way, and they're sure to comb the district around the town. They always do. The amateurs start by looking near home."

"They're more generally right than the professionals, then. But Caswell is one of these crafty fellows. He starts right in to get inside my mind, find out what I'm thinking about, and then outguess me." He laughed softly. "Caswell follers me as if he was a general; as if I was an army with a board of strategy—and here I am, plain Jess Dreer. All I do is to act simple, and that always fools him."

"Listen to me."

"Yes."

"Jess Dreer, why have you come back?"

"Partly I've told you why. Partly because I left in such a terrible hurry that I forgot something. After all you done for me, I plumb forgot to thank you. So I come back to tell you now that you're the finest girl I've ever knowed, Mary Valentine."

"Hush!" she whispered. And to cover her emotion and the tremor of her voice, she added: "Isn't that someone listening at the door?"

"Not a soul. They ain't anybody near. And they's another reason why I had to come back. Like as not you'll be hearing considerable talk about me the next few days. You'll be hearing about Jess Dreer the murderer, Jess Dreer the gambler, Jess Dreer the robber, Jess Dreer the no-good hound. Well, mostly I don't care what people think about me after I've gone by. My trail fades out, and what they think about me don't reach my ears, so why should I care? But this is different."

He turned more fully toward her and looked up. She could see him frown with the effort of hard thought.

"I ain't much good with words. I'm out of practice, too. But this is the way I feel. When I come to this house I struck soft dirt, and I've left a trail that's going to last. I mean—I mean—I got an idea that maybe you won't forget me for quite a while, you see?"

He spoke very apologetically.

"I shall never forget you," said the girl.

He paused.

"No," he said carefully, "I don't think you ever will."

It would have been disgusting assurance on the part of another man; but it seemed perfectly natural coming from Jess Dreer.

"And here's the way I feel," he went on, "that if ever you should get your head filled full of wrong ideas about me, I'd know it if I was a thousand miles away. I'd know it, and I'd feel like someone had stuck a knife in me—and then—turned the knife. It would hurt, you see?"

She could not answer.

"Maybe this'll sound all foolish to you," said Jess Drecr, "but what I say now I say because you're the first human being that's ever gone a step out of his way to help me since the law turned me out. You took a chance. You risked something. You got me a chance to get clear. And so what I say now I say for you and God and me to hear. That's a fact!

"I ain't going to pile up a lot of excuses. All I say is this: That first a wrong was done, and that I took the law into my own hands, and then the law threw me out. And since that time, no matter what liars say, I've never lifted my hand except to defend myself. They's another thing. I've took the money of other people. I'll tell you why. When they run me away from my home, they run me away from my own cattle and my own land. It was a good-paying ranch and I figure that the world owes me as much as I'd have made clear off that ranch. And that's what I take every year—or less. And I've never yet taken it from nobody who couldn't afford to lose it. Mostly I've taken it across card tables, but some—I've taken at the end of a gun."

He paused.

Suddenly she was aware that he was in an agony; that he had spoken in an agony; that he sat now, waiting in a silent torment, for her judgment. And a great humility rushed over Mary Valentine. An ache came in the hollow of her throat. And somehow—she herself did not know how—she had taken both his hands.

"I'm talking the same way," she said, "for you and God to hear me; and I swear that I'll never believe harm of you, Jess Dreer."

He raised her hands suddenly to his face; her finger tips touched hot, pounding pulses in his temples; and his hands were quivering.

"God bless you!" he said.

Was it possible that he had kissed her hands?

"For eight years I've been riding on a lone trail," said Jess Dreer. "I've had the spur dug into me for eight years. And a spur leaves scars. And now, for the first time, I've reached a stopping place."

"If you can stay," she was whispering, "oh, Jess, we'll find a way to clear you!"

"Girl, you don't know men! But wherever I may go on the outtrail, night and morning, I'll send my thoughts back to you."

"Are you going? No, no! Not yet. I have something to say—I—"

She could not finish the sentence.

"But if you should ever need me; then send for me. I'm a gambler, as I've said. And they's a string of places through the mountains where they know me. In Salt Springs they's one. Dan Carrol knows me, and he can get word to me wherever I am—by underground wires. Good-by."

"Not yet, Jess."

"It ain't right for me to stay. Is there something troubling you, girl?"

At length she said: "Go now; quickly."

He stared at her in wonder. She stood erect; her face was buried in her hands. And then Jess Dreer slipped down from the window.

Afterward, she cried out, or thought she cried out, but

he did not turn again. After a while she saw him pass on Angelina over the top of the hill, and across the moon.

CHAPTER 14

Next to the rooster in the chicken yards, the cook is generally the first living thing to waken on a ranch. Even during the short nights and long days of early summer he is in his kitchen while the dawn is still chilly and gray. But on the ranch of Morgan Valentine there was always one person up even before the cook began to rattle at the lids of his big stove, and that person was the owner. He was like one of those old-fashioned skippers who keeps only one eye closed even during the dogwatch. Usually Morgan Valentine employed the early hour in a walk among the ranch buildings. He enjoyed that morning stroll while the light grew brighter and brighter on the mountaintops and the mists became thin in the lower valleys. Each day he watched his big domain unroll before his eye, and the first pride of the possessor flowed back upon him.

But this morning he went into the living room and knocked up a fire over the coals which remained from the night before. It burned poorly. There were charred ends of logs from which the smoldering heat had been eating the life all night, and now they glowed like charcoal, but would not flame. A thick smoke rose toward the chimney, and some of it rolled out and curled around the mantelpiece and filled the room with pungent scent.

Morgan Valentine remained hanging over this dreary blaze. A man, if fifty, is generally fat enough to content himself with the present, but when he turns back to the past, it is dangerous. And Valentine was thinking of the past. There had been something in Jess Dreer which made him reminiscent of the days when he and his brother became empire builders in this valley. Sitting before the fire, the rancher recalled how the tall man had sat back in the shadow and watched the others with bright, uneasy eyes. Like a wild animal, thought Valentine, which has come out of the night, and even in captivity carries with it an air of the freedom of the outer spaces.

That was the thing which tormented him. Jess Dreer was free. Free and penniless, no doubt, but freedom was worth poverty. Here was he, the rich man, tied down by his wealth. What had it brought him except an unloved wife and children who were hardly more than names to him? To Jess Dreer the whole mountain desert was synonymous with the word "home."

There was something infinitely attractive to Valentine in the character of the outlaw. There was an honesty—if that word could be used with a thief—that drew the rancher as he had never been drawn before to any man except his dead brother.

Someone was coughing in the hall; he recognized his wife even before she appeared in the door.

"Why, Morgan, I thought the house was on fire," she said, and straightway she went to a window and opened it. "The house was that full of smoke," she added, coughing again.

He returned no answer to this, but kicked the log fragments again, and this time a yellow tongue of fire leaped out and hung for a moment quivering in the mist of smoke as though it had a life of its own. After that, the blaze began, and the smoke diminished. There had been a touch of irritation in that kick at the smoldering wood, but now he was able to turn his usual calm face toward his wife.

"You look kind of tired," he said kindly.

"How could I look any other way after last night?"

"Bear up for a little while, Mother. Mary is leaving in a few days and then you can have a long rest."

Maude Valentine regarded her husband critically. She had studied this silent man with profound attention for many years and knew less about him now than she had at the beginning.

"I been thinking something," she said slowly, and folded her hands before her. "After Mary goes, every time you miss her, you'll look to me and be angry."

"I'm never angry, Mother."

At this a little spot of color came up in each cheek.

"I wish you'd talk straight out to me once in a while, Morgan. I wish you'd talk man talk to me now and then."

He shrugged his shoulders, but she went on in spite of this danger sign: "Even if you was to storm at me, Morgan, I'd like it better than—this!"

"I try to be kind, Mother."

"Kind?" she said. "Kind?" And there was a breathless little check in her voice. It suddenly occurred to the man that she was acting as if she had been enduring for a long time and had now reached the limit of her strength. He braced himself with that chilly feeling in his back which a man usually has when he faces the hysteria of a woman.

"Well," she said at length, so calmly that his nerves gradually began to relax, "we won't talk any more about her. We'll talk about—you, Morgan."

And she made a step toward him as timid as a girl approaching her new lover who has not yet completed his avowal. Now and then a sort of youthful beauty would flush across this middle-aged woman's face.

"Just now," said he, "I'd kind of like to talk about her. You ain't apt to admire her, Mother, but you got to admit that what she did last night was pretty fine."

Maude Valentine blinked.

"Fine?" she gasped. "Getting a murdering outlaw away from a sheriff. Fine?"

"Two sheriffs," corrected her husband grimly.

"Are you laughing at me, Morgan?"

"I mean, she took a bad job off my hands, Mother."

"Off your hands?"

"Would you of had me let them take my guest under my roof, when he come here by my invitation?"

She found no ready answer to this, but nevertheless she instinctively shook her head.

"If it hadn't been for Mary, I'd of had to stand back to back with that Jess Dreer and fought 'em off."

He sighed.

"I think we'd of cleaned 'em up. Then it would of meant that I'd be riding this minute beside Jess Dreer on the long outtrail, no matter where it takes him, and every man's hand agin' us. That's what it would of meant."

"Morgan, I actually believe that you almost regret it!"

"Sometimes—I dunno. But it's Mary that's kept me here."

"Ah, but you don't look down deep and get the reasons why she done it, dear. Do you know what they were?"

"Well?"

She bore the patient, neglectful tone.

"Because she saw that Dreer was paying a lot of attention to Elizabeth. She was not being talked to. She was jealous! That's the whole fact of it!"

"Maude," said her husband after a moment of silence, "here comes the sheriffs. Maybe you better meet 'em and make 'em at home."

At that, she regretted what she had said, for she saw the mouth of Morgan Valentine setting in a way she knew very well. But he had closed the conversation too definitely and pointedly for her to attempt to reopen it.

The sheriffs were at least good losers. They made only laughing comments on their futile chase of Jess Dreer the night before. And they kept up the same cheery talk all during the breakfast. When Mary Valentine came down with Elizabeth beside her, they neither frowned at the girl who had broken through their trap nor openly reproached her. If anyone were estranged by the events of the night before, it seemed, oddly enough, to be the three women. For Elizabeth studiously avoided the eye of Mary and paid strict attention to eating, and as for Maude Valentine, it seemed that her niece was not in the room for all the attention that she paid her.

Charlie and Louis were full of open admiration for the manner in which the outlaw had broken through.

"But it must of been a lucky shot that he got in," said Charlie. "It ain't hardly likely that it was aimed, the shot that dropped Sam."

"D'you see where it hit him?" asked Sheriff John Caswell, raising his head at this point in the conversation.

"Clean through the thigh. He'll be on his feet ag'in inside three weeks and riding after Jess Dreer."

At this the sheriff smiled pityingly.

"Son," he said, "Claney tells me you're kind of handy with a gun yourself; but you fasten onto this. If Dreer had wanted to kill Sam he would of done it. That *was* an aimed shot, son. And don't make no mistake."

"But it was night, Mr. Caswell, and besides, he was on a galloping hoss."

"Sure he was, but all Dreer needs is enough light to see what he's shooting at. He's a snap shot, son, and he shoots with a gun the way other men point with their finger. No, sir; he planted that shot on purpose not to kill Sam, but to drop him off'n his hoss. And here's another thing. Sam won't take the trail after Jess as soon as he can ride a hoss ag'in. Not him! It's a queer thing, but them that's ever faced Jess don't generally have any hankering to see him ag'in. And them that's seen him swing a gun jest natcherally lose all appetite for seeing the same show all over ag'in."

"But you've been on the trail a long time, Sheriff," said Charlie.

"It's different with me, son. I'll tell you how it is. Jess Dreer has made a fool out of me more times than you can count on your two fingers. And I don't mind much of anything except to have a man laugh at me. Well, they's been other men take after Jess that was a heap smarter men than I'll ever be, and they's been some that was faster fighters and straighter shots. Jess has fooled 'em all. He may keep right on fooling me, but he'll never shake me off'n his trail. I stay there till I come up with him and one of us goes down. I ain't fast, I ain't smart, but I'm a tolerable patient man, son. Tolerable patient!"

For some reason there was little talk at the breakfast table after this moment.

CHAPTER 15

It was the patient man who said to Sheriff Claney of Salt Springs, a little later: "Claney, have you been looking around over the ground this morning?"

"What ground, Caswell?"

"Around the house, where Dreer got away."

"Yep. I ran over a little of the sign."

"What'd you think about it?"

"It was all pretty clear reading, I thought. I seen the place where he dropped out of the window and camped

84

for a minute waiting, before he whistled to that hoss of his, that Angelina you're always talking about."

"I'll tell you something then, pardner. They's some new sign this morning. Something added on top of what they was last night. I seen where that long-stepping Angelina went away—and I seen where she come back."

"Dreer came back?"

"Unless that hoss traveled alone, which ain't likely, I'd say."

Sheriff Claney cursed fluently.

"He come back to the house, with you and me inside it?"

"Yep, with you and me inside it, asleep. And he didn't only come back and look things over. He come back and went inside the house."

Claney gasped. "Are you sure?"

"Positive certain. And now, Claney, I think my hard work is over."

"How comes that?"

"It's the first time that ever Dreer took a back step on a trail. It's the first time that ever he took a useless chance. What was they for him to gain by coming back here?"

"Nothing except to sass us."

"Dreer wouldn't even sass a two-year-old kid. It means that he ain't the same man that he used to be. It means that he ain't working alone. Well, Claney, you know it's a hundred times easier to catch two men that travels together than it is to catch one."

"I don't foller you, pardner."

"I don't mean that they's really another man with Jess Dreer. What I mean is that he's found something in this house that he came back to. And I'd even talk up and say what it is."

"Well?"

"It's the black-haired girl, I figure."

"And if he come back to her once, he'll come back to her ag'in. It's his nature."

"Soft on women?"

"Never looked twice at one before, so far as I know. That's why I'm sure that this means something. Dreer has played a lone hand, but now that he's got somebody besides himself to think about, he's lost. Claney, you write this down in red and remember it. As sure as they's rain and sunshine, I'm going to get Jess Dreer, and where I get him ain't going to be far away from this house."

"You're going to camp here and wait for him to come back?" asked Claney, smiling.

"I'm going to camp near here," replied the sheriff from the southland, "and I'm going to wait. Time and the black-haired girl, Claney, will win for me in the end."

And the two men parted.

It happened that at this moment Charlie Valentine and his brother Louis were standing on the veranda together and overlooking this scene.

"What beats me," said Charlie, "is the idea of a gent like this Caswell taking a crack at Jess Dreer. Why, big Dreer would bust him in two with one hand."

"I dunno," replied Louis in his mild way, "they's something about Caswell. Speaking personal, I'd sort of hate to have him on my trail."

"That's another one of your hunches," Charlie said in good-natured banter. And they watched the two sheriffs ride side by side up the road.

They had hardly disappeared around the hill when another horseman galloped into view from the opposite direction.

"It's Tom Waite," said Charlie Valentine after a moment.

"How d'you tell?" asked his brother.

"By the way he rides, slanting. They ain't anybody has the same seat as Tommy."

"Well," murmured Louis, "I'll tell you another thing. Tom Waite is bringing us bad news."

"And how d'you tell that?"

Louis Valentine scratched his head.

"I dunno, Charlie. Look at the way he keeps his head down and the brim of his hat blowing across his eyes. Take a gent that's just riding, and he'd be riding with his head up. But Tom comes as if he was trying to get away from something behind him."

His brother looked askance at Louis. He constantly felt his superiority as the better fighter, stronger man, sharper wit; but all of these qualities were being continually discounted by a singular power in Louis. It might have been called second sight, these odd premonitions. It often made him laughed at, ridiculed; but there was an undercurrent of respect for the superstitions of the youngest Valentine. For instance, though he was a capable broncobuster, he had been known several times to refuse positively to mount a horse considered by no means dangerous; and it had been noted, on these occasions, that the horse was exceedingly apt to develop a bad streak after Louis Valentine refused to take the saddle. Not that Louis was considered a prophet, but he was widely known as "a gent that's got hunches."

Accordingly, Charlie looked sidewise at his younger brother on this day and frowned uneasily. Indeed, the prophecy was instantly verified, for Tom Waite ran up the steps and came to a panting halt before them. He wasted no words.

"Charlie, you're going to Salt Springs tomorrow?"

"Yep. To get that saddle I won at the bucking contest last month."

"Then lemme give you some advice. Keep away from Salt Springs tomorrow. Keep right here at home. It ain't healthy for you to go into town."

The brothers exchanged significant glances, but Louis showed no pleasure at seeing his "hunch" come true.

"Talk sharp, Tom," said the elder of the Valentine boys. "What's up?"

"The Normans are up," replied Tom Waite, drawing his first easy breath after the ride and the run up the steps.

"That news ain't altogether news."

"Not about the Normans at the ranch, but now they's another twist to things."

"Go ahead. Are they going to mob me when I come in?"

"Some say that the Normans was thinking of that very thing, but they found out mighty quick that around Salt Springs we wouldn't stand for any crowd jumping on one man. No matter what you've done, Charlie—and between you and me they's a good many think you're too free with a gun play—but no matter what you've done, it's always been man to man, a clean break, and a fair chance all around."

"Thanks, Tommy."

"Oh, I'm with you, solid enough; and they's a lot more of us younger gents that's all behind you. But with some of the older men it's different. They figure that you've got a lesson coming, or something like that. The long and short of it is, Charlie, that if somebody was to jump you single-handed, they wouldn't be many men that would go out to help you."

"Thanks again," remarked Charlie coldly. "I don't ask for no help agin' one man, Tommy."

At this, the young fellow shook his head.

"They's men and men," he said, with a probably quoted wisdom. "Stack you up agin' a common kind of fighter, and you'd come off first rate. But they's some that makes a business of fighting. Even with most of them you'd have a good chance, Charlie, because you've got a good idea of the hang of a gun. You shoot fast, and you shoot straight. You got plenty of nerve, too. But they's some you wouldn't have a chance agin'. And the Normans have found a gent like that."

"What's his name? What's the name of this pet murderer of theirs?" asked Charlie, sneering, but a little white about the lips.

"Hired murderer is the right thing to call him," said Tom Waite. "And his name is Jud Boone!"

He paused, expectant, and the results were not such as would disappoint him. The pallor which had begun on the face of Charlie now swept completely over it. Yet he maintained a steady front while Louis Valentine, as though it were he whom the danger threatened, fairly collapsed against the railing of the veranda and stared at Tom Waite.

For the name of Jud Boone was far known and known as a man of evil. A fighter and gamester by instinct and profession, he was one of those men about whose past few know many details, but regarding whom there is a general murmur of suspicion. One death near Salt Springs was charged already to his account, but that one killing was the sort whose mention would strike a whole circle of men silent.

"Seems he's some sort of relation to the Normans, and they've looked him up. I suppose they've paid him a bunch of money. Anyway, there's gossip around the town that the plan is for Jud Boone to be somewheres around Carrol's saloon when you go in there for the saddle. And then, of course, he'll pick a fight. So the thing for you to do is to stay home, Charlie."

The latter stood motionless. Plainly he was badly frightened, but he had not yet made up his mind. It seemed that Louis was in fear of some rash decision.

"Don't be a fool, now," he pleaded. "Do what Tommy says!"

"I dunno," muttered Charlie. "I know I got no chance agin' a man like Jud Boone. But—since folks expect me to be in Salt Springs tomorrow—if I stay home—"

"Folks will say you got good sense, that's all."

"I got to see Dad about that," replied Charlie.

He led the others into the house, and finding his father, he related to him briefly the news which Tom Waite had brought. In the distance Mrs. Valentine heard and said nothing save with her eyes.

CHAPTER 16

"First thing," said Morgan Valentine, when the story was completed, "is this: How d'you feel about it yourself, Charlie?"

His son was disturbed and showed it.

"I dunno," he said cautiously, and he watched his father with troubled eye. "Point is, if I don't go in, folks maybe will think I'm afraid of Jud Boone."

"You'd be a fool if you weren't," answered his father. "I know Jud Boone. I've seen him work. I'm afraid of him myself."

"Then you think I'm right to stay home?" And Charlie sighed, immensely relieved.

"I leave it to you," said his father with his usual unperturbed manner. "When it comes to life and death, every man is his own best judge."

"If he was an ordinary kind of man," complained Charlie, "I'd take a chance as quick as anybody. But a professional murderer—" He shuddered. "You say you're afraid of him, and I guess it ain't wrong for me to say the same thing."

"All right, son. You stay here tomorrow, and I'll go in and get the saddle for you."

"Dad, if you go, they'll most likely take it out on you!"

"Most likely they'd try to."

"And you've already said that you wouldn't like to meet Jud Boone."

"I wouldn't like to, but I'd do it."

Silence fell on the group. Charlie Valentine moistened his colorless lips.

"I'll tell you something," went on the father in his calm manner, which had now a deadly interest for the younger men. "One time my brother John got mixed up with a ruffian in the early days."

He paused to collect his thoughts, and the hush upon the others became deeper; for when Morgan Valentine, once in a year, mentioned the name of his brother, it became a breathless moment.

"I forget the name of the gun fighter. He was a gent with his notches in his gun—and he was the kind that talked about 'em. Well, John crossed him. The gunman was drunk, and he was too clever to fight while he was drunk. He waited till he was all sobered up and then he sent word to John that he was waiting for him.

"I was with John when the news came.

"Well, John waited for an hour or so, thinking. Then he sat down and wrote out his will as good as any lawyer could have done. Then he climbed on his horse and went down to the town. I tried to go with him, but he wouldn't let me.

"He didn't come back that night. I waited until dark and then I follered him. When I come to town, it was full of the fight. John had met the gunman, and the gunman had beat him to the draw. He knocked John down with the first bullet through the shoulder—the left shoulder. And while he lay on the floor, he shot John again, and the bullet ripped up the flesh along his ribs. But John lay there and lifted his own gun, slow, took a good aim, and then he fired. That bullet went through the gunman's heart."

There was a pause, but no one spoke, for it was evident from the lifted, tense face of Morgan Valentine that he would speak again.

At length: "When I see John, he was pretty badly done up. He took my hand. 'Thank Heaven it's over, Morgan,' he says to me. I says: 'John, it was a glorious thing to do. The whole town is talking about how brave you are.'

" 'It wasn't bravery. It was fear,' says John. 'I was afraid of that fellow as if he was death. But I'm more afraid of shame than I am of death.'

"I ain't asking you to follow the example of John, Charlie. I'm simply showing you the way one man faced the same sort of thing that you've got to face."

Charlie was white, as though the bullet of Jud Boone had already pierced him.

"All right," he said huskily, "then I'll—"

"Don't make up your mind now," said his father gently. "Go off and sit down by yourself and think it over. If you go into Salt Springs, you'll meet Jud Boone. If you meet him, the chances are one out of four that you'll kill him and four to one that he'll kill you. You're a young man, Charlie. You got a lot of things ahead of you. It's hard to pay that price. But keep this thing in your head, too. That if you don't meet Jud Boone, the time may come, sooner or later, when you'll have another thing to face. It may be different. And when that time comes, you may say to yourself, 'Is it worth it? Is what people may say about me worth the money that I'll have to pay to keep my name clean?' And you may remember how you kept away from Jud Boone and then lived down the shame of it. But go off by yourself and think this thing out."

He left them, and the moment he was gone, Mrs. Valentine, staggering, ran to her oldest son.

"You ain't going to go, Charlie. Oh, tell me you ain't going to go?"

He pushed her away, almost rudely.

"You take my nerve when you talk like that," he said. "Gimme a chance to play the man, Mother! Gimme a chance to think it over!"

He went his way, and Mrs. Valentine, after standing a moment with her hands clasped, looking after him, cast a frantic glance over Tom Waite and Louis, and then hurried from the room.

She had remembered that source of comfort which had many times aided her in her problems with advice keen and to the point even if it came out of a younger head. In a word, she went to the room of Mary Valentine, and there she found not only Mary, but her daughter Elizabeth. They had been laughing together, whispering over some small secret. They started up at the sight of the smaller woman. Mrs. Valentine hardly saw her daughter.

"Mary," she said, "I've got to see you alone."

And Mary took Elizabeth to the door and then faced her aunt, turning slowly and nerving herself as if for a shock. Not that there was an actual anger existing between the two, but each was from a separate world, and they always looked on one another as from a distance. Mary, now, was forcing a faint smile of interest, but Mrs. Valentine was too distressed to even pretend to disguise her emotion.

"Like as not," she said, and her voice was softer than her words were bitter, "like as not Elizabeth has been telling you things that only her mother should know."

"I give you my word, Aunt Maude, that if there were anything really important about it, I'd tell you myself."

The wan smile of Aunt Maude had no mirth in it.

"It's the same with Elizabeth as it is with the boys. You come first, Mary. And you come first with—Morgan—I think."

"Hush! Hush! What are you saying?"

"A man likes spirit. Decision. All the things that you have and that I haven't."

"Aunt Maude!"

"It's true. You see, I've watched and understood. They come to me just to be around. But when it's a big happiness or maybe a secret or maybe a sorrow—then they go to you. As if they felt I couldn't hold a big thing."

"I'm only a shock absorber. I simply take the shock of silly things that would bother you."

"Ah, Mary," said Mrs. Valentine, and she made a singular gesture of drawing imperceptible things toward her heart. "Don't you know that a mother wants to be troubled by them that she loves? You'll know someday, Mary. The treasures of a woman are the troubles that her family bring to her. It's her secret life. I've got no such life, Mary! They pass by me. They go to you!"

Mary Valentine watched the head of her aunt bow with grief. She made a little movement as though she would go to her and strive to cherish her, but the movement was checked. Between the two was a barrier which even the smiles of Mary and all her ways could not break down.

"I don't complain," said her aunt faintly. "After all, I suppose it's the call of blood to blood. You're a Valentine —and I'm just about—nothing. I'm on the outside.

"But I haven't come to rake up old troubles. I dunno

why I always say these things to you, Mary. You've been fair and square to me, honey. You've never gone about behind my back. You've never repeated things. You've never tried to make bad blood between me and the rest. And Lord knows you could of done it many's the time. They ain't a small part about you, Mary. And—and now I've come the way Elizabeth comes to you, and the way Morgan comes to you, and the way Charlie and Louis come to you. I've come to ask for your help, Mary!"

After what she had said before, there could not have been a sadder confession.

"It's about Charlie. The old trouble that started over Joe Norman. Now the Normans have hired Jud Boone, and he's going to lay for Charlie when Charlie goes into Salt Springs to get the prize saddle tomorrow."

"Then it all comes back to me. It was for my sake that Charlie fought Joe Norman."

"But I'm not casting that in your face. I'm only asking you what we can do, Mary."

"Sit down. You're all of a tremble. Sit down—here—let me hold your hands. Is that better?"

"Yes. You sort of steady me, Mary."

"I'll tell you what we must do. We must keep Charlie at home."

"I thought of that. Everybody thought of that first thing. But—Morgan won't have it that way."

"His own father!"

"He says it's better to die than to be shamed."

"Ah, that sounds like him! But—I'll go and try to persuade him."

At this, Aunt Maude winced.

"You could always do more with him than anybody else could, Mary. But this time you can't budge Morgan. Because he's following an example."

"Whose?"

"Your father's, dear."

The girl was silent.

"But you'll try to think of something to do, Mary? You'll try to find some way to keep Charlie from Jud Boone? Ain't there anybody among all the men you know that would help Charlie? You could ask someone—Morgan wouldn't lift his finger to get help."

Mary Valentine sat very stiff and straight in her chair and stared fixedly at her window, as though she saw a ghost forming against the bright rectangle.

"I've thought of a thing to do," she said at last. "It won't be easy. Maybe it won't work. But—I'll try!"

CHAPTER 17

Silence lay over the house of Morgan Valentine. No one had asked Charlie for his ultimate decision, but Louis stole down to the family that afternoon and reported that Charlie was in his room upstairs working busily over two revolvers, oiling them, cleaning them, testing their balance with nervous care.

That report was more forcible than the most violent affirmation, on the part of young Valentine, of his determination to face Jud Boone and fight him man to man. Even the hand of Morgan Valentine was unsteady as he lighted his pipe. His wife had dropped her head upon her hands with a moan; and Elizabeth cried out.

One would have thought that a death had been announced.

But as for Mary, she still turned in her mind the gambling chance which she had determined to take. It was no less than a purpose of leaving the house and going to Salt Springs to speak with Dan Carrol and through him send to the outlaw, Jess Dreer, an appeal for help.

Yet it was not easy to do this. If she stated that she wished to go to town, some one of the family would accompany her; and if she wished to see Dan Carrol, questions would certainly be asked. For the repute of Carrol was a sooty thing and contaminated all who touched him. Even if she slipped away during the day and reached Salt Springs unknown to the family, it would be impossible to see Carrol without letting half of Salt Springs know to whom she made her visit. Not that she really cared what public opinion murmured about her, but if her visit were a public matter, there was very little chance that Carrol would tell her where she could find Jess Dreer.

It was a trip that must be completed between dark and dawn, and for this she laid her plans.

One thing favored her. The family did not sit up late in the living room, for it was a gloomy matter to stare from face to face and read in each eye the same foreboding which filled one's own mind. Mrs. Valentine, close to tears, was the first to leave. Then Charlie, who had remained white-faced, sullenly defiant, apparently decided that he dare not risk the complete breakdown of his nerves. He rose, muttered his good night huskily, and hurried from the room.

The others trooped away one by one, leaving Morgan Valentine alone beside the fire. The report of Louis had made him show one touch of emotion, but neither before nor since had he appeared to be in the slightest degree concerned.

As soon as she was in her room, Mary hurried into her riding clothes before she put out the light and crept into bed. For she feared that visitors might come. And they did. First, Elizabeth. And then Mrs. Valentine came in and leaned over her. But when she heard the regular breathing, she apparently decided that the girl was asleep. She leaned and touched Mary's forehead with her lips and then stole from the room.

Mary was deeply moved, for it had been years since her aunt had showed any true affection. And when, a little after this, the house was quiet, she got up, pressed her hat on her head, and slipped out by the rear of the house. Five minutes later she was speeding down the road on her sturdy little Morgan mare, docile as a pet dog and durable as leather.

Midnight brought her to Salt Springs, with the dust of the street squirting up around the hoofs of the mare. She rode on between the rows of black, silent houses until she was close to Carrol's place. Then she swung her horse between two dwellings and came out directly in the rear of the big saloon.

The midnight of Salt Springs was the noon of Dan Carrol. His saloon burst with light and voices, and through the open windows, across the shafts of light, clouds of tobacco smoke rose, cut briefly away by the darkness.

But how could she come to Dan Carrol?

A man came to the screen door at the rear of the building and opened it. She saw the faint arc of light as he tossed his cigarette butt away.

"Halloo!" called Mary, roughening her voice. "Send Danny out to me, will you?"

"Can't you walk?" cried the man, who apparently did not recognize the voice of a woman. "Go get him yourself, son."

She waited. A skulking figure slipped out of the darkness and hurried across the open toward the gaming house. She reined her mare across and touched his shoulder with her quirt. At that, the man leaped sidewise, very agile. He was a small fellow.

"Pardner," said Mary, "I've got a word to say to Dan Carrol. Will you take it in to him?"

"Me?" said a harsh, shrill voice, the voice of a Chinaman. "Dan Carrol?"

"Never mind," and she reined her horse back, for she had recognized the accent of Kong Li, her father's cook.

This was the explanation, then, of Kong's periods of sudden affluence and sudden poverty. But now the little man followed her.

"Never mind," she repeated. "I don't need you!"

"Miss Mary," said the Chinaman, whining his astonishment. "Miss Mary!"

She writhed in the saddle. To be recognized in full daylight would have been bad enough; but to be recognized at the door of Carrol's gaming house and saloon in the middle of night was infinitely worse.

"Listen to me, Kong Li," she said fiercely. "I have to see Dan Carrol. I want you to see that he's brought out here, but I don't want you to tell him my name before any other man. Understand?"

"I savvy."

"And if you ever tell anyone that I've been here—I—I'll tie you by your queue to the limb of a tree till you starve to death, Kong Li. Understand?"

"I savvy," said Kong, and he shuddered. It was not the first time in her life that Mary had threatened him, and he considered her quite capable of anything she named.

"But," he murmured, "Dan Carrol very bad man, Miss Mary."

"Don't I know that? I'll take care of myself. You hurry along."

He hesitated a moment longer, but dread of Miss

Mary's tongue at length made him whirl and shuffle away toward the gaming house. At the door he paused and looked back again, but he went on, the screen door banging loudly behind him.

There followed a long pause. Her mind filled up the vacancy of Kong Li approaching the table of the gambler, touching his arm, and being cursed for a no-good chink. But eventually there was a sound of scuffling, the screen door burst violently open, and Kong Li leaped from the lighted interior into the darkness, sprawling, his arms and legs stretched out before him, and the pigtail whipped straight out behind.

Dan Carrol sprang into the doorway and poured a hurricane of abuse and profanity after his victim while Kong Li darted by, crying to Mary as he passed: "Bad man! Very bad man, Miss Mary!"

"Mr. Carrol!" called the girl, guarding her voice.

Carrol fell silent; at the very sound of the voice he had touched the hat which was never off his head. Now he stepped cautiously outside. There were a hundred men who would have welcomed a chance to shoot Carrol securely, by night.

"Who's there?"

She rode close to him.

"I suppose you know me; but my name really doesn't matter. I've come on important business, Mr. Carrol."

Slowly he took off his hat and spun it in his hands; she could feel his astonishment even though darkness quite covered his face.

"You're Mary Valentine!"

"Hush! I'm Mary Valentine. I want you to tell me where to find Jess Dreer. Can you?"

The gambler started, drew back, and then stepped close to the horse.

"How should I know Jess Dreer?" he muttered very softly. "You mean the outlaw?"

"He said you did."

Carrol drew in his breath with a hissing sound.

"Dreer said that?"

"He did."

"Well—he lied. That's straight talk, and it's true. What would I be doing with Dreer, eh?"

"He's a man whom I am proud to know," said the girl. "Does that make it any easier for you to talk?"

"Listen," said Carrol. "The gent that knows where Jess Dreer is can take down several thousand for telling the sheriff. They's a price on him that would stock a ranch."

"That," said she, "is the reason why he can't trust any except men who are above money, Mr. Carrol. Will you tell me where he is?"

"Did he say I was above money?" asked the gambler curiously, after a pause.

"He didn't. But he said you could send me to him. And I infer the rest of it."

"You infer too much. I can't do it."

"I thought that perhaps you couldn't. So I've written out what I have to say to him. I have it here in this envelope. If I give it to you, do you think that you could get it to Jess Dreer?"

"I don't know nothing about him."

"Of course you don't." She extended the letter. "But maybe you'd keep it for him on the chance that he might call in someday?"

"I don't know anything about him," repeated the gambler, "but if you ask me to keep this for you—why, I'll hang onto it."

"Thank you, and—good night. One thing, Mr. Carrol. I haven't seen you tonight."

"Lady, the gent that was to say that you'd seen me tonight would have to chew up his talk and swaller it ag'in. Good night, and good luck!"

And he remained standing with his hat in his hand until she was gone into the darkness with a quick patter of hoofs.

CHAPTER 18

In the days of his youth, someone in the midst of a barroom brawl had stood on Dan Carrol's nose, and the result was that the rest of his life it remained sadly crushed in the center. The nostrils flared out disagreeably from the same cause, over a wide, thin-lipped, sinister mouth and just such a jaw as brings admiration to the bull terrier. For Dan Carrol was the fighting type. Not brawny. But his body made up for flesh by bones and sinews. When he turned his head, the cords stood out on his neck. In spite of his little more than average weight, there were tales of Dan Carrol performing prodigious feats of strength.

In fact, he rarely used a gun in the brawls that often developed in his barroom, but was far more apt to trust to his naked hands. And it was known that more than one obstreperous drunkard, no matter what his size, had been lifted and swung crashing through the swinging doors of Dan's domain.

He was not a pretty man to look at. Aside from his ugly face, his shoulders sloped forward so as to give an unhealthy look to his chest, and he was remarkably bowlegged.

"When most kids was flat on their backs sucking their

thumbs," Dan used to say, "I was on my feet trying to get places. That's how it come I overstrained my legs."

Dan's moral character was as deformed as his body. But it would require a book by itself to deal with his past; and as for the name of Dan Carrol in Salt Springs, it was an offense. However, so long as no one aired his opinion in the hearing of Dan Carrol, he was indifferent to private judgments. He was known to run the squarest game in Salt Springs and to sell the cleanest liquor; and for that reason his prosperity waxed and his purse grew fat.

As he passed through the rooms with the letter stuffed into his hip pocket, someone hailed him to rejoin the game which he had just left, but he consigned them to another table and went on. To the second story of his rambling building he climbed and came to a room in the rear with this sign in great letters upon it: "Storeroom. Keep out!"

Upon this he tapped—three short taps, a pause, and then three more.

Whereupon, after a moment's pause, but with no preliminary sound of the knob being turned, the door was opened swiftly.

There was no sign of an occupant, at first, though the storeroom was fitted up as a bedroom, and the cigarette smoke was still curling slowly from an ash tray toward the shaded lamp. But as Dan Carrol stepped in, the inhabitant, who had been standing directly behind the door, now closed it and turned to his host. It was Jess Dreer.

"Neat little trick, that," said Dan Carrol.

"Sit down," Jess invited.

"I ain't got a minute. I been wondering if you was getting lonely up here?"

"Me? I'm never lonely. Besides, I hear the boys soaking up the laughter and the booze downstairs, and I enjoy a jag at second hand. It's cheaper, and it don't give you no morning after."

"That's the first economical thing I ever heard you say. Well, Jess, it's a shame you can't pry your way downstairs and take in some of the loose coin. It's floating in in oceans. I hate to take it away. They come up and pour it into my pockets."

"I don't have to play with the crowd," murmured Jess. "I got it down to a finer system. You take the stuff from the boys, and then I get it from you. Nothing easier or simpler, Dan."

The face of the gambler clouded, and he cast an expressive glance at the table as though it recalled gloomy scenes to him.

"You got all the luck," he declared, "that a man was ever born with."

"Nope," said Jess. "I work on a system."

"What?" His eyes gleamed while he asked.

"I wait for a hunch and then plunge to the limit."

The gambler leaned back with a growl of disgust.

"Well, if you're all right up here, I'll go back."

"Go ahead. But, first, ain't you forgetting something?"

Dan Carrol squinted narrowly at his friend, for of all the men in the world he would, perhaps, have named Jess Dreer first in this capacity.

"What d'you mean?" he asked sharply.

"I mean, ain't you forgot the thing that brought you up here? Talk short. What's up?"

"A girl come here and wanted to see you, Jess."

"She's here?" cried the big man in an indescribable tone.

"She was here."

"Carrol, you turned her away?"

There was something so sinister in his manner, so quietly grim, that the gambler gave back a little.

"Pardner, would you have wanted me to bring her in? Where a dozen men might have seen her? Where they'd been a hundred chances for folks to start talking about her? This ain't no ladies' seminary where they can come calling, is it?"

At this, Jess Dreer wiped his forehead.

"You're right."

"She gimme this letter for you, Jess."

He extended the letter, and then—a rare act of delicacy —lest he should see an unwonted emotion in the face of the big man, Carrol bowed his head and left the room without another glance at his guest.

But Jess Dreer, when the door closed, stood for a long moment with the letter unopened. At length, nervously, he ripped the envelope open and shook out the folded paper. He read:

DEAR JESS DREER: I thought at the time that it was not a farewell, but I never dreamed that I would have to remember your offer. And now I have to come to you for help. I have thought and thought, but there is really nobody else. Others might be willing to try, but you are the only one who could accomplish it.

It is an ugly thing out of my past. I hurt the feelings of young Joe Norman; and he said something indiscreet about me, and my cousin, Charlie Valentine, shot him—only a slight wound. The Normans were furious. They had no one to put up against Charlie, so they hunted until they found a professional fighter —the low cowards!—and that man is the notorious Jud Boone. Charlie has to go to Salt Springs tomorrow for a saddle he won in the bucking contest, and the plan as we hear it is for Jud Boone to meet him and bring on a fight.

What can I do? You see that Charlie is really in grave danger for my sake, for it all began with me. If I were a man—but I'm not a man, and I have to turn to the bravest and strongest man I know, and appeal to Jess Dreer for help.

Can you stop Jud Boone before he murders Charlie?

MARY VALENTINE.

CHAPTER 19

The whole theory of Dreer's strategy in remaining in Salt Springs was the theory of the rabbit which cowers in a hole while the hunters sweep on along the probable trail. But if the rabbit raises its head before the hunt has driven by, its trick is worse than useless—it is suicidal. And if Jess Dreer, while half a dozen headhunters were scouring distant mountains around Salt Springs in pursuit of him, should appear in the center of danger he would be fully in the role of the silly rabbit.

Yet he was called upon to act, and from the first moment of that call he had not the slightest hesitancy. The only question was: how he should strike at Jud Boone.

One possibility presented itself at once. Aside from the people on the Valentine ranch, and they would not be apt to be in Salt Springs, there was only one man who was apt to recognize him, and that was the sheriff of the southland —Caswell. Suppose, therefore, that he boldly walked into the bar of Carrol's saloon at the time when Charlie Valentine arrived for the saddle, and if matters reached a crisis, stepped between Charlie and danger. The repute of Jud Boone had reached his ears even in the distant south, yet he was perfectly willing to take a chance against the bad man. The thing that troubled him was that if he entered into a shooting fracas with Boone, he would certainly be detained for an inquiry after the affair was over. And in that case Caswell or someone else was certain to recognize him.

It was suicidal, therefore, to face Boone in the saloon. It remained to stop him even before he entered the saloon. And that was the plan of the outlaw.

The first thing he had done when he took refuge with Carrol was to secure from the gambler a rudely sketched map of Salt Springs, the trails around it and the location, and the alleys branching from the main street, as well as the position of each house and the name of the owner— a task far from complicated. To this plan he now had reference, and having located his goal, he left his room.

It was not difficult to escape from Carrol's gambling house without attracting attention. In the first place, the men within the building were occupied with interesting affairs of their own. In the second place, there was an easy "back door" for Jess Dreer. He had only to slip from his window out onto the broad, shelving roof; along this he worked to the lowest corner over the rear of the house, and having made sure that no one was in sight, he dropped noiselessly to the ground and remained where he fell, bunched and moveless, while he examined again everything around him.

No living thing moved within range of his eye. Behind him, the gaming house still bustled softly with humming voices and the occasional clink of glasses; but all the rest of Salt Springs was gathered in a black sleep.

So he went boldly down the main street until, coming opposite the house he wanted, he walked to the front door of it and knocked. Luckily, there was someone still up even at this hour, for a light flickered yellow in an upper window.

In answer to the knock, after a moment, a window was flung up noisily. Jess Dreer stepped back from the flat face of the shack, for in spite of its two stories there was no sign of a veranda, and he could look straight up to the second level of the building. There he saw that the window had been opened in the lighted room but the occupant was not standing in view. He remained to one side, and his bulky shadow wavered across the curtain above him.

"Who's there?" he called in a rather guarded voice.

"A friend with news."

"Who d'you want to see?"

Dreer made swift calculations and then took his chance. "Why, I want to see you, Jud."

A silence. He could not tell how that announcement was taken, and yet by the change in the shadow he had no doubt that the other was striving to reconnoiter the midnight visitor and at the same time remain himself in covert. Law-abiding citizens were not apt to show such remarkable discretion, and Dreer's belief that his guess was right was growing stronger when the voice went on: "Well, and who are you that wants to see me?"

"Look down," said Jess, knowing perfectly that the other could not distinguish his face by the starlight. "Look down and you'll recognize me, Jud."

"I ain't a bat. How can I see in the dark? What's your name?"

"Don't you even know my voice?" said Jess in aggrieved tones. "Then lemme come up and surprise you, Jud."

The other did not reply for a moment. Then he reached a decision.

"Come tomorrow. Too late now. Come tomorrow."

"Whist!" Jess Dreer whispered. He stepped closer to the wall and cupped his hands about his whisper: "Tomorrow'll be too late, Jud!"

At this, the shadow swerved on the curtain; then a whisper answered.

"Come on up, pardner. The front door's open. This end of the hall—door on the right!"

So Jess Dreer entered the house and went up hurriedly over the uncarpeted stairs that creaked at every step, and down the hall until he tapped at the designated door.

"Come in," said the other.

And Jess, entering, found on the other side of the room a blocky fellow, prematurely bald, perhaps thirty-five years old, with the small, chunky hands and the little feet which often denote a man of agility. He stood beyond a little deal table, with his hands resting lightly on his hips and an expression of face and attitude which betokened the utmost readiness for action.

All of these things Jess Dreer noted with a familiar eye, and while he closed the door without turning away from the stranger, he allowed a broad grin to spread over his face. The hands of Jud Boone slipped a little farther down his thighs.

"A fake, eh?" he said grimly.

"It's the first time, Jud, that I've ever been called a fake."

"And who the devil might you be?"

"My name is something that I handle real tender. As a matter of fact, of late years every time I have to mention my name, I most generally have got to mention my gun at the same time. You know how it is?"

This amiability seemed by no means to the liking of Jud Boone. He studied his man from beneath a deepening frown, and by the twitching of his lips it was easy to tell that he was of two minds whether to pitch the stranger headlong through the door or let him continue to talk. Perhaps it was the width of the shoulders of Jess that discouraged the first notion.

"I don't know nothing," averred Jud Boone. "But I'd like to know what you want out of me."

"Talk," said Jess, helping himself to a chair by hooking a foot under it and swinging it dexterously behind him. "Talk is my prime reason for coming here, Jud."

"You know me, eh?"

"I never seen you before," said Jess, smiling again.

The face of the other grew tense for an instant. He made half a step sidewise toward the window, and then seemed to realize that he could not look out of it without relinquishing his watch upon his visitor.

"I ain't got any friends with me," said Jess. "If that's what's bothering you. I ain't got the sheriff down below waiting for me to bring you out."

"And what's any sheriff got to do with me, eh?"

"I leave that to you," said Jess with a careless gesture. But the gesture was with his left hand; the right remained resting easily upon his thigh. All of which Jud Boone took into careful consideration.

"Come short with me, stranger," he said. "What you want? I'm a tolerable peevish man, and I need sleep just now."

"I'm agreeable. What I want is a promise."

Jud Boone gasped.

"If I had my pick between a million and a nerve like yours," he declared with wondering admiration, "I dunno which I'd take. You want a promise out of me?"

"Gentleman's agreement. I want you to keep your hands off Charlie Valentine when he comes in tomorrow."

"They's been a lot of fool talk floating around this town," declared the gunman, "about what I figure on with Charlie Valentine. I ain't never seen him, and I don't never want to. But first I want to know what is the point you knife in at?"

"Jud, I'll tell you. I'll double the ante you got from the Normans. I'll give you a thousand bucks in cold cash if you just fade out of Salt Springs and make no noise."

In response, the latter merely stared with narrowed eyes.

"I see," nodded Jess. "You ain't so cheap as I figured. What's your price?"

"I dunno what you mean," declared Jud Boone, "but if I did know, I reckon I'd have to bust you in two, pardner, and throw the loose ends out the window."

"If that's the way of it," and Jess smiled, "then maybe you know enough. Think again, Jud. What's your price?"

"I'll tell you the price of a whole hide for you," said the gunfighter, "and that's to get up and back out of this joint mighty quick. I'm tired of your funny chatter, friend."

"My money don't talk?"

"It don't."

"My, my. Now you're getting real cross. But listen to reason. You get hired for one job—to bump off Valentine. But now it's a different job. You got two men on your hands."

"Meaning you're the other?"

"Meaning just that."

"And d'you think that'd stop me, pardner?"

"That's what I think." He lowered his voice to the volume of a whisper: "I'm Dreer, Jud."

CHAPTER 20

It caused an astonishing change in the face of the other. Dreer saw a desperate thought balancing in the eyes of Boone, but then the glitter died away.

It was a slow death, and for a time either fought the other with his eyes. Just as two men try grips until the hand of one weakens—crumbles. In such a manner the nerve of Jud Boone, keyed up to the point of fighting, broke and weakened. In the first moment, had Jess Dreer made the slightest motion toward a weapon, gun play would have resulted. And Dreer knew it perfectly well. His hands did not stir, but the faint sneer was stamped upon his face, and his eyes never wavered until the mouth of Jud Boone sagged open a little and his glance grew dull.

"You're Dreer?" he said huskily.

"I'm Dreer."

Jud Boone raised an uncertain hand and wiped his dry lips. Then he shrugged his shoulders and managed to chuckle.

"I might of known you," he said with an attempt at cheeriness. "As a matter of fact, I've heard old Tom Le Sand talk a pile about you. Put her there!"

He crossed the room with a swagger and extended a hand which Dreer instantly took. But on the part of Boone it was unconditional surrender, and both men knew it. Just as some promising prize fighter, who would beat an ordinary man to a pulp, is suddenly frozen to helplessness when he is placed in the ring with a champion in his class, so Boone collapsed under the eye of his companion. And he hated Dreer for his superiority.

"What I don't figure," he said, "is why you didn't tell me your name the minute you come in?"

"I knew I could trust you, Jud," the other lied smoothly, "but I've sort of formed a habit of keeping my name in the dark. Mostly, it don't do no good but a lot of harm. You know how it is?"

"Sure, sure. Have a drink?"

"I'm keeping clear of the booze. Thanks."

Jud Boone flushed and then sat down in turn. During the rest of the talk his eyes were mostly lowered, only flashing up for instants at the face of Dreer when the latter spoke.

"Now we'll talk turkey. Let's go back to the matter of the coin, Jud. I know how it is. A gent will get in a hole so that he needs a bit of coin, and—"

"Money ain't got nothing to do with it," cried Jud Boone. He writhed in his chair. "I'll tell you the straight of it. I'm busting loose from the old game, Dreer. You know me. You know I ain't been any little tin angel. But you don't have anything on me—nothing cold. They ain't a man living that could put me behind the bars!"

How many of the dead could have given that evidence, was the thought of Jess Dreer.

"And now I've found some blood kin of mine. These Normans. They want me to settle down with 'em. They need me. And if I'm to go straight, I need them. It ain't easy to go straight. A gent's past is apt to come up and turn him wrong any time. Besides—"

He choked.

"They's a girl, Jud?" suggested Jess Dreer with singular emotion.

"Maybe," admitted the other, flushing. "Here's my point: This Charlie Valentine is a bad one. He's got the makings of a gunman. He'd ought to be stopped before he gets going real good. You see?"

He was arguing desperately; and Jess Dreer sat back with a vague pity beginning to work in his heart—pity and contempt. This hardened rascal to talk of stopping the career of a gun fighter! But he saw that there was a grain of sincerity buried in the talk of Jud Boone. The man meant it. He wanted to go straight, to break away from his past. The whole story came out as he talked.

He had been passing through that section of the country. He had stopped in at the house of Joel Norman, a distant cousin. He had fallen desperately in love with Joel's daughter May. The girl had liked him, she had shown it, and he had tried to play the game straight by going to Joel and asking his consent to the marriage. But Joel put him away with horror.

And Jud Boone left the country with hatred for his whole clan in his heart. Then they sent after him, and Joel put up the proposition to him. He was to right the affair of Valentine and avenge the shooting of Joe Norman. That done, no cash would change hands but Jud—if May was still willing—could marry her and settle down on a piece of land which Joel would stock for him. His past would be forgotten. The family power of the Normans would be used to the utmost to restore Jud's standing as a law-abiding citizen.

Not that this tale flowed smoothly from the lips of Jud. It came brokenly. Illuminating phrases told whole episodes in a second.

"That's how I'm fixed," he concluded. "I don't aim to kill Valentine, I just want to—"

"Wait a minute," said Jess Dreer. "If Charlie was a common cowhand, you wouldn't need to kill him. You could drill him through an arm, or a leg, and let him go. But he ain't that kind. He's a fast boy, Jud, and you know what that means just as well as I know it. If you meet him, you'll have to shoot to kill. So would I, if I met him. Just the same as we'd have to shoot to kill if we got tangled up with each other."

Once more Jud Boone met the eye of Dreer and quailed.

"Put it short," he said at length. "How far'll you go for this Valentine?"

"To the limit."

"They must of paid you high," said Jud bitterly. "They's no other way out?"

"They ain't a single way. We got to give way, one of us, Jud. And that one ain't going to be me!"

A gray color invaded the face of Jud Boone. He rose slowly from his chair with his arms hanging stiffly at his sides.

"Dreer, I can't step out. I've give my word. I—I'd rather go to hell than to face her—after running out on my promise."

He swayed himself a little back and forth and set his teeth. With every scruple of energy in his soul and body he was striving to call up the fighting passion, but the result was only a dull glare, and the mouth of the gun fighter was twitching loosely.

"If you're going to stop me, Dreer, you got to stop me now!"

The sneer deepened on the thin lips of Dreer.

"You poor fool," he said contemptuously. "Look down at your hand! A Chinaman could beat you to your gun, Boone, and shoot you full of holes."

As one fascinated by a superior power, Boone looked down, saw the quaking fingers of his hands, and dropped back in his chair. His face was buried and he groaned. Jess Dreer walked to him and touched the trembling, massive shoulders. The gun fighter dared not look up.

"Listen to me. Jud, I'm sorry for you. I ain't your confessor, but I tell you I've heard some awful things about you. About what you done to your pardner that found that claim for you back of Angelville. About a pile of other things I've heard, too. But I'll say now that I don't believe them.

"I'm going to do my part by you. How do I know that this Charlie Valentine is enough of a man to be worth all this trouble and pain saving? Maybe in a pinch he'd show yeller. I've seen it done. He's done nothing but clean up on a bunch of kids. How'd he act facing a real fighting gent like you? That's the question! Well, Jud, we'll try him out.

"You go to that saloon tomorrow and you hang around until Charlie Valentine comes in. Then give him a try. Walk up to him and see if he's got the nerve to meet you. Laugh at him, mock him, tell him what you're going to do in the line of filling him full of lead, and when you're done with that, just tell him to get out of the saloon; and then stand still and look him in the eye.

"They ain't one chance in ten that he'll come through. Most likely he'll try to grin and then back out. And if he does that, you're through. You've done your part better than the Normans could of asked, because you'll have shamed the boy.

"Aye, it would be worse than shooting him, in a way. But I'll stand by and give you the chance. And I tell you straight it costs me more'n you guess to do it. But you go ahead. Try his nerve.

"But if he don't buckle and quit—if he don't walk out of the saloon—if he stands ready for a fight—then, Jud, you won't be fighting him. You'll be fighting me. Because I'll be standing by, and the minute the test comes, I'm going to call your name out, and you and me'll finish what you and him begun."

"D'you mean it?" cried Jud Boone, leaping to his feet, exultant.

"I mean it."

"But how can you stand around in Carrol's place? What if you're seen?"

"I won't be seen, but I'll be seeing."

"Then, pardner, you'll see this Charlie Valentine crumple up like wet paper when I get my eye on him. And—I know how to work it!"

His face went savage. Indeed, he had had a practical demonstration that night of the power which one eye may exert upon another.

"They's one thing more," said Jess Dreer slowly. "You know my name. You know I'm wanted. If you was to spread the news around that I was in town, it might be kind of bad for me. I'll leave it to your honor, Jud."

"Gimme your hand," cried Jud. "You've met me half-way, and you can trust me to go square with you, pardner!"

"S'long, then."

And the outlaw backed to the door, waved his hand, and was gone.

CHAPTER 21

But the moment he was alone, shame threw Jud Boone into a perfect frenzy of rage and self-hatred. He ran to the door with the revolver naked in his hand, as if even now he would call back Dreer and face him. But he heard the door close downstairs and he hurried back to the window. Across the street below him the tall figure was passing, and he raised his weapon for a chance shot, balanced it a moment—and then dropped it into the holster with a groan. He sank into a chair, grinding his knuckles into his forehead, then leaped up as though under a spur and paced the room. But the thought of Jess Dreer followed him like a ghost, and like a ghost kept the calm eye upon him.

At length he made up his mind. It was a shameful thing, perhaps, to betray the word which he had pledged to Jess Dreer, but to Jud Boone this was a matter of life and death; and where he was vitally concerned, he had never been in the habit of consulting the requirements of honor.

He went straight to the bedroom of his host, Sol Norman, and slipped in without knocking at the door. He found the lamp on the table by dint of fumbling and lighted it, looking up to find Sol Norman rising in bed on one elbow and blinking rapidly at the light. Sol Norman was prodigiously long of nose and chin and was considered the saddest-faced man on the ranges. His face was now even longer than usual while he gaped at the gun fighter.

"The game's off," declared Jud, frowning at the other.

"What game?"

"Me and Charlie Valentine. I'm through."

At this, Sol Norman swung out of bed and plunged his bony legs into trousers. Sol was preeminently a man of action. Half a minute later he was strapping on a gun, and all these vital seconds he had not asked a single question.

"Now," he said, catching up his hat, "what's wrong?"

"I took on one man, not two," declared the gunman sullenly. "I took on Charlie Valentine for you folks. You all figured that Charlie was too fast with his gun for any of you to tackle, and I was willing to have a try at him. But the new man—"

"What new man?"

"Jess Dreer."

There was a foul oath from Sol Norman.

"What's he got to do with it?"

"This: That if I jump Charlie, Dreer will jump me."

"Two to one, eh? Don't worry, Jud. That's just what we

want. If we can get this down to mob action, everything is dead easy. We got the numbers."

Jud Boone flushed.

"It ain't the numbers, Sol. He ain't going to work with Charlie. He'll work by himself."

"Then you'll send him the same way you send Charlie Valentine, Jud, and you'll collect the price for him. Not a bad day's work, eh?"

He made his voice hearty as he said this, but Jud failed to show enthusiasm. He flushed as he approached the shameful truth.

"Sol, don't you know nothing about Jess Dreer?"

"Well?"

"He's the fastest man with a gun that ever sunk a spur into a hoss, Sol. Why, it was him that killed 'Salty' Moore —and—I've seen Salty work!"

He had turned gray while he recalled Salty, and now Sol Norman nodded slowly; he understood.

"But they's one way around it. We'll keep Dreer from coming anywheres near Carrol's saloon. He's an outlaw. Nobody don't need to wait for an invitation before they plug Dreer. We'll pass the word around. We'll get all our boys out with something on the hip."

Jud Boone mopped his forehead.

"It's a rotten job," he muttered. "I don't feel no ways right about it. Keep him away if you can. But—somehow I figure he'll get through. He'll be somewheres near watching when I face Charlie Valentine. But—"

"Have a drink," urged Sol, studying the face of the fighter with his little, shrewd eyes. "Have a drink. Then you tumble into bed and have a snooze. I'm going to make the rounds and get the boys together. They'd be on hand, anyway; I'm going to make sure of having them here early. But what does this Dreer look like? I've never seen him; none of the rest of the boys have."

"He's tall—big shoulders, narrow waist, long arms—like a gorilla. He ain't very good to look at. Kind of lean in the face. Got a straight-looking eye." He shuddered slightly as he remembered that eye. He concluded: "You just tell the boys what I've told you. And when they see Jess Dreer—they'll know him well enough."

He stepped closer and clutched the arms of Sol with his pudgy hands.

"Sol, you got to keep him away!"

And he turned to the whisky bottle.

Sol Norman left the room with three huge strides, went down the stairs with as many leaps, and burst into the night on his errand; and Jud Boone, turning the whisky glass nervously, was comforted by the beat of hoofs that swept down the street.

There was no sleep for Jud that night. Most of the time he spent in recalling the most minute details of his interview with Dreer. And then he focused the eye of the memory on the personal appearance of the outlaw—and most of all he dwelt upon the long, capable, deft fingers of the man. In those fingers a revolver would become a living thing, he felt.

In the meantime, before dawn was well up in the sky the first arrivals appeared at the house of Sol Norman, for this was the rallying place for the clan. And their coming, also, cheered Jud Boone. He could hear the front door slamming more and more frequently and their noisy stamping through the lower hall to the kitchen.

When he went down, they gave him a noisy reception. He was their champion, and they treated him like a king. Eagerly, to the circle of attentive faces, Jud described the outlaw, and the necessity of keeping him away from the saloon. They were to shoot at sight, ask their questions later, for if Dreer ever got the drop on them or even a fair warning of his danger, he would probably escape through a thousand of them. Jud was willing to exaggerate the prowess of Dreer. It made his fear of the outlaw less cowardly, and more like a man's dread of any power in nature. Jess Dreer became, under his painting, a cyclone against which one man or even two would be foolish to stand. And the result of the speech was that every man of the Norman clan looked to his weapons and then went out prepared for desperate battle.

By the time it was full day they had already laid their preparations and their plans of battle. And by the time it was full day Dan Carrol went up to the room of Dreer.

The big man, like Jud Boone, had not slept during the small remainder of the night, and at a signal from the gambler he went to the window.

"Look yonder."

"Well?" asked Jess Dreer.

"What d'you see?"

"A bald old boy scratching his head."

"That bald old boy is Tom Norman—the old man himself."

He led the way to another window.

"What d'you see?"

"Why, the same thing you do. Three gents sitting on a log playing dice."

"Them three are Walter Norman and his two cousins, Garry and Wally. Now, Jess, d'you begin to do a little thinking?"

"I begin to think that they's a considerable heap of Normans in this town. Anything else I'd ought to think?"

"Why d'you think they're there?"

"Why, they're going to hang around and wait for the fight to come off. They're waiting to see Jud Boone kill Charlie Valentine. Wouldn't take much brains to figure that out."

"Don't it strike you that they're a wee mite early?"

"They don't want to get caught in the rush. Go on, Danny, and tell me what it all means—if it does mean anything queer."

"Kind of queer, pardner. Them gents ain't the only ones. They's others all around the saloon. They're sitting on front porches. They're loafing around in the alleys. They's a couple of 'em down in the barroom now. Not talking much. Just standing and sipping their drink like they didn't like it, and looking, looking, looking. Jess, they're out there to keep you from getting to the saloon!"

It made the outlaw whirl on him.

"What the devil do they mean by that?"

"They's a whisper going the rounds that you intend to show up when it comes to the pinch between Jud and Charlie Valentine, you're going to step in and take a crack at Jud. They ain't anything in it, Jess, is there?"

The tall man was stunned, but he gradually recovered.

"It's Boone," he said huskily. "The skunk has started talking. He gave me his word. Danny, I could of killed the hound dog and got away clean without nobody knowing I was ever near him. And now he's double-crossed me!"

"He told what?" gasped Carrol. "D'you mean to say that you *were* going to step in between Boone and young Valentine?"

"I was—and I am."

"Jess, you're hanging yourself!"

"I'd only be hurrying up something that's sure to happen sooner or later. But—I still got one chance."

"What's that?"

"If I can get back to my room after the fracas—"

"No good, Jess. They'll search every inch of the house."

"That's right." He fell silent. "They's only one chance, then. If I have to make a play agin' Jud Boone with all this gang around, I'm done. But if jud bluffs down Charlie—why, then my neck's saved."

122

"But what'll I do? Where can I help, Jess?"

"Nothing you can do. These here things, Danny, just up and happens."

CHAPTER 22

Public opinion in Salt Springs was strictly neutral. On the one hand it was felt that Charlie Valentine had overstepped the bounds within which a peaceful man should walk by his various shooting scrapes. On the other hand there were not many who entirely approved of the Normans. They were a clannish tribe. They carried into the mountain desert the spirit with which they had lived in the Kentucky back hills. And the spirit of the clan is not wanted west of the Rockies in the large spaces where a man's malice should dissolve before he had spread it like a poison into the blood of his relations. Therefore, when Salt Springs found out that if the toes of one Norman were stepped upon, the fists of fifty Normans avenged the hurt, the townsmen put their heads together, marveled at this new spirit, and then began to frown. The Westerner does not make up his mind suddenly. He really is more conservative than the most hidebound New Englander. He is taught from his childhood to look on the better side of a man, and if the man has not a better side, then to avoid him altogether. The reason is simple. It is dangerous to disapprove of a man who wears a gun; it is far better to keep away from him, and above all, it is best to say nothing about him lest tidings of what you have said be brought to his ear.

Accordingly, Salt Springs saw the Normans, disapproved of them, and then waited in silence for something to happen. But on this day, when the Normans gathered in the streets of the town, every man armed, every man silently ugly, it was felt that they had overstepped the bounds of decorum. Salt Springs, in a word, disapproved, and hitched at its gun belt. And if the opposite party had not been a young mischief-maker himself, there was every probability that the neutrals would have risen en masse and run the Normans out of the town.

But as it was, it was felt that this private war had best run its own course, though many public-spirited men shook their heads with the knowledge that, if Charlie Valentine fell, it would be merely the beginning of constant warfare—for Morgan Valentine himself would then take up arms, and when Morgan Valentine stirred, society was shaken to the roots. As for the other rumor—that Jess Dreer was mixed up in this matter and was on the side of the Valentines, most people were inclined to disbelieve it. Besides, Dreer was to most of them a semi-mythical spirit. He came from the southland. His crimes were not of their region. And the man himself was discounted. Compared with Jud Boone, a known force, he was nothing.

But there was something so set and staged about this affair that Salt Springs began to grow excited before the morning was old. It drifted more and more thickly toward Danny Carrol's saloon, where the meeting was to take place. And all eyes, turning upon Jud Boone, who sat at a table in the corner, would then flick over to the prize saddle, which now lay at the other end of the bar waiting for Charlie Valentine.

Obviously, no one could look at the saddle and then at Jud Boone without picturing the gun fight which was coming.

But where was Jess Dreer? He had not been seen. The loose-flung circle of the Normans had espied no one even distantly resembling the descriptions of the outlaw. Of course, no one dreamed of looking into the saloon. And in the saloon, least of all, would they have looked into the old closet at one end of the room. But here stood Jess Dreer, with the door ajar a fraction of an inch. From this he could not see the barroom, but he could look down the long mirror behind the bar, and in this mirror he saw perfectly at second hand all that happened. He saw the crowd filter through the door, a silent crowd, lining up before the bar, and then breaking swiftly into groups that gathered along the wall—always hurrying across the line between the chair of Jud Boone and the door, as if at any moment Charlie Valentine might appear in this doorway and the guns be drawn.

Jud Boone drank with a deep relish of the excitement which his presence roused. The number of the mustered Normans soothed his nerves. And if Jess Dreer were kept away from the saloon, this day his triumph would never be threatened.

There was a sudden flurry around the door of the saloon. Everyone stood up—except Jud Boone.

Then the whisper passed down the room, rose to a murmur, to a deep voice: "Charlie Valentine is riding down the street—and he's coming alone!"

Alone, and into the very teeth of all this savage clan of Normans!

All at once the men of Salt Springs began to remember that Charlie Valentine was young, handsome, of good family. That in his quarrels he had never taken an unfair advantage; that he had never actually killed. And then they looked from the open doorway to the face of Jud Boone, killer. The contrast was perfect.

Not even Valentine's brother—not even his father had come with the boy. It was as though the whole family trusted everything to the sense of fair play in Salt Springs.

And that was the reason for the deep, stern hum that went about the saloon. Sheriff Claney, of course, was not there. His habit was to attend such affairs after and not before.

But Steve Harrison made himself spokesman when he went up to Gus Norman.

"Look here, Gus," he said, "they ain't any mystery about why you got all your men out here today. But you take my advice. Stay clear of trouble. Don't start no mob action. It ain't popular around these parts. And write this down in red—Charlie Valentine is going to get a square deal!"

And as he stepped back, once more the murmur passed up and down the barroom approving.

It was possible for Jess Dreer, in the closet, to watch the approach of Charlie Valentine down the street. Distant voices were calling from the outdoors, small at first and then growing in volume. Were they murmurs of admiration? Of sympathy?

Jud Boone, at his table, finished his drink, and then leaned back in his chair. It was a careless attitude, but the hand which hung by the gunman's side was clenched until the skin whitened across the knuckles. Jess Dreer saw all this in the mirror.

Then he heard, at the very door of the saloon, a woman's voice pitched high and shrill. It was calling: "Oh, Charlie Valentine, don't go inside. They're going to murder you, Charlie!"

Every man in the saloon stopped in the midst of gesture or spoken word. What a thrill in that girl's voice! Perhaps she was some old friend. She had danced with Charlie Valentine. She had known him when he was a child. She had even loved him, perhaps, and now she cried this warning.

The affair had been grim before. It now suddenly became filled with horror.

Then followed a heartbreaking pause, a dead silence outside the saloon. No voice within. What was happening? Had Charlie Valentine paused? Had the cry of this girl broken his nerve? Was he taking her advice and turning away? Was it this that accounted for the silence?

Jess Dreer, believing this, sighed with relief—and then Charlie Valentine stepped into the doorway.

It was the thing for which everyone in the saloon had been waiting and priming himself during the past hour or more.

And here stood Charlie Valentine, dark against the white sunlight beyond. Being the center of attention, he seemed hardly more than a child. Defiantly he had put on a shirt of blue silk, and he had a scarlet handkerchief around his neck. Poor fellow! His very gaudiness accentuated his deadly pallor. Purple circles surrounded his eyes. His mouth was set until the red of the lips disappeared. One could understand at a glance that this youngster had not slept in expectation of the fight.

Now he looked over the barroom, with its crowd of faces, and smiled. There was no mistaking it. Every ounce of power in his soul and body was given to make that smile. His lips parted; he tried to speak.

He had to moisten his lips and try again before the sound would come.

Very faintly: "Hello, boys! I—I've come for that saddle, Danny."

Dan Carrol from behind the bar looked somberly at him. As much as to say: "Poor devil, you've come to be killed!"

Aloud he said: "It's yours, Charlie. And a beauty, too. Bring in the buckboard for it?"

"Yep."

And Charlie Valentine walked to the saddle and put his hand on the horn of it.

With one accord, every eye in the room turned upon Jud Boone. Yes, he was slowly rising; he had pulled down his hat a little; he was sauntering forward carelessly with his hands dropped lightly upon his hips.

Jess Dreer heard, near his door, a whisper which said: "It's plain murder. That kid agin' Boone! It ought to be stopped!"

But who would stop it? Jud Boone was a known man.

"Kind of a fine-looking saddle, Valentine, ain't it?" Jud remarked.

At the voice, a shock went through Charlie Valentine; a shudder as though a powerful current of electricity had been flung through him. Then, slowly, fighting himself to make his movements calm, he turned his head. His face was like death, yet he forced a wan smile. A little whisper of admiration went up and down the saloon. The combatants were at length face to face. And what a contrast! As well send a stripling two-year-old to try his horns against the scarred front of some bull who has long lorded it over his range.

The sneering smile of Jud Boone was a silent token of his knowledge of superior strength. And the head of Valentine, held desperately high, was an equally eloquent token that he knew he was approaching his death.

CHAPTER 23

"A fine saddle, kid, eh?" repeated Jud Boone, who after pausing a few paces now went a stride nearer.

The eyes of Valentine widened a little, fascinated, and

then, by degrees, he was able to look away from his enemy to the prize. He touched it with a shaking hand.

"Pretty nice," he admitted.

"Yep, and they've wasted a pile of silver in fixing it up, I'd say."

It was an obvious opening for an insult, if Charlie Valentine chose to follow it up. But it was instantly clear that he would avoid the issue if that were possible.

"I guess I'll have time to keep the silver shined up, Jud."

It seemed somehow that a subtle appeal were conveyed by this use of the man-killer's first name. Something of appeal, too, in the faint smile which the boy now turned on his antagonist.

As though he was mutely saying: "For Heaven's sake, Jud Boone, be merciful. Don't push me to the limit; give me a chance!"

Salt Springs noted all this, and the face of Salt Springs took on a sick look of pain and horror.

Then the same girl's voice, shriller than before, and closer to the door of the saloon:

"I will get in there, I tell you. I *will* get in! They're getting ready to fight now. I can tell it by the silence!"

A muttering of men's voices followed. Those were the Normans, no doubt, who were keeping the poor creature away.

And then her voice, pitched higher still: "Oh, if any of you are half men, go in and stop them! Save Charlie Valentine! He's only a boy!"

Somehow that girl's voice was the crowning horror.

Charlie Valentine, shaking like a hysterical woman, turned his head with jerks and stared at the silent crowd along the wall.

"Won't some of you—go out—and stop that noise?" he murmured gaspingly.

But the brutal Boone had seen another opening and instantly took advantage of it.

"What's the matter, Charlie? Does the lady think you're sick? Or about to get sick? That's Nan Tucker, ain't it?"

But he had whipped down the pride of the boy too much. Now a touch of color came in young Valentine's face.

"My dad taught me one little thing," he said, "and that was never to name ladies when I was having a drink. Around these parts, Boone, we most generally keep our womenfolk outside of saloons."

"But," said Boone, furious at the murmur of approbation along the wall, "I ain't seen any drinking going on."

"We'll start in now then." He turned to the others. "Step up, boys, and have one on me."

Not a man stirred from the wall. The pale, interested faces stared as if these two had been on a stage, and the others were sitting behind footlights watching the drama of unreal lives. Charlie Valentine swung back again with an attempted smile, which only served to show his set teeth, flashing. "Nobody ain't particular dry, I guess," remarked Jud Boone.

"I guess not," whispered Charlie.

"Speaking of saddles, son, I hear that you ain't really got any right to that one."

"I got no right to it? Well, what d'you mean by that?"

Obviously the crisis was coming. There would be no escaping from the quarrel which Jud Boone was urging on.

"I'll tell you what I mean—it's what I hear pretty general around Salt Springs. They say that young Tolliver really ought to be taking off this saddle today."

"And how comes that?" queried Charlie Valentine in the same ghastly, faint voice.

"It comes this way. Bud Tolliver rides straight up and

won't pull the leather, and he sticks on every horse but the last one. And then you come out and stick through all the horses. But when you come to the one that throwed young Tolliver, you sneak a grip that the judges don't see and pull the leather, and that's how you happen to be here today taking off the prize saddle."

Once more Charlie Valentine moistened his colorless lips.

"Somebody has been joking with you, Jud. I didn't pull no leather that day."

Jud Boone raised his head and laughed derisively. And the fire was in his eyes. Plainly he was drinking deep of pleasure in this torture scene.

"Ask the boys, Jud," gasped Charlie Valentine. "They'll tell you I didn't pull leather."

Jud Boone rolled his keen glance up and down the line —and not a man stepped forward—not a voice was raised.

Once more the gun fighter laughed. His confidence was mounting to great heights by this time. No attempt had been made so far by Jess Dreer to break through the cordon of the Normans around the saloon; and apparently the game was in his hand. And even if Charlie Valentine mustered courage enough to draw his gun, he would be worse than helpless with such shaking hands. Yet Jud was determined to avoid a shooting affair if possible. He was set on breaking the nerve of this boy and making him "take water." Because there was one chance in ten that even though Jess Dreer were not here today, he might make it a point to look up the slayer later on. And Jud was distinctly desirous of avoiding that future meeting.

"You see," he said, "they ain't any volunteers for information. Kind of looks as though they were agin' you, Charlie. Look 'em over yourself."

Obediently Charlie cast a wild glance down that line. Not a man would stir or speak. He looked back to Jud.

"I dunno how it is," he said.

Suddenly Jud shouted: "Well, how do you think it is?"

Charlie Valentine trembled. Perspiration poured out on his forehead.

"Maybe," he whispered very faintly, "I'm wrong. Maybe—I've forgotten—just what I did—that day!"

Gratification flooded the face of Jud Boone. Plainly the nerve of the boy was breaking; he was about to take water. And in the closet at the rear of the room Jess Dreer, though he was quivering with horror, muttered to himself: "Thank Heaven. They ain't going to come to a showdown. I won't have to step in!" But a great desire to spring at Boone and break him in his hands was sweeping over the outlaw.

"Yep," sneered Jud Boone, "I figure that you got a pretty handy memory. But I'll tell you what you do, son, to put yourself in right ag'in. You just leave this saddle here for young Tolliver, and I'll see that he gets it."

The head of Charlie Valentine dropped; his hand which had been twisted around the horn of the saddle loosened and fell nervelessly away. He seemed about to turn back toward the door, and a breath of relief came from the onlookers.

It may have been that breath that changed the mind of Charlie Valentine; it may have been that little whispering sound which made him recall the stern words of his father when he set out that morning.

He whipped himself together with an effort and looked Jud Boone in the eye.

"Jud Boone," he said, "the saddle's mine!"

The other was shaken by the sudden change. On his brow gathered his most ferocious frown.

"Son," he said ominously, "watch what you're saying. I'm a tolerable peaceful man—till I get riled up. And you're riling me a whole pile. If you take this saddle, it's just the same as calling me a liar!"

"Then—Heaven help me—that's what I call you, Boone!"

It was done. Even Boone could hardly believe that he had heard it.

"Think twice, Valentine. I ain't a man to stand such talk!"

"I—I've done my thinking," cried the young fellow, trembling like a girl. "And now—have it over with!"

He stood perfectly straight, his chin up; and it was patent that he could never get his gun out of the holster in time to meet the lightning draw of the other. And Jud Boone had forgotten all scruples, forgotten even Jess Dreer. The fighting lust was on him, and his upper lip was drawing back over his teeth in that bestial manner which needs to be seen only once to be remembered forever.

Then a voice cried from the other end of the room—a deep, mellow voice: "Boone! Jud Boone! You're facing the wrong way!"

Those who saw the change that came in the face of Boone were haunted by it. They looked down the saloon, and there stood a big man, broad-shouldered, long-armed, with his gun hanging far down on his thigh. There was something negligent in his attitude, and negligently alert.

Yet for a long instant Jud Boone did not turn. When he whirled, it was with a shrill, animal cry, the gun coming into his hand as he veered.

Two reports. Two drifts of thin smoke, like two small puffs from a cigarette which is being deeply inhaled. The smoke went upward slowly. Jess Dreer had dropped his gun to his side again. But Jud Boone stood with a dazed expression, his revolver still extended. First the weapon crashed on the floor. Then he reached his left hand along the rail of the bar. His head dropped over, and he lowered himself slowly to the floor.

When they reached him, he was dead.

CHAPTER 24

The group on the veranda of the Valentine house had remained there for close to two hours. Mary sat halfway down the steps with her hands clasped about her knees. Elizabeth was above her, leaning against the railing. Morgan Valentine and his wife were in chairs on the veranda itself.

He was smoking his short-stemmed pipe steadily. Mrs. Valentine had abandoned her knitting some half an hour before, and now sat stiffly erect, with her chin drawn in, her mouth tight, her color ashen.

And every eye of the four was bent fixedly upon that point where the road swerved around the shoulder of the western hill and dipped toward the house in a long, swift curve. No one had spoken—hours, ages of silence, it seemed. But now and then the glance of Mrs. Valentine lowered upon Mary, and her lips stirred with bitter, soundless words. And once when Mary turned and looked up, she met the glance of Elizabeth fixed on her as though she were a snake.

All this trouble rested on the head of the girl, and only the eye of Morgan Valentine was kind and clear. But even he, toward the end, was abstracted.

Now, over the hill, a horseman darted. And the four rose to their feet at the signal. It was Louis Valentine. He was spurring his horse to a mad gallop down the slope.

His hat off, he was waving it frantically. Every inch of his body spoke joy.

And a cry came from the watchers.

"Thank God, thank God!" whispered Mrs. Valentine, and fumbling blindly, she found the hand of her husband and clung to it.

Elizabeth was weeping soundlessly.

Now the courier plunged up to the house and flung himself out of the saddle.

"I seen him!" he cried. "I seen Charlie coming over the next rise! I seen him! He's all right! He's coming alone!"

"But you don't know," said Mrs. Valentine. "He may be—"

"Not a scratch on him. I can tell by the way he's riding. Coming like sixty. Spurring every jump. He's got Baldy stretched out straighter'n a string. No wounded man could ride like that."

Then Morgan Valentine spoke: "Did you see the saddle? How's it come that he drives in in the buckboard and comes riding a hossback? He drives Baldy in and rides him back? Where's the saddle?"

A gasp from Louis; half of his joy disappeared.

"You mean—you think Charlie took water—you—"

"I don't care what he did!" cried the boy's mother. "He's alive—he's safe—in spite of you, Morgan!"

"But his honor," said the indomitable rancher. "How about that?"

There was no opportunity for further surmise. Over the hill came a second rider, and this time it was Charlie who appeared, spurring hard, as Louis had said. He did not wave his hat as he saw the waiting family. At their joyous shout that went tingling to him, he returned no answer.

"Rides like they was someone behind him," muttered the ominous voice of Morgan Valentine, and for the first time he removed the pipe from between his teeth, and shaking himself clear from the hands of his wife, he stepped to the head of the stairs and waited.

Charlie Valentine dismounted less hastily than his brother had done and was caught in four pairs of arms; showered with exclamations from four pairs of lips. Only his father remained aloof.

"The saddle, Charlie!" he cried at length, even his iron nerve breaking under the strain. "Did you bring it out?"

At this the women and Louis released the boy and turned; his face could be seen clearly for the first time, and it was notable that there was not the slightest sign of exultation. He seemed to have aged many years; he had gone in hardly more than a child; he came out to the ranch from Salt Springs carrying his manhood stamped upon his face.

"There's the prize saddle on the hoss," he said tersely.

"And Jud Boone?" breathed his brother Louis, half abashed before this new Charlie Valentine.

"Jud Boone is dead."

Dead silence. Had their own Charlie killed the man? Did that explain the gravity, the joylessness of his manner?

But Morgan Valentine came down the steps with gleaming eyes. He stretched out his hand.

"Son," he said, "you live up to the blood that runs in you. I'll tell you now that when you left the house this morning, I thought you were riding to your death. I've had you dead in my thoughts, Charlie!"

"I can't shake your hand," replied the son. "It wasn't me that killed Jud Boone."

Another caught breath from the crowd. The arm of Morgan Valentine fell slowly to his side.

"I'll tell you how it was," said Charlie slowly. He frowned and recalled the bitter picture in detail.

"When I faced Jud Boone, my nerve left me. I was like —like I was standing in a cold wind. That's the way his eye got on my nerves. I kept thinking—about death—and being young. And—I near crumpled up. I—I near took water. Along comes the last minute. I was just swaying between being a coward—and then something snapped in me. I called Jud Boone a liar, and then waited for the draw. But I knew I was simply waiting to be killed. My hand was shaking so I couldn't of hit the other side of the room. And Jud Boone was as cool as if he was getting ready to shoot at a target.

"And then—I heard a big voice call: 'Boone! Jud Boone! You're facing the wrong way!' "

He imitated that deep tone, that full voice, and a quiver ran through the listeners.

"Jud turned with a yell, with his gun out before he was clear around. Wasn't till he was clear around that the stranger made a move. Then it was just a jerk of his hand, a flash of light as the gun jumped into it—and he shot Jud Boone dead! And that's why I'm here—alive."

"God bless him! Who did it, Charlie?"

But still Charlie showed no joy. He lifted his arm and pointed sternly at Mary Valentine. The others followed that pointing hand and saw her standing with a white face and great, staring eyes.

"I reckon you know, Mary. When it was over, he says to me: 'Tell her that she don't owe me nothing. That the account is just squared up, that's all.' I reckon you know who he was speaking about, Mary!"

"It was Jess Dreer," said the girl faintly. "And—he got away, Charlie?"

"You must of known when you asked him to help me that there wasn't any way for him to get loose. Not with a whole line of men stretched around the saloon waiting for him—and Normans, all of them! You must of knowed you was asking him to step in and die! And him being that kind of a gent"—the voice of Charlie trembled—"he wouldn't say no to a woman."

"Charlie, you aren't speaking true? He isn't caught?"

She had broken through the circle now and was clinging to him, pleading with him.

"Don't hold onto me, Mary," said the boy coldly. "I swear that I'd rather be back there lying dead on the floor of Dan Carrol's place than to have Dreer die for me."

"Hush," broke in Morgan Valentine.

He was looking at Mary, not at his rescued son.

"Mother, take Mary inside."

"Oh, Mary! That was what you done for us? Oh, Mary, and all the bitter things I been thinking of you!"

"I won't go, Aunt Maude," said the girl steadily. "I want to know just what happened. After Boone dropped, what did Jess Dreer do?"

"He turned his gun in his hand and caught it by the barrel.

" 'Boys,' he says, just as quiet as I'm talking now. 'Boys, I guess you know who I am. I'm Jess Dreer. They's about one chance in three that I could rush the lines outside and get clear. But I'm sort of tired. So I give myself up. Who'll take my gun?'

"Nobody moved. I called out: 'Jess, I'm with you. I'm at your back. We'll try it together.' I meant it. I'd of died for him. I still would! But he says: 'Go easy, boy. I know you're white, but don't you go making a mess of things for yourself.' "

"Charlie," said Mary Valentine in the same calm voice in which she had spoken before, "I'll never forget what you said to Jess Dreer and the offer that you made."

He went on, unheeding: "Then he goes up to Harrison and puts out his gun: 'Pardner,' he says, 'I figure you for a man-sized man. Take my gun and lead me to the lockup.

They's a pretty fat little price on my head. It's all yours
—and you can give it to charity.'

"But Harrison took Dreer's hand, not his gun. 'You've
done a mighty fine thing,' he said. 'I dunno what your
record is, Dreer, but here's one that would back you. And
we'll see that you get a clean deal in Salt Springs.'

"But just then Sheriff Claney comes through the door.

" 'Will you make the same offer to me, Dreer?' he says,
with his hand on his gun.

"I could see something flicker in the eyes of Dreer. He
had his gun in a bad position—by the muzzle—but I
thought for a minute that he was going to flip it and try
to get Claney first—and I think he could of done it.

"But he says: 'It ain't such a pretty party with you on
the receiving end, Sheriff. Speaking personal, sheriffs
ain't been my bunkies, generally. But here's the gun,
Claney.'

" 'How d'you know me?' asked the sheriff.

" 'I can tell you by the scar on your forehead,' says Jess."
There was a cry of pain from Mary Valentine.

"Aye," said the boy fiercely, "cry and wring your
hands, Mary Valentine, but that won't save Jess Dreer.
And he's going to be saved!"

"Charlie," pleaded the girl, "let me have a chance to
help!"

"Keep away, Mary. I'll tell you why. I been thinking
about you all the way home. I been thinking about you
ever since Jess Dreer talked to me that way and gave me
that message for you. It was on account of you that he
done it.

"And who was the cause of the whole thing? It was you!
You made the fight between me and Joe Norman. And
that fight laid the plan for this. It's on account of you that
Jud Boone is dead just when he was trying to get a new
start and be a decent man. It's on account of you that the

finest man that ever wore a gun is waiting in jail for a rope. And I say that you ought to be punished some way for it."

He had risen on tiptoe; his whole body had swelled to a greater size as he poured out the denunciation. "I don't know how, but—"

Morgan Valentine stepped in between them.

"You've talked enough," he interrupted.

"Let him talk," said the girl, and she smiled in a singular manner. "But I want you to know that I'm punished already, Charlie. More than I can bear. Because I love Jess Dreer!"

There was a stifled exclamation from Elizabeth.

But Charlie turned his rage into a sneer.

"You love him?" he said scornfully. "Well, you've had considerable practice loving men!"

And Mary bowed her head.

CHAPTER 25

"You see," was the manner in which Claney greeted his brother sheriff from the southland, "that you was wrong, Caswell, and that Jess Dreer wasn't taken near the Valentine ranch."

"But the theory was right enough," protested Caswell. "And it was on account of the Valentines that he got into this mix-up."

Sheriff Claney smiled benevolently on his companion.

"Theory is one way, but practice may be a mighty long ways off from it. It was this time."

"Well, I'm free to say that you're right. I ain't one that

falls in love with my mistakes, pardner. Besides, you're a gent with a pretty good head, Claney, which makes it a whole pile easier to be beaten out by you."

It was a very neat little tribute, and it was delivered in a voice so sincere that Sheriff Claney had the grace to blush.

"Here I was," pursued Caswell, "after follering this Jess Dreer for years, and knowing him like I knew myself, almost, and yet you step in at the right minute and grab him. It's a pretty piece of work. I thought you'd be miles away from Salt Springs hunting for the trail of him."

Sheriff Claney cleared his throat; it would be long before he explained the purely adventitious circumstances which had brought him to Salt Springs that day.

"But," ran on the man from the southland, "now that you got him, you want to look sharp that you keep him. I looked over your jail and it don't look none too manproof, to say nothing of being Dreer-proof!"

"Leave all that worry to me, pardner, because I ain't going to let my bird get away ag'in."

"What you doing to him?"

"Got an iron on his feet and got his hands shackled in front of him."

Sheriff Caswell whistled.

"That's kind of harsh."

"The hound tried to make a mock of me, Caswell. He had worse'n the irons coming to him. But—tomorrow morning I start south with him, so I won't have to bother with him long in that paper-walled jail. And while he's there he's got to grin and bear the irons."

Sheriff Caswell was deep in thought.

"Well," and he sighed, "I wouldn't be in your boots for considerable money if he was to get away. He'd most likely drop in for a call."

"Let him call," replied the sheriff stoutly, though his

mouth tightened a little. "I ain't been a sheriff such a short time that I'm afraid of lawbreakers. They ain't none of them that can get the jump on an honest man."

"H'm," remarked Sheriff Caswell.

At this, the other became markedly uneasy.

"Matter of fact," he said, "I'd like to have you look him over. You know him better'n I do. You might look him over in the cell and see if you think he's safe there. I got to go out in the country now, but this afternoon—"

"I'll be on my way south this afternoon maybe."

"Well, go over by yourself, Caswell."

"All right. But they ain't any real call for it, I guess."

"I'd like to have you."

And that was the reason that Sheriff Caswell entered the Salt Springs jail that day.

It was a little square, squat building of homemade brick. It looked like a fort of the primitive days. Through such narrow, barred windows the defenders could have fired at Indians, say. A battered old fort, for the weather had nicked and chipped and scarred it as much as a prolonged musketry fire. In reality it was not ten years old. The sheriff had his office here. Behind the two rooms which served for that purpose, there were two rooms fenced with the finest tool-proof steel both on the sides and above. Sheriff Claney had refused to run for reelection unless he was given the proper cage for his prisoners, and Claney was so valued as a man catcher in Salt Springs that the citizens provided him with his man-proof trap. Beyond these two cells was a narrow passageway in which the citizens could flock to look over the captives.

There were not many on this day, for Claney feared that some one of the sympathizers—and for some reason Salt Springs was singularly interested in the southland outlaw who had killed Jud Boone—might convey to Dreer a tool with which he could effect his escape. For this reason he allowed only those who carried special passes signed by himself to enter the jail today. The mob stayed outside.

Sheriff Caswell found one of the favored coming out as he entered. It was Mary Valentine, whose father was too powerful near Salt Springs for the requests of his children to be denied. She walked with her head high, her face white, her eyes starry, and her mouth so firmly set that the sheriff knew she would burst into tears as soon as she was beyond the public eye.

But at sight of the sheriff the tears were whipped from her eyes and a color of anger mounted into her cheeks.

"You're one of those who've hounded him down to this," she said softly and fiercely. "And I want you to know one woman's opinion—that he's worth a thousand of men like you—ten thousand!"

The sheriff looked mildly upon her. He took off his hat and turned it thoughtfully in his hands while she spoke. Then he said with his one-sided, whimsical smile: "My dear, you're not alone. You'll find Salt Springs full of people who agree with you about Jess Dreer. And all of them aren't girls."

She was about to break out in a storm of scorn again, but something in the patient eyes of Sheriff Caswell made her stop, look at him very closely, and then go on without another word. At the end of the passage she turned again —he had not moved foot or hand—and looked back at him. One might have said that there was a misty appeal in the eyes of Mary Valentine.

For some time longer the sheriff remained in this singularly devout attitude—just as if he were standing before the painting of some difficult and high-priced master. At length he sighed, and replacing his hat on his head, far back, he sauntered on into the interior of the jail.

He was amazed at the precautions with which this rare

prisoner was surrounded. At the door to the inner passage past the cells were two guards, each with a pair of revolvers swung at his belt and each with a sawed-off shotgun.

That was intended, no doubt, to check a rush which might be made by friends of Dreer—other outlaws, perhaps, though it was known that Dreer usually rode alone. The sheriff looked with a bright eye on those shotguns. In his experience with men of action he had never found anything with quite such a sedative effect as the sawed-off shotgun with its big bullets and scattering murder at short range.

These two guards examined the slip of paper which Sheriff Claney had signed. They both had seen Caswell before, but they were exceedingly strict in their surveillance. Finally, when he was admitted, the sheriff remarked two other guards walking up and down in the passageway, both equally armed to the teeth.

And all this on account of a man lodged behind tool-proof steel bars and beneath bars of the same nature, with a floor beneath him of closely set stones of huge size. Suppose a man could loosen one of those stones, he would have to call for help before he could budge it. But even if he budged it, there was still a trick remaining; the outer edge of the walls were projected deep into the ground with the same tool-proof steel, covered with tar paint.

One might have turned a giant loose in such a prison and scoffed at his attempts to escape. No human force could either cut that steel or bend it, and unless one of these things were done, the only possible means of entering or leaving that cell was through the door with its ponderous lock which only one key could turn.

Yet Sheriff Claney was not satisfied with surety. He added something more. He had locked the ankles of Jess Dreer to a hundred-and-fifty-pound iron ball and his hands were shackled before him with the most approved manacles. And in this wise Dreer sat on his cot smoking a cigarette of his own making. It was an odd thing to see him raise both ironed hands and laboriously place that little cigarette between his lips and remove it again.

"So," said the sheriff, "here you are, Jess!"

Jess Dreer started; then his long, lean face wrinkled into a kindly smile.

"Why, Caswell, I'm glad to see you again. Wait till I work my way over to the bars, and we'll shake hands."

"Never mind, Jess. I'll come inside."

"No, you won't," put in one of the guards.

"Look here," explained the patient sheriff. "I'm Sheriff Caswell. I've followed that man for years. Do you think they's any danger of me helping him to get loose?"

"Pardner," said the guard, scratching his head, "I dunno but what you're right, but orders is orders, and Claney was downright positive about what he said. Nobody is to go into that cell. Nobody, not even to take him grub. It's all got to be passed through the bars."

Jess Dreer was already standing up. The manacles on his ankles gave him a play of about four inches, and that was the length of his step. Moreover, every time he took a step, the weight of the iron pried at him and often nearly toppled him to the floor. Only the exercise of the greatest leg power enabled him to struggle painfully across the floor. Yet he maintained the greatest good nature. And though the perspiration started on his forehead, he chuckled whenever the tug of the iron ball nearly threw him off his balance.

Sheriff Caswell cursed softly, and the guard, flushing, declared that this was none of his work.

"Claney ain't taking no chances," he declared. "And the sheriff says that if anybody can get something to Dreer with four of us gents looking on, he's welcome to it."

At this Sheriff Caswell grinned.

"I'm glad to see Claney has the sporting spirit," he said. "A little chance is better'n none at all."

CHAPTER 26

With this, since Dreer was now close to the bars, the sheriff went forward and held out his hand. But he was caught at the same time by either shoulder and flung strongly backward.

"None of that!" cried the two guards who paced the passage. "None of that, Caswell! Nobody's to pass nothing through them bars."

The sheriff remained silent for a moment. His hat had been knocked down over one eye by the violence of that jerk, and now the muscles at the angle of his jaw bulged. But at length he smiled and quietly straightened his sombrero.

"Not even a bare hand?" he asked, showing that inoffensive member.

Sheriff Caswell looked from the face of one guard to the other. Something about his look appeared to be intensely interesting to Jess Dreer.

"Well," said the sheriff, "I see you boys are a mighty smart pair. Claney must of picked you out real special. And if that's the way you work it, I'll play with the same rules."

He turned to the prisoner.

"I dunno just why I came, Jess. It wasn't sure to look you over and gloat on seeing you behind the bars. You believe that?"

"Pardner, I know it."

"Matter of fact," and the sheriff nodded, gratified by this admission, "I'm mighty sorry for you, old man. Wish it had been a different end. Wish you'd gone down for the last time with your boots on, and two guns working."

"You forget, Caswell. I'm not a two-gun man. I ain't got that many talents."

The sheriff grinned again.

"You got enough talent to pass," he declared. "But when I think of what lies in front of you, Jess—" He stopped abruptly. "I suppose I shouldn't talk about them things, though."

"It's all right. No harm done. I'll tell you how it was. I might of busted through the boys, but I didn't have the nerve. I got sort of tired. Didn't seem like it was worthwhile taking the long chance—and killing a pile of boys I'd never had a grudge agin'. But here I am, and no whining, Caswell. But I'm sorry for you."

At this the patient man gasped. He was openly astonished.

"Sorry for me. Now, is that a joke, Dreer?"

"It ain't. You hear me talk straight talk today, pardner. Of all the gents that ever took my trail, you're the squarest shooter, the cleanest hand, the best head. Of the whole gang I'd rather of been taken by you. Caswell, I mean that so much that I sort of hanker to shake hands on it!"

"Claney had his own ideas about that," said the sheriff very quietly.

"Speak up, gents!" exclaimed one of the guards. "Speak up so the four of us can hear you."

The sheriff turned deliberately and looked them one by one in the eye; then he said to Jess Dreer: "You must be pretty young, Jess; they got you chaperoned to a finish."

"Yep," nodded Dreer, and he also looked with singular attention at the four, "they got a lot of thoughtful gents around Salt Springs. I'll try to remember 'em all. Well, I don't kick. This is a pile drier night than the time you run me through the hills down by Lawson, Sheriff."

"Speaking of Lawson, I've always wondered how you got past me through them hills, Jess."

"Didn't go through the hills, Sheriff. I tried to twice and then I found that you'd got your posse strung out about one man every hundred feet."

"Well, that made it sure you couldn't come through, Jess."

"Sure it did. I couldn't come through as myself, so I come through as somebody else. You know how you had your scouts out ahead of the rest? I rode right back to the line like I was one of the scouts. It was along about evening; pretty dim. I sings out that you want 'em to close up—rode back part ways with 'em—and then ducked away. Went straight on through Lawson with Angelina trotting or walking, and nobody even looked crosswise at me. They expected I'd be going the other way as fast as the old hoss would take me."

Sheriff Caswell swore again, and his eyes lighted.

"You're a fox, Dreer."

"Fox or no fox, you've give me a great run for the money—and I wish you had it coming into your money bags, Sheriff."

Caswell flushed. "I was never on your trail for the price, Jess."

"I believe it, pardner."

"But seems like I'll have a pretty empty kind of life, Jess, with you gone. The old days is ended. I'll hang up my guns and let 'em rust."

Here, after a brief consultation with one of his companions, a guard approached them.

"Claney ordered that if any gent come in and got real friendly with Dreer, we was to run him out. I guess that goes with you, Caswell."

"Ain't you stepping kind of hard?"

"I'm taking no chances. Well, if you two want to swap lies about old times, go ahead for five minutes more."

The sheriff nodded. He turned to Jess Dreer and for a moment looked at him without a word.

"Seeing this here jail, Jess," he began at length, "reminds me of an old shack I used to run down the country. Full of holes that jail was. Remember Garry Smith? I had him three times, and every time he got clean off. Then I sent him up, and when he'd come through with his term, I swore him in as a deputy and got him to show me how he used to get clear of the irons. Man, man, it was a sight to watch Garry work! Nothing in the shape of an iron could stick on him. He had long hands like yours, and he showed me how he could bunch up his hands and make them smaller'n his wrists and shake the bracelets off'n him."

"Never tried leg irons on him, eh?" said Jess.

"I never believed in treating a man like a dog," said the sheriff with a side glance at the guards, "but after Garry was my deputy, I put on the ankle irons for fun. Didn't see how he could make his feet smaller'n his ankles."

"But he did?"

"Sure, he *didn't*. But after he got his hands loose, he'd take out a little bit of a watch spring and go to work on the lock of his leg irons. He tried to show me how it was done, but I couldn't get the hang of it. I don't suppose you know how to work a lock like that, eh?"

Jess Dreer looked the sheriff straight between the eyes.

"No," he said slowly, drawling the word.

There was just a twinkle in the eyes of the sheriff.

"I thought not," he remarked.

"But where did Garry keep the watch spring? Didn't you search him?"

"Clean down to the skin, after the first time, but the

second time he'd put it in his hair, and the third time he'd put it between his big toe and the second toe—they was sort of hammered together and didn't spread out when he walked around barefooted. That was how he got the watch spring into the jail."

"Then you didn't give him the kind of a search Claney gave me," said Jess Dreer. His jaw set like iron. Then he went on: "He even combed my hair, Sheriff, if you can believe that."

"Somehow," said the sheriff, "I can."

He was fumbling in his vest pocket with thumb and forefinger. He brought out a toothpick.

"Time's up, Caswell," called the guard who had last spoken.

"All right, friend." And the sheriff turned.

The cells were dimly lighted from a skylight, brown back above the passage where the guards walked up and down on their beat. Jess Dreer, to relax the suspicious interest with which the guards watched him while he talked with Caswell, had gone back to his bunk. And now, by the dim light, something glittered faintly in an arc that disappeared at the feet of Dreer. Also, there was a tinkle of metal on stone.

"What's that?" cried the guard.

"What?" asked Dreer, lifting his head.

Sheriff Caswell had completed the motion of raising his hand to his mouth and now had a toothpick between his teeth.

"Something jingled, sort of. Something near you, Dreer."

"I tell you, son," drawled the outlaw, "when you get older, you'll find out that chains rattle now and then."

At this the guard flushed. In reality he did not wish to persecute this silent, gentle-appearing man with too many suspicions.

"Sounded sort of smaller and lighter than the chains," he grumbled.

Jess Dreer had moved one of his feet and now kept it still.

"S'long, Sheriff," he said.

"S'long, Jess."

"If they's a slip, Sheriff, and I get loose ag'in, I'll be glad to have you back on my trail."

"Jess, don't you make no mistake. If you was to get free, I'd foller you to the end of the world and drop you if I got the chance."

"Same here, Sheriff. Thanks for looking me up. Good-by."

He tried to make a gesture of farewell, but the manacles checked him, and the best he could do was to rouse a harsh rattling of the chain.

"Now, there's what I call a friendly man," said Jess to one of the guards, and he began to roll a cigarette.

"He talks too much," answered two of the guards in chorus.

"Well, sir," said Jess, "most generally when he talks a lot he's got something to say."

At this point the cigarette paper fluttered down out of his hand and came to a rest beside his foot. He leaned over, moved his foot, and when he sat up again, the paper was in the tips of his fingers, and against the palm of his hand was a little strip of strong steel, a watch spring.

CHAPTER 27

There were other visits on that afternoon.

One by one the Valentine family came in, for two were not allowed to be present at once.

Charlie was first straight as a soldier before the tool-proof bars, and as white as when he faced Jud Boone in Dan Carrol's place. He tried to speak.

"Son," said Jess Dreer very gently, "you run along. You're a clean one, Charlie. I know everything you want to say. I'd a lot rather have you think it than say it. So long, old man!"

And the boy blundered out. Even the guards were moved by him and his silent anguish.

Then Mrs. Valentine and Elizabeth, for the exception was made that the two women might come and stand huddled against the wall and stare at Jess Dreer. It was dusk now; but two big lanterns with powerful reflectors behind them were trained upon Dreer and made his face appear older, more seamed, paler than before. Also, it kept his eyes altering between black shadow as he lowered his head and a flash of the pupils as he looked up.

And these, also, said nothing; they thought that speech was forbidden. But the mother looked on Jess Dreer as some woman of the old days might have looked on a knight of the Holy Grail—a man unapproachable.

Tenderhearted Louis was next to last; and he wept like a child. The guards smiled and nudged one another.

"Pardner," said Dreer in a voice that the boy never forgot. "You ain't got any call to be ashamed even if these gents grin at you. The day'll come when you'll be a harder-handed man than any of 'em—a harder-handed man than Charlie, even. Good luck to you, pardner."

And Louis went out with his head high, and he looked the guards fiercely in the face.

Last of all the father came. He was such a man that even the guards stood back from him. They knew Morgan Valentine. He spoke with a ring in his voice that had never been there since his brother died.

"I've sent East for a lawyer," he said. "And I've started to get at the governor. I know him myself and I know he'll listen. You're going to get every chance that exists, Dreer."

Then he outlined briefly exactly how his influence would be brought to bear—all the little cogs that would be turned.

But in the end Dreer said: "Valentine, you're wasting your time and your money. I thank you for it, but it won't do any good. Law is law, and a dead man is a dead man. Why, looking at it impersonal, I'd say the law was a joke if it didn't hang me. So long."

After that, it was night. But just before the complete dark Sheriff Claney came in from the country. He looked over his guards and noted their readiness with words of approbation. They were chosen men. He told them what their duties were, just as a good general keeps repeating his instructions to his subordinates on the day of the battle.

Tomorrow, he said, they would have him on the way south to the county seat, surrounded by men day and night, and well on the way to the gallows—unless he were lynched on the way when he reached his own country. In the meantime the thing to watch for was an attempt from the outside. He might have friends in Salt Springs who would make an attempt. The Valentines were indirectly struck at in this. Four choice men patrolled the outside walls of the jail, and they would keep off any surprise. Yet in spite of bars and shackles, there must always be at least one man in the passage, walking up and down and keeping an eye on the prisoner himself.

"And if he acts queer, don't take no chances. Shoot him down. I'll be your warrant for it."

He faced Jess Dreer when he said this, and the tall man rose and elaborately bowed.

"Mr. Murderer Claney," he said, as though acknowledging an introduction.

And Claney showed his teeth when he grinned.

To be sure, his part in the actual taking of Dreer had been almost nothing, but the very fact that he was intimately connected with such a man would make him a household word throughout the mountain desert. He would willingly have sacrificed ten years out of his life rather than see this man go free.

He heard himself talked of; in the eye of his mind he saw future thousands point at him. "There's the man who sent Jess Dreer to the gallows."

And the thought was sweet to Claney.

After this visit, the night watch began.

Not that Sheriff Claney retired for the night. He kept coming back at half-hour or hour intervals, and fastened his keen glance on his prisoner, almost as though he feared the famous outlaw would evaporate.

For a time Jess Dreer smoked, talked with the guards, who grunted their answers, and hummed softly to himself.

But after a while, weary but unable to get onto the little couch comfortably because of the leg chain and ball, he slouched over in a corner with one shoulder against the wall. The weight of the manacles seemed to pull his long arms straight down so that they almost touched the floor. At least, it brought his hands upon the leg irons.

As the guards saw him take this position of rest, they were inclined to show one bit of mercy by letting him sleep out the remainder of the night if he could. But the sheriff, the next time he made his rounds, cursed them for their tender-heartedness. Let Dreer sleep with the light in his face. And did they not know that if this devil were able, he'd kill them all in order to get away?

So the guards changed the direction of the light from the two big reflectors, and focused it carefully on the outlaw.

And in that position he was forced to work, with the light flashing full upon him.

In a way it was a help, for even the most suspicious person would not suspect a man of trying to free himself in the glow of such a radiance, with four pairs of eyes turned on him again and again, a dozen times a minute.

Joe Chalmers alone would have been enough. He was the most trusted of the sheriff's henchmen. To him had been given the priceless key to the door of the cell. It hung at his cartridge belt. He had discarded his heavy, sawed-off shotgun, and instead of standing post he walked up and down the passage steadily, hour after hour, and the little eyes never lagged for a moment in their wariness. There was something terrible, something of the animal in this endless patience. To understand it one would only have to watch the wolf slinking ceaselessly up and down behind the bars of the cage.

In sheer bulk of muscle he might have been a match, single-handed, for the sinewy strength of Jess Dreer. And he had the facial conformation of a bulldog, the nose flattened away and the mouth and jaw huge, while his head was that bullet type which is incapable of holding more than one idea at a time. Yet for all his bulk Joe Chalmers was an agile man.

He was proud of the precedence which the sheriff had given to him. His pacing up and down kept him in the center of attraction as he walked in a narrow ellipse, turning toward the cell at one end of his path, and turning away at the farther end. And the other three interior guards naturally fell back and allowed Joe Chalmers to carry the main burden of responsibility. After all, it was he who had been reproved for not following the new position of Dreer with the lantern light, and it would be he who would be praised for their united vigilance.

He was a host of watchfulness in himself. During all his pacing he never took his eye from the prisoner except for the moment when, at the end of his beat nearest Dreer, he turned his back to take the back track down the passageway.

And during this half second, as the big man was turning, the active, strong fingers of Jess Dreer made a single deft movement, and between his fingers the stout little piece of watch spring turned in the lock.

Yet when the guard bent his eye on the prisoner again, the hands were once more motionless. Even if a guard had seen that motion of fingers, he would probably have thought it a convulsive movement, a twitch of the nerves as the man slept. For his head was fallen, and only through the long, sunburned eyelashes did he watch his guards and time the play of that watch spring.

It was tedious work. His arms ached from the awkward position. He had only a second of contact through the spring with the lock within. And after that contact he had to wait, studying the lock in his mind, remembering what he had done before, guessing at the mechanism, and ready with some new movement when the next opportunity came.

Still nothing happened; the lock held firmly; the iron crushed into his ankles, for the manacles were too small.

He had really given up hope some time before. His arms were numb and the nerves asleep from the shoulders down, yet he kept mechanically to his effort—one twitch of the spring each time the guard turned at the near end of his beat.

And then—he hardly knew what happened, except that the spring encountered something which resisted and yet yielded. And suddenly he felt the pressure of the iron about his ankles relax.

His legs were free! They were free, but not yet useful. From having kept off his feet for so long a time, the pressure of the iron had shut off the flow of the blood, and now they were numb, paralyzed.

He looked down; the irons remained apparently in place. Was it the weight of his hand that kept them there? He lifted his fingers—the manacles still stayed in place. But what if some unguarded movement should make the iron fall off with a rattle?

Now that the blood began to flow once more, his feet tingled, and it was almost impossible to keep them motionless. He set his teeth, and the perspiration burst out on his face.

CHAPTER 28

A movement with his arms was now necessary. He covered it adroitly by openly yawning—a sound that made every one of the guards whirl toward him. But they saw him straighten a little and drop his hands so that the manacles rested exactly between his knees. And then the pacing of Joe Chalmers began again, and the others relaxed. They were beginning to envy the resting figure of the prisoner.

Once more Jess Dreer began the subtle, careful movements. Of a different kind this time and necessarily more open. For each time that Joe Chalmers turned his back, he had to fold his hands together and strive to draw them back through the handcuffs. But the manacles fitted close, and these tugs were far more obvious. Yet the looseness of the sleeves of his shirt covered the careful movements of his arms to some extent. Also, the four guards were convinced that the man was now asleep.

Only Joe Chalmers continued to keep his eye on the figure under the brilliant light.

Still that patient work went on—until his hands were wet with perspiration and the skin was chafed from his wrists. Indeed, it was the perspiration which made the thing possible. The bruised wrist bones suddenly slipped through—the broad part of the hand was crushed together under the strain, and now—oddly light—his hands lay free upon his knees. He thrust them quickly down between his knees and waited. Though what he waited for, he could not tell. At least, it was impossible to do anything with four men waiting there in the passage. He suddenly realized how foolish, how futile, all his work had been.

Yet a great happiness was surging through his veins. His hands were free! Strength seemed to be descending upon him, showered out of the air.

And then—it came like a bolt on him: "Hey, Jess Dreer!"

He looked up. There stood the sheriff outside the bars, grinning at him. Had the sheriff seen all those futile efforts and now come to mock the prisoner with his knowledge? Or, worse still, was it dawn, and time for the journey to begin?

He looked up beyond the brilliance of the shaft of lantern light and saw that the square of the trapdoor onto the roof of the passage was indeed gray. The early light of day! Despair fell upon him. He was suddenly weak with it.

And this was what Sheriff Claney said: "Dreer, I forgot to tell you: Angelina gets a slug through her head as soon as it's light enough for me to see her."

The outlaw was stunned.

"The boys tried to ride her yesterday, and she pitched Gaston and then tried to eat him. We're going to put her out of trouble, seeing that you won't have no more use for her."

"Claney," said Jess, when he could speak, "give the old hoss a chance. Take her out into the hills and turn her loose."

The sheriff laughed.

"Sort of riles you, don't it, Dreer?"

And the tall man studied him.

"Why do you hate me, Claney?"

"Why does any honest man hate a man-killing thief?" returned the sheriff.

There was a long pause. Even the guards were stirred. Joe Chalmers stood scratching his head, and his face was troubled. Plainly he felt that all was not right, but he could not discover just why. Only something did not please him.

"I'll tell you why you hate me," said Dreer. "You're one of them small-souled skunks that hate a man they're afraid of."

The sheriff burst into a torrent of curses.

"I'll find ways of making this up to you, Dreer!"

But the big man did not hear him. He said at length: "Well, good-by, Angelina. And Heaven help you, Claney, if I ever get clear of the jail!"

The sheriff smiled again. He had a most evil smile.

"It'll be over behind Carrol's place in the corral," he said as he went out. "If you listen sharp, maybe you'll hear

159

the shot. It'll be in about half an hour." And he was gone.

The guards for a moment muttered together, but their commiseration of Dreer was interrupted by a clangor of tin in the outer office of the jail, and then a cheery voice calling: "Chuck, boys. Leave one of you gents to keep watch, and the others tumble out here and have doughnuts and coffee."

It brought a shout from the three, but Joe Chalmers shook his head.

"I ain't hungry," he said. "This is meat and drink for me!" he gestured at the prisoner in the cage.

So the three went out. They left the door wide. One of them came back and stood in the lighted opening, tempting their companion with the steaming cup and a handful of doughnuts. But Joe Chalmers shook his head doggedly and went on.

"What if something happens?" he said. "Who'll get the blame? You gents have your lunch. I don't need none."

He took a tug at his belt and continued the pacing, grumbling in his deep voice. He vented his anger by pausing at the bars and glaring at the prisoner. Then he resumed his pacing, but the moment he was on his way, a change began to take place in Jess Dreer's position. He did not wait now for the guard to have his back turned before he began to move. He had not time. For his plan was formed, and in that plan the saving of every available second was essential.

He began to move, but very slowly, gradually, steadily. He drew his hands back, he straightened by fractions of inches, he pushed himself forward on the bed so that his weight fell more and more on his feet.

Then, when he had gone as far as he dared, he began to gather himself for the attempt. If it failed, there would be either instant death, or else a certain death in the future. But he was ready for the chance. He began to gather his muscles under him as the football linesman crouches and grows tense as he hears his quarterback calling the signal and knows that the next play is coming his way. His way, and the goal inches ahead!

Down the passage swung the bulky form of Joe Chalmers. He paused halfway. Had he seen? No, he went on again; he turned at the end, and the moment his eyes had swung away, Dreer sprang.

One leap swept him out of the shaft of light, across the cell, and up to the bars. The back of Joe Chalmers was squarely turned, but as though he had eyes in the back of his head—perhaps some play of shadows had startled him —he whirled.

It was too late for the outlaw to swing the handcuffs with which he had intended to strike down the guard. In midair literally he saw the big man swerve and changed his plan. His feet struck the stone floor; he bounded forward again, and just as Chalmers swung fairly about, the fist of Dreer drove out the length of his sinewy arm with two hundred pounds of plunging weight behind it.

The blow struck Chalmers fairly on the point of the chin and flung him back against the wall. *Back* against the wall. That was the thing that broke the heart of Dreer, for if he fell there, Chalmers' body would be out of reach.

And it was even doubtful if he would fall. The brutal jaw might have absorbed the shock without transmitting enough of it to daze that brutal mind. Now Chalmers stood with sagging mouth, his shoulders against the wall, his eyes utterly senseless.

His knees buckled; he sank gradually, and then rolled on the floor.

"Heh, Joe, fall down?"

Dreer waited, his heart knocked at his teeth. But the question was not repeated. Looking through the open door he saw big, shapeless shadows brushing across the farther wall. He could make out the caricature of a head.

Then he dropped to his knees and stretched out his arm. His fingers fell short of the senseless body. He tried again, grinding the flesh of his shoulder against the iron, and this time his fingertips reached the shirt. He gathered it into a handful, cautiously, and when his grip was sound, tugged the big body slowly toward the bars. The shirt began to give way under the strain, and before it should tear with a loud noise, he shifted his hold, and this time he barely was able to reach the belt. Now the body came easily enough, the legs and the head trailing back. It was near; it was close to the bars. One moment of fumbling and the key was in the hand of the outlaw.

Now a door opened into the outer office. There was a tumult of shadows on the wall as Jess ran silently to the door.

"Chalmers! Booze!"

That call could not go without an answer.

"To the devil with the booze," Jess Dreer answered, deepening his voice as close as possible to the tone of the guard.

And in the excitement of the moment in the office they did not note the difference.

Now the lock gave under the key silently, for it was well oiled and new. A moment later Jess Dreer stood with the belt of Chalmers buckled around his waist and a gun in his hand.

Well for the guards in the outer room that one of them did not look in on the prisoner at that moment!

Yet he was still far from liberty. Far, indeed, for the only two exits lay either through the office itself or through the skylight and out onto the roof. He turned the chances swiftly in his mind. He might rush through that outer office and escape without being shot in the flurry of excitement, but the chances were large against him. On the other hand, if he gained the roof, there were the four men who walked their posts, one for each side of the prison. Yet the dull light of the dawn would make for bad shooting.

He made up his mind, and drew back for a run and a jump at the edge of the trapdoor.

CHAPTER 29

It was a big jump, and the great danger was that, in missing, his impact on the floor would surely alarm the men in the office, so he gathered himself, ran swiftly on his toes, and sprang. His hands slapped on the edge of the framing, the fingers slipped—and held.

He was swinging like a pendulum from the impetus of the leap, and taking advantage of the backward sway, he drew himself with a lunge through the skylight, and his knee rested on the roof.

Only now did he realize what freedom would mean. The gallows which had been his familiar thought, the death which he had been nerving himself to die, became dim, misted ghosts behind his conscious mind. And he saw, to the east, a long streak of white light, and the black hills tumbled away under it. There was his freedom!

He skirted across the flat roof, and at an angle looked down. Beneath him paced two men, meeting at the corner on each beat, and then turning their backs, like soldiers, and swinging off in opposite directions. Within three paces they were out of sight of each other, so Dreer drew back along one side and crouched to wait.

They were calling inside, thunderously loud: "Chalmers, Chalmers!"

Seconds would tell the story now, and how slow that fellow dragged along his beat, met his companion at the corner, and turned back. Half a dozen steps—a yell tore up from the inside of the prison, and the guard halted abruptly and looked behind him.

At that instant, like a black panther from an overhanging bough, Dreer dropped. His knees struck the fellow at the nape of the neck, and the blow stunned him. He was pitched upon his face, and Jess rolled half a dozen steps away, and came to his feet again, running low and fast across the clearing toward the nearest house, his revolver in his hand.

But not a shot followed him. The yell from the prison had dissolved into a shouting of many voices, and no doubt the other outer guards had hurried inside the jail at the very moment when they were needed on the outside. A moment later Jess was in the black shadow behind the first house.

It was his right direction, luckily, and he cut straight ahead at full speed, running as he had never run before. And how the absence of those irons gave wings to his heels! Behind him the uproar burst out of the jail and crashed through the open air. Doors began to slam open down the street; windows were smashed up. Other voices were calling here and there.

He had never dreamed that an entire town could be alarmed so quickly. It seemed to him that the noise spelled one syllable to the town: "Dreer!"

He whirled in at the saloon, vaulted the bars of the corral, and raced through the barn. His saddle was hanging on the very peg where he had left it. He reached

Angelina, standing with her sleepy head hanging far down, and cast the creaking burden on her back.

Angelina did not even raise her head; she did not even stir an ear. Such scenes as this were old indeed to her.

Jess Dreer could have burst into song. His own saddle, his own horse. Angelina of all others. With her stubborn sides between his knees he felt that he could mock the world. There was only one thing lacking, and that was the old revolver which hung on the wall of the office of Sheriff Claney in the jail. For that matter, he had two better guns hanging now from his belt.

But he would not have traded the original revolver for a thousand of the newest. It belonged to him, and he felt his luck was inextricably wrapped up in it. For a moment, sitting in the saddle, he hesitated; then he determined on the venture. Instead of cutting out of the corral of Carrol's place and heading for the hills, he jogged up the alley and swung onto the main street of Salt Springs. Almost instantly a volley of a dozen horses thundered down at him. Two of them swung off with a yell as he came into the road.

"Go it, boys! I'm with you!" yelled Jess Dreer, and waved his hat at the diminishing line of riders.

But now the gray dawn was growing every moment, and in a short time people would be able to recognize him. Up the street he went at the same slow trot, feeling Angelina unlimber beneath him and begin to come up on the bit, for the unaccustomed rest of the last few days had filled her full of running.

Straight to the jail went Jess Dreer again.

From a distance he could see single horsemen and horsemen in groups radiating from the open door of the sheriff like rays of light from a lantern, and he knew that the sheriff, the master mind, was directing the pursuit.

Why did the sheriff himself abstain from taking part? Like a wise general, perhaps, he preferred by far to remain behind the lines of action and view his troops at a distance, measuring chances and results.

There was a dwindling group of saddled horses in front of the jail, and now and again out burst a man, flung himself on his mount, and rushed headlong off.

Jess Dreer reined in Angelina and waited a little uneasily. For now the daylight was increasing with every moment, and his stay in Salt Springs became with each second doubly perilous. But it seemed to him that to the very tips of his fingers his hands ached for the familiar touch of his old revolver.

Still he delayed. A secondary purpose was beginning to form in his mind, a sort of delicate mental dessert, and he rolled the anticipation of it over the roots of his tongue, and grinned to himself in the dim dawn. Far away, he heard the pursuit splashing through the hills around Salt Springs, voices, even gunshots.

Yet he remained there at the center of his danger until there was left, before the jail, only a single horse. The moment he saw this, he sent Angelina into full gallop with a touch of his knees. Sheriff Claney came and stood in the doorway.

"Who's there? Down to the old fort, pardner, and ride mighty fast! But who are you?"

This as, instead of obeying, the new horseman flung himself out of the saddle.

"An old friend," said Jess Dreer, and thrust a gun under the chin of Claney.

The sheriff stiffened, as if suddenly petrified.

"Dreer!" he whispered.

"Don't beg," said the big man. "I got a sneaking idea that maybe you'll be on your knees in a minute, begging for your life. It gives me the creeps to see the yaller come

166

out in a gent, Sheriff. So I'll tell you beforehand that I ain't going to send a slug through you. Got two reasons for letting you off. First, because a shot would bring some callers, most like. Second, because I can do worse'n kill you, Claney. I can shame you so's you'll be the laughing-stock of the ranges. And that's what I'll do. Now turn your back."

The sheriff obeyed without a word.

"Step inside."

Inside went the sheriff. When the light struck him, one could see that he was quaking. His head and shoulders were sinking. Indeed, he seemed to be wilting away, as slugs will when salt is sprinkled on them.

"I had an idea you was a skunk," said Dreer, making a face as though he were swallowing a bitter pill. "But I didn't know the yaller streak was so wide."

The sheriff seemed tongue-tied. Dreer took from the wall of the room a long rope and spun it dexterously around Claney, weaving him, hand, foot, and body to the neck, in a tight coil of horsehair.

The sheriff's own wadded handkerchief made the gag, and it was wedged deep into his throat.

After this, Dreer looked around the room. It was in the wildest confusion. Chairs, overturned, lay here and there, even including the sheriff's own priceless leather-seated throne. And in his mind's eye the outlaw pictured the excitement when the yell of the first discoverer sent the guards rushing into the jail.

It was perfectly quiet in Salt Springs; but a ring of noise rolled farther and farther away around it. Dreer stepped to the door, looked out, and then came back and poured himself a drink from the uncorked bottle. He found his own revolver—already by the industry of the sheriff enclosed in a glass case with an inscription burned into the wood below it.

"Taken from the celebrated desperado, Jess Dreer, by Sheriff Claney."

"The dead come back to life," and Dreer grinned as he threw aside the two guns, unstrapped one useless holster, and slipped his ancient weapon into the other.

Instantly he felt a double reliance.

Going out, he paused by the sheriff, smiled contemptuously into the man's face, and seeing the eyes widen with fear, he turned on his heel and went out.

He was climbing into the saddle when three men plunged up to the jail.

"What's orders?" they called, still from a distance.

"Down to the Six-Bar Ranch," directed Jess.

"Are you going that way? Show us down!"

"What's the matter? Strangers?"

"Yep."

"Never seen Dreer?"

"Just got in last night. Heard about him, but never seen him. What's he look like, before we start?"

"I'll tell you as we go along. I'll be your guide, boys, and when I see him, I'll tell you what's what. Take him all in all, he looks a good deal like me."

"Thought he was a pile bigger."

"Come to think of it, I reckon he is. Let's start!"

And the four comrades raced off into the early daylight.

CHAPTER 30

Salt Springs was quick to rise to an occasion. It was equally quick to settle down after the crisis. For a week or so every man over fifteen years of age rode his horse to gauntness on the trail of Jess Dreer and then, as though by a sudden mutual agreement, every man returned to his habitual occupation. Jess Dreer, in a single day, was relegated to the past along with the raid of the Brown brothers, the fire of ten years back, and a few other upheavals which had wrecked the mental peace of Salt Springs for a fortnight.

Indeed, though each man would have given half of his life to gain the honor of capturing the outlaw, there was no personal bitterness to keep them on the trail; and as for the price on the head of Dreer, such money is not esteemed in the mountain desert.

Yet in spite of the numbers who had ridden their horses to a staggering condition during the past ten days, no one had been so busy as Morgan Valentine. Sheriff Caswell, seeing him come down the main street of the town this day, went out from the veranda of the hotel and stopped him. Purple pouches lay beneath the eyes of the rancher, and beside his mouth were deep grooves, and his cheeks were flattened.

The sheriff remarked these things aloud, and concluded: "Didn't know you'd been sick, Valentine."

"Not sick; busy," said the other. He added, looking closely at the sheriff: "You're staying with the old theory, Caswell? You're not following Dreer? You're waiting for him to travel in a circle and come back here?"

The sheriff shook his head.

"Takes nerve for a gent to change his mind," and he

smiled. "I've got nerve. After the last little party, Jess won't come back to Salt Springs. His face is too well known."

"You're taking your time about following him."

"I've been hunting around for a new hoss, and I've got a beauty at last. Look yonder."

He pointed to a pony chestnut with ratty mane and tail.

"Don't look particular like a picture hoss," said Valentine, controlling a smile. "But they's a nice set of legs and plenty of size around the girth."

"Yep; it ain't a picture hoss, but it's the nearest thing to Angelina that I could find. I tried him out a couple of days back, and he done fine."

He added: "But sounds like you're set on having me catch Dreer, pardner?"

He was surprised to find that this question did not bring an indignant denial from the rancher. The latter merely rubbed his chin thoughtfully with his fist.

"Maybe I am," he admitted openly.

"That don't sound nacheral, Valentine."

"After what he's done for my boy, Charlie?"

"Yep. And then, him being the sort of a gent he is all around. I didn't figure you'd be hot on his trail."

"I'll tell you," said the rancher. "If he was square in the eyes of the law, he's the sort of a gent that I'd work my hands to the bone for. I'd set him up in life and ask no questions, and he could have what he wanted for the asking. Maybe you think I'm talking extravagant?"

"I don't. In your boots, I'd do the same things."

"But," said Morgan Valentine, "the point is this: he's not square in the eyes of the law, and he never will be. I have wires through which I can reach some of the political heads, and I've been working night and day at two governors, Sheriff. I've been trying to get them to call off the dogs and let this man live his life without being forced into harm to himself and the rest of the world. But they won't do it. In fact, they know what Jess Dreer is. He has a character that makes good talking, and every one of 'em knows that Jess would go straight if he had the chance— and that he never would have gone wrong if it hadn't been that he fell into a bad hole with no way out except by breaking the law."

"That's what I've told a thousand people, most like."

"Well, they know all these things as well as you and I do. But Dreer is too big a gun. He's too notorious. Here and there and the other place he's shot up the second son of some rich family. Or he's made a fool out of some sheriff who's strong in politics. I'm not hitting at you, Caswell."

"It's all right if you are. I'd rather be made a fool of by Dreer than praised by most men."

"The end of the story is that the governor who pardoned Dreer would be ruined in politics. He'd have a host of enemies, and most like he'd be accused of having taken a bribe. They'll hear reason. They'd even be glad to have Dreer taken in some state outside of their own. But when it comes to a pardon, they won't hear of it. I've tried 'em all."

"You look worked out, Valentine; they ain't any doubt of that."

"Yes. Because I've worked harder for him than I would have worked for myself. But he can't be saved. And besides—"

He stopped.

Now Sheriff Caswell was by no means an old acquaintance of the rancher, but he knew him well enough to understand that Valentine was not a man of many words. For that reason this sudden outburst of talk surprised him, made him suspicious. After the first moment he had begun to wait for some unusual climax to the talk, and now he said frankly: "Valentine, what is it?"

"I'm talking pretty free," said the other.

"You're talking free to a man that keeps things to himself."

"Well, it's this: If I can't save Dreer, I'm going to ruin him."

The blow had fallen, but though the sheriff was prepared to be startled, he was nevertheless aghast at this revelation.

"That's free talk, and it's queer talk," he said slowly. "I'm a sheriff and my chief job is to get Dreer. But I sort of think that I'd rather you hadn't said that, Valentine."

"Do I sound like an ungrateful hound, Sheriff?"

The latter shook his head.

"A gent like you has reasons for what he does. They ain't any yaller streak in you. But maybe some of your reasons is wrong, Valentine. And why do you tell me all this? What's behind it?"

"Because I can't very well touch Dreer with my own hand."

"I'll tell a man!"

"And I have to use someone else."

"That's clear."

"And you, Sheriff, are the man!"

Once more the sheriff gasped.

Then: "Go on, Valentine. This sounds like a fairy tale."

"Walk on down the street with me. I get nervous standing still. First, tell me your plans about Dreer."

As they sauntered along, Caswell outlined his theory briefly. Dreer had headed north, in spite of the fact that other people were sure he was then riding south. He was heading north into a fresh country where his face was still unknown. He would travel slowly, not anxious to cover a great distance, for a man traveling too fast would be sure to excite suspicion. He might even stop here and there and work a few days. Such were the habits of Jess Dreer when he was on the road. Caswell intended to follow alone, weaving across the country loosely, like the line of a lariat tossed carelessly on the ground, until he found some traces of a tall man with exceptional arms, wide shoulders, and a long, lean face.

"Once seen, Dreer is never forgotten. And that's why I'll get him in the end—unless he gets me."

The rancher waited until he was through and then said: "Caswell, you're wrong. Your first theory was right. Dreer will come back."

He explained: "Out at my house my niece, Mary Valentine, is a changed girl. She doesn't go out to parties. She doesn't play around the house with the boys. When she's inside, she sits by herself with her hands in her lap, very grave. When she goes out, she rides alone."

"She's grieving for Dreer, Valentine."

"I know that. She gave up the trip East. When I pressed her, she said that rather than go she'd open up her father's house and live by herself, if I didn't want her.

"I was telling you that she spends a good deal of time out by herself on her horse. I thought at first that she was out to meet Dreer, who might be in hiding somewhere in the hills. So I had her trailed a few times. But she never met anybody. She'd get to the top of a high crest and sit her horse without budging for an hour. Always looking one way."

"North?"

"North," the rancher nodded, surprised by this interruption.

"I knew it."

"She acts, Caswell, like a half-breed wolf you've tried to raise as a dog. Tame while they're young, but some spring when they begin to rove around at night and stay away from the other dogs. And then one day they're gone, and you find a fine calf or two with its throat cut. You know what I mean?"

"That she's going to cut loose and go after Dreer?"

"That, or he'll come back to her. The two of 'em are a good deal alike in ways. The way one acts tells you what's going on in the other. Why, the girl is as silent as though her mind were a hundred miles away."

He grew excited, but graver than ever, and his face, as he talked, withered into the face of an old man.

"She's got to be stopped, Caswell, and you're the man who must do it. You have the hand of the law. I tell you, if the girl were mine—I don't know—I might let her follow her own nature. But she's not mine. She was given to me as a trust, and I'll give her a chance at happiness in spite of herself. There's the spirit of her father in her, Caswell. He was a man of whims and impulses. His first thought was his last thought. I was the only living human being who could change him.

"But nothing on earth can change the girl. She's like fire when she sets her mind on a thing."

They walked on again through a moment of silence. Both of them were thinking hard.

"I'll tell you," said Caswell. "They may be fate behind all this. I ain't seen much of that girl, pardner, but what I've seen, I've liked. Just the way I like a hoss that may of throwed a dozen men. Along comes the right gent, and when he can ride that hoss he's got something to keep for life. Now, look at the way that girl's flirted around. They ain't anything else to call it. They say she's made eyes at everything that wears pants inside of fifty miles and fifty years. One hour—she's tired of that gent and throws him for another. And she keeps right on. Then along comes Jess Dreer. She sees him—more'n half an hour. But she's still interested. After a while he's gone, and she sits down and mourns for him. Or else she goes out on her hoss and waits to see if Jess won't come sloping over the hills. Valentine, if I wasn't so old, that'd put a tear in my eye!"

But the face of the rancher was set.

"Fate or no fate," he said, "it can't happen. Go to a man like Dreer—lead the life of a wolf—hunted. No home— no children—my brother'd rise out of the grave, friend! Caswell, it's between Mary and Dreer, and Dreer has to go down. I'll strike him with you, if I can. If you fail, I'll try my own hand. But if she sees the man once more, it's fatal. Nothing'll hold 'em!"

CHAPTER 31

Between the dusk and the dark of this night a lone horse-man halted on a cattle path which led to low lands, and in the midst of the hollow was a broad, low barn. Even by that uncertain light the traveler could see that one end of the structure had fallen in. He shook out a white strip of cloth which he had kept in his pocket until this time, he tied the rag around his left arm close to the shoulder, peered about him as though he feared this simple action might have been seen, and rode his horse to the barn.

It was a gingerly progress. Coming a little closer, he saw that a faint light was burning in the barn. It made the structure seem huger than before and vastly more ruin-ous. At this discovery he checked his horse completely and studied the place.

At length, as though summoning his resolution, he pulled his sombrero so low that it quite covered the upper part of his face and raised the flap of his neckerchief so that it equally concealed his mouth and chin. This done, he pushed on briskly.

Not until he had dismounted before the great door of the barn did his former diffidence return. He slipped to the door and pressed his ear against a crack, but he could hear nothing.

Finally he knocked in a peculiar manner. Twice close together, a pause, and then three short raps. With this, the big door was seen to move slowly, a voice said softly from within: "Who's there in need?"

The first man started.

"A friend in need," he said in a low and hurried voice.

"And your name?"

"Gus Norman."

"Come in. And bring the hoss."

He now pushed the door wide open, so that Gus Norman could see, far in the interior of the huge, empty mow of the building, a scattered group of men and their horses around a single lantern.

Gus Norman went in, leading his horse, and looked sharply at the doorman. The latter was similarly disguised by means of a lowered hat and raised neckcloth, but now he lifted his hat for an instant.

"Sam!" said Gus Norman. Then: "What's up?"

But the doorman made a gesture commanding silence and Gus went on toward the group.

They were equipped, like him, each with masklike neckcloth and each with the strip of white cloth around the left arm, close to the shoulder. None of them seemed eager to stand close to the lantern, but each had drawn back beside his horse so that he was wrapped in the shadows as with a cloak. There was a general turning of heads toward the newcomer, but no one spoke. And Gus Norman seemed as undesirous of having the others know his face as he was eager to learn their own. He paused at a considerable distance from the lantern and leaned silently against the shoulder of his horse.

There were twenty men present, so far as he could count, and each was armed to the teeth. Now and then one of them spoke softly to a restive horse, but these deep murmurs only accentuated the common silence.

Presently, after an intermission of some five or ten minutes, another horseman advanced from the door, leading his mount, and this time the doorman, Sam Norman, came with the last arrival. He went gravely to the middle of the empty space from which the lantern light had driven the others, and he looked from side to side.

"I've counted as you come in," he said, "and they's no one left out. Every Norman that's old enough to carry a gun and shoot from a hoss is here." He kept his voice so low that there was a general cautious approach from all sides to hear him. "Now," he said, "I've done my duty. I've kept the door that I was called on to keep, and him that's to speak next, according to custom, let him step out —the man that called this meeting of the family."

He waited, turning slowly from side to side, but no one stirred.

Finally a voice called guarded from the rear circle: "The leader can't speak till the roll is called. Call the roll, doorman."

"Right," and Sam Norman nodded. He closed his eyes, as if to summon the list into his mind, and then began calling the names—first names only. One by one there was a deep murmur of "Here!" from the listeners.

When this was finished, the doorman paused again and looked expectantly about, but still no one spoke or moved.

"Brothers," said Sam Norman, "him that called this meeting has got to stand out. Fifteen years has gone since the last meeting was called by these signs, and they's some here that knows the signs but never seen a meeting before.

And I've been hoping that they would never come such a meeting as long as I lived. Him that called us, let him talk now."

Still only the heavy silence prevailed. There was a restless movement, then a murmur through the circle.

"Someone may of known the signs and called us for a joke."

"Brother," said the doorman sternly, "him that made that joke'll never make another. Still, him that called the meeting is wrong, because the law stands that they was never to be another called until a Norman was killed by wrong. That law was made while we was still living in Kentucky—before some of you was born. And they ain't any Norman been killed by numbers or by wrong since we come to the West. Remembering all that, let him that called the meeting stand out and say why he called it."

So intently had the circle attended these words that no one noticed, near the beginning of the speech, that the big door of the barn had been softly opened, and another member had come in. But now this stranger approached, leading a horse. The figure was in every respect like those of the others, but there was a general murmur, a general movement of weapons at its approach.

Sam Norman went farther than the rest. He whipped out a revolver and went a few steps to meet the newcomer.

"Who's there?" he called.

"A friend in need," answered the other faintly.

"Halt, friend. The number's been counted, and it's full up, and every face has been seen by me. Halt, I say!"

For the other, abandoning the horse, had refused to halt and had come straight on—a slender, short figure of boyish outline, and now, in the immediate circle of the lantern light, the hat was snatched off and hair tumbled across the shoulders of a girl. The neckerchief was lowered, and the circle found itself looking into the face of

May Norman. Her father uttered an exclamation of dismay.

"That law," said the girl, "was spoke wrong. The meeting can be called for any Norman that's killed by wrong. And it can be called for any man that dies for the Normans. And that's why this meeting is here. That's why the signs was sent. They's a man dead, brothers!"

She was a pale, round-faced girl, all her features diminutive except the mouth and chin. Her tone was a disagreeably harsh nasal. Neither in voice nor in face was she attractive, but there was an air of such dignity about her, and the raising of her hand was so solemn, that for a moment no one replied.

Then, from her father: "What man is dead?"

"What man is dead?" she cried, turning fiercely on him. "D'you stand there and ask me that? Well, speak up, Gus Norman. You tell 'em what man is dead that died for us!"

Gus Norman stirred, advanced a step, then shook his head.

At that she cried out: "It's Jud Boone that's dead fighting for our cause. I was the price that bought him to fight for us. You know that, Dad. The rest of you know it. He fought and died, and I seen him put in the ground. I waited while you was trailing him, but when I seen you all stop the trail, I called this meeting. It's my right, because I'm the one that was most hurt by a killing. Now I call for the law of the family to help me!"

She swayed them with her vehemence.

Yet her own father said: "He died, but he was killed in a fair fight."

"Does that change it?" she answered hotly. "If he was one of us and fought his own fight, it would be different. But he wasn't one of us. He fought our fight. Where was you-all when a man was wanted to face Charlie Valentine? You wasn't home. You was away. They wasn't nobody would do it. Then you went out and got a better man than you—you got Jud Boone. And Jud come and fought your fight and done what was asked of him—and now he's dead. He's dead! And I'm here calling to you and saying I want a death for a death!"

Her shrill voice filled the great spaces of the barn.

And in the pause, while the echo whispered back from distant recesses, she added: "I want Jess Dreer!"

Every man stood with his head bowed, thoughtful. At length Gus Norman came forward and stood beside the girl.

"She's right," he said gloomily, turning his hairy, wolfish face from man to man. "It means a feud, maybe. And maybe it don't. Dreer is an outlaw. We got a right to hunt him. And May is right. Come in, brothers. We need your heads, all of 'em. Step in and show your faces. This ain't work that'll be done tonight, but the plans for it has got to be laid. Sam, you're the doorman. Take charge."

Without a word the circle closed. And the hats were raised, the neckerchief flaps lowered from mouth and chin. Many a time in the past there had been gatherings such as these in the hills of Kentucky—the same dark, lean faces, the same bright eyes and savage mouths. The tie of blood was law to them—a deathless fealty to one another, a suspicion of all strangers.

Each, as he came into the circle of the lantern light, took the hand of May Norman and spoke the solemn formula: "Your cause is my cause; my hand is your hand."

And the younger men spoke the phrase eagerly. Something they had learned and spoken in whispers before. But all the older men, who had one time spoken the phrase aloud, were grave and downhearted.

180

CHAPTER 32

Sheriff Claney had one virtue worth ten ordinary qualities. This virtue was that he hated his enemies with a truly Old Testament virulence. Personal hatred, indeed, for another man, had been the reason that he first sought election as sheriff. And once in office he had very cleverly so arranged it that his personal enemy was found to be an offender of the law. Whereupon an arrest was made, resisted, and the sheriff in the exercise of his legal functions had shot the other squarely between the eyes and washed his hands of the old grievance.

For the sheriff improved on the word of the Scripture. Instead of tooth for tooth he was apt to extract two. But Claney loved his labors and loved his office. He loved to watch the face of a man upon whose shoulder the heavy hand of the law had fallen. Whether the fellow were defiant, sullen, pitiful, venomous, or despairing, the sheriff found a part of his palate which could relish any and all of these moods.

So he had been continued in his office. He was known to be fairly courageous; very deft with a gun and very free in the use of it; and indefatigable in the pursuit of his duties. Never before had Salt Springs enjoyed the ministrations of a man who seemed in love with his work.

He was elected; he was reelected. The men of Salt Springs were fond of showing off the industry of their sheriff compared with the sheriffs of neighboring counties.

But all this changed.

It was not that a prisoner had escaped. Not at all. Salt Springs was even rather glad that Jess Dreer was not to hang. But Salt Springs saw itself in the role of a town that has talked too soon and boasted too often. The invincible jail of which they had so often vaunted had been treated as a mule would treat a paper barn. Holes had been kicked in it, locks had been magically opened, and a man under special guard had been whisked away from beneath the noses of the sawed-off shotguns.

From the first this thing was not pleasant. It became more distinctly annoying when men from neighboring villages drifted in in the course of the next few days and dropped random remarks, such as offers of a loan so that Salt Springs could build a really effective jail; and offers of the loan of a man who would make a real sheriff.

This was putting the bur under the saddle, and Salt Springs began to buck. Every time it came down out of the air with bunched feet and humped back, it jolted on the thought of Sheriff Claney, the man who had been tied hand and foot by a prisoner and turned into a joke. Moreover, other murmurs were added to the rising tide. Men who had been wrongfully accused of various crimes came out with dark testimonies of the third degree harshly applied by the sheriff.

In fact, things reached such a point that in Carrol's saloon a man in the heat of liquor suggested that they tie the feet of the sheriff under the belly of a bucking horse and send him out to explore regions unknown. Others advocated a ride upon a rail to give him a new start in life. But though these proposals never got past the stage of talk, one and all agreed that strangers in Salt Springs would never lack subject of conversation as long as Sheriff Claney was in office.

And to make matters worse, his new term was but newly begun!

Friends called on the sheriff and suggested that he resign and go elsewhere to places where his undoubted talents could be employed and appreciated. But they did not know the sheriff. It was not that he wished to restore the affection of Salt Springs. He hated and despised them all, but he wanted to teach them to fear him again. He knew they were laughing at him and writhing because strangers joined in the mirth. It was dust and ashes upon the head of Claney.

Every day be bowed his heart in prayer that some gigantic crime would wipe out nine tenths of Salt Springs so that he could demonstrate his efficiency to the remaining one tenth. His dreams at night were filled with prodigies of shooting, and he walked the streets of the town hounding every man he met with a hungry eye that dared the other to smile.

And no one smiled. A man who is drunk is dangerous; a man who is justly enraged will keep a whole town indoors; but a man who has been shamed is a devil incarnate.

So he remained in Salt Springs, tormented by a dearth of crime, and burned away to a shadow by his shame and his hate.

Gus Norman, entering the office in the jail one day, found Claney sitting bowed at his desk with his head buried on his arms and his fingers sunk in his hair.

Gus Norman was not a fool.

He retreated on tiptoe, and when he came again, he was whistling discordantly, but in great volume. This time he found the sheriff seated with hair neatly smoothed, rolling a cigarette. He finished licking and lighting the cigarette before he spoke. He wanted to know just what brought a man that ought to be honest to the jail.

It was not a diplomatic opening to a prominent citizen, but the sheriff was far past diplomacy.

"I've come," said Gus Norman, "about something that's partly my business and partly yours."

"You're one of the thickheads that wants a new jail, eh?"

Gus Norman set his teeth and his bushy face was like a cartoon of the devil—one of those child-book pictures. "I want a man in the jail, not a new jail," he said.

The sheriff snapped his cigarette across the room. It struck the wall in a shower of fire that was dead before the ashes fluttered to the floor. He leaned across his desk.

"They's something doing? You got something on somebody?" he whispered.

Even Gus Norman was a little daunted by such ghoulish eagerness.

"It's something you already know. Jess Dreer."

The sheriff turned white.

"Go on," he said faintly.

"I think I got a line on him."

At this, Claney literally leaped to his feet.

"Norman, have a drink—no, talk—no, drink, and then you'll talk better!"

But the rancher was methodical. He wanted to show all his strength.

"First," he said, "I got twenty men who'll pack a gun in a posse that goes after Jess Dreer."

"Get to the point, man—where's Dreer?"

"Go easy, Sheriff, go easy. You ain't the first that's tried to hunt down Dreer with a public posse that everybody knows about. You ain't the first, and all the rest have failed. Why? Because every one of 'em worked in the open. And Dreer has friends who let him know when the law is on his heels. He's got a lot of friends. He's got friends in this here town!"

"D'you think I'm fool enough not to know that? Someday I'll get the hound that gave Dreer the watch spring, and I'll rope him to a tree. But—go on!"

In an ecstasy of impatience he dashed himself back into his chair and thrust his nervous hands into his pockets.

"You found a watch spring?" asked the curious cattleman.

"Yes—but go on!"

"My point is, that what you need is a gang that'll work secret. When we get Dreer spotted, they'll slip out of town one by one and collect wherever you say."

"I know that, don't I? But men who have to be paid publicly have to be hired publicly. How can I work a secret posse?"

"You don't have to work it. I've worked it for you. And the gang don't have to be hired. They'll pay their way."

The sheriff stared.

"What's more, when you nail this gent, Sheriff, we don't want none of the price that's on his head. You get it all."

The sheriff was not mercenary exactly, but this generosity made him gasp.

"What *do* you and your men get?"

"I'll tell you. We get the fun."

And there was such a collected, cold malevolence in his voice that even Sheriff Claney was moved.

"Norman," he said at length, "they's a lot more to you than I guess I've seen before. Now we'll get our heads together and talk business."

"Not yet," replied the cattleman.

He left the office and went to his horse. He returned carrying a small canvas sack, black with oil stains. He tossed this on the desk, and the desk shook under the impact.

"That's dust, Sheriff. They's about five thousand dollars in that sack."

By this time the sheriff was worked up to a high point of excitement. He touched the sack gingerly and snatched his fingers back as though they had been burned.

"Five thousand dollars!" he murmured, and his eyes went from the sack to the stolid face of Gus Norman. "Go on!" he ordered abruptly.

"That money is yours to use to get Jess Dreer. Me and my men have raised it. It didn't come easy. Nobody give us that coin for the asking. We earned it, and we dug into money that we got with sweat to give it to the cause."

He squinted his eyes, recalling the long deliberation at the meeting before the money had been raised.

"I don't quite foller you," murmured the sheriff, now quite humble. "I don't just see why we need this much money if your boys will work without hire."

"I'm coming to that, slow and sure. First, our line on Dreer."

"Yes, that's first!"

"You know on the day of the shooting of Jud Boone we tried to keep Dreer away from the saloon?"

"Yes."

"And you know that somehow he slipped through us?"

"Yes?"

"The fact was, Sheriff, that he was living right there in the saloon all the time."

"Then Carrol was in cahoots with him? What a fool I've been not to think of that!"

"We all was fools," said Gus Norman, showing his yellow teeth at the thought. "But here's the point: Carrol kept him while he was in Salt Springs. Maybe Carrol knows where he is now. They ain't any doubt of it to my mind. He travels free and easy up and down the ranges. They must be a reason for it. They's places where he

186

makes his money outside of what he steals. Carrol's is one of them. They're friends. Carrol knows where he is, and all we've got to do is to make Carrol talk."

"I'll get him here and use some little tricks I know," said the sheriff ominously.

"Lemme talk," said Norman. "He won't be an easy gent to persuade. But they's a way, Sheriff. I've figured it out. Carrol has a price."

"How d'you know that? His place makes a pile of money."

"But he puts it back in the game. Can't keep away from the cards. Right lately somebody's taken a pile of money from him. I know, because he borrowed money from me. He's near broke, right now. And I've figured up that his price is just what you've got in that sack now. Sheriff, I'd go and talk to him myself, but he's a hard man. I wouldn't have a chance to get talking. It'll be a pile different with you. He'll have to listen. You'll find out what you want to know, and after you find it out, you'll have me and my gang to work on the trail. Good-by."

And without waiting for a word of reply he rose and left the office.

CHAPTER 33

Suppose one were to lead a starved beggar to a loaded banquet table and then give him ten dollars to persuade him to sit down. The mood of Sheriff Claney as he stared at the canvas sack was the mood of the beggar. He had his first clue to the whereabouts of a criminal whose apprehension would not only restore his vanished prestige, but would even raise him up on a higher pedestal than before. To try and fail is human; to try again and then succeed is glory.

Sheriff Claney felt that his lean strong hand was extending toward the green wreath.

This time there would be no question of escape. If he came in range of the outlaw again it would be a matter of lead and powder and buzzard food left behind. Dead, he was worth as much as he was worth alive.

But in addition to all this, to have a sack of five thousand dollars added for his personal use! He rubbed his hands; for the first time since the jailbreak the heart of the sheriff was warmed.

But as for going to the saloonkeeper and gambler and thrusting the five thousand into his hands, this was not at all to the liking of the sheriff. He had another idea which was fully as good. As long as the correct information were exacted from Carrol, there was no good reason why the money should not remain in hands which would use it to far better advantage.

He went straight to the saloon with the gold in a valise.

"What's in it?" was the gambler's first question.

"Something I can't get here. Good booze."

The quip did not please Carrol. But he regarded the sheriff with a calm eye. If Claney had known parts of the gambler's past—certain parts which Jess Dreer, for instance, could have told him—he would have put a gun to his head before he would have taunted such a man.

But he ran on: "I've come on an unpleasant errand today, Carrol."

"Mostly you don't come on no other kind of errands. What's on your mind?"

"To put it to you straight; your games are on my mind."

"My games are straight."

"Of course you've got to say that."

"It's true, Sheriff."

"I been hearing stories. Lemme see. There was a gent that blew through town—little squat, fat, half-breed sort he was. Said you was working something that looked like a brake on your wheel. What about it?"

The gambler flushed.

"I had a fool working for me—that was six months ago. He come to me and showed me how he could fix up the wheel so it would make a pile of money for me. I told him I wasn't running that sort of a game. He thought I was kidding. I told him straight. But I took him on and give him a job; he was busted.

"Well, he was a snake. He knew how much I'd been used to making on the wheel. He fixes up a brake on the wheel, and of course he busts the boys for a great big percentage. He gives me what the house used to make right along, and he sneaks the rest of it into his pocket. In about a week I went over and watched the wheel one day. Seemed to me it was running queer. That night I looked it over and found the brake.

"I called in Tommy, gave him the licking of his life and a hundred dollars for luck, and sent him on his way.

"That's the only crooked thing that they's ever been about my house. I would of paid back the boys that lost their money. But how could I find 'em? And if they knew I was paying, would they of told me just how much they lost? No, they was nothing I could do. Besides, I didn't get the coin. It was the thief that done that. So there you are, Sheriff, and that's the truth."

There was no escaping from the sincerity of the man.

"It's the first time that I've ever been even questioned," he said gloomily.

"That's the point," said the sheriff hastily. "You been going on so long that some of the boys are kind of suspicious."

189

At this Carrol rose from his chair.

"Look here," he said quietly, "what are you here for, trouble?"

"Sit down, Danny. Sit down. I'm a reasonable man, and I got your interests at heart. You'll see that I have in a minute. Right off, I'm going to tell you that what some folks is kind of riled about. They don't like the sort of gents that you bring in and put up at your rooms, Danny."

"My friends is my friends," declared the saloonkeeper grimly, "and if you and the rest of the town don't like 'em, you and the rest of the town can go to the devil. That's straight!"

"Is that fishing for trouble?" said the sheriff coldly.

"You know it ain't—but you can take it any way you want. Name some of the gents that ain't been liked?"

"Jess Dreer!"

It shook Dan Carrol to his feet. Coming so smoothly, so unexpectedly, it was utterly impossible for him to control his expression, and his staring eyes had in a moment admitted everything.

He saw at once that he was exposed. The sheriff had tilted himself back in his chair and was grinning complacently at the other.

"It's a lie," was all he could say, more angrily than effectively.

"Hush up, Danny. You done it smooth, all right, and I wouldn't never have guessed it if it hadn't been for one thing—Dreer himself."

"Jess done that?" muttered the saloonkeeper. "He told?"

"I put him through the third degree, Danny, and he busted down and told."

Slowly, as though the strength were gradually melting from his legs, Danny Carrol sank into the chair.

"He done that!" was all he could murmur.

And he stared at the floor.

"But I didn't want to ride you about it," went on the sheriff smoothly. "I'll tell you why: I like you, Carrol. You look square to me, and I didn't see no good in making trouble for you for shielding an outlaw."

He paused to let the words soak in, then went on: "But now things are different. Dreer is gone from jail; I've got to find him; and I come to you and say: 'Dan Carrol, you know where Jess Dreer is. Tell me!' "

As he spoke the last words, he leaned over and thrust his fingers under the nose of the other. Dan Carrol raised his eyes slowly from the floor.

"Sheriff," he said, "I dunno. But—if Jess is a hound, then I'm worse'n a hound. And no matter what he's done to me, I still got to stand behind him. And if I knew where he was today, you couldn't drag it out of me."

"Carrol, go easy. I could bust you. It'd be a black case agin' you. First, a charge of using a brake on the wheel."

"Would you scrape that up?"

"Business is business. First the brake. Then this shielding of an outlaw."

"You can't prove it."

"I'll swear you've admitted it. Besides, I can prove anything on a gambler and saloonkeeper. You ain't got a chance."

Perspiration broke out on the forehead of Carrol, but he shook his head stubbornly.

"Me and Jess has been pals. Go ahead with your dirty work. I won't blab on him. Besides—I'm tired of talk, Sheriff. I need a drink."

"So do I," admitted the sheriff. "But I'm not through."

Carrol sighed and settled again into his chair. The strain had been great, and he was weary.

"They's one other thing I want to bring up in your

mind, Danny. If you lose this place, you lose a lot. You wasn't no church-attending saint a few years back. But you reformed. You settled down. You played square. You got a place for yourself in Salt Springs and people trust you. You're willing to risk all that in order to shield Dreer. I'll tell you why. It's because you've had some bad luck, Danny, and you've blowed so much coin that now you ain't got any more than a fingernail grip on your saloon."

Inspiration struck across the mind of the sheriff.

"Carrol, who brought you the bad luck? Who busted you, mighty near? It was Dreer playing with you every night!"

And the gambler nodded gloomily.

"Now listen to me, pardner. Will you talk turkey?"

"Not in a thousand years, Sheriff; I'm busted, any-ways."

The sheriff paused. He had worked hard to save the money for himself; but Dreer meant more than money to him.

He pointed to the satchel.

"Pick that up."

The gambler obeyed.

"It's dust. Five thousand. Carrol, that coin belongs to you—if you talk!"

The big hand of the other tightened on the grip of the satchel.

"He's north," he said huskily. "Windville."

Then realization of what he had done rushed on him. He hurled the bribe to the floor.

"You skunk," he cried. "Take the coin. I don't want it. Besides, I told you wrong. He ain't in a thousand miles of Windville!"

But the sheriff stood at the door smiling.

"Keep the money, Danny, and I'll keep my word. So long."

He was gone, and Dan Carrol dropped into a chair.

"Jess," he whispered. "It kind of busted out. I couldn't help it. Forgive me!"

CHAPTER 34

But the retirement of Sheriff Claney was purely a feint. He understood perfectly that if he had remained another moment in the room he would have had the money hurled at his head with a bullet behind it perhaps. He knew, also, that temptation is like whisky. It needs time to work. It goes down raw and makes one shudder with repulsion at first taste. Afterward, a glow runs through the body and fire mounts to the head. The world is seen awry.

In other words, the sheriff waited until the gambler had had time to estimate the value of that gold; he waited until Carrol, having finished the count, would have made up his mind to retain the satchel and its contents, for the sheriff was sure that once the man had actually fingered the contents, he could never let them go.

In exactly one hour the sheriff returned, and at a single glance he knew that his purpose was accomplished. The glance of Dan Carrol was no longer straight and solemn. It flicked here and there, and there was a glitter in his eyes that pleased the sheriff enormously. Dan Carrol had no word to greet Claney. But the latter had seen at once that the satchel had been removed; it was locked in the gambler's safe. It was also locked in his heart. He had estimated the sum. He had counted it. It was already a part of his life. Before the sheriff he backed into a corner and stood there like a savage animal, able to tear its keeper to shreds but held in awe of the trainer's whip.

This simile occurred to Sheriff Claney and made him smile. He enjoyed such scenes as this. Just as a chemist loves to watch some sturdy amalgam melt under the touch of an acid, so the sheriff looked through the eyes of Carrol and saw the disintegration of his soul and his honor.

After the opening pause the sheriff laid his cards frankly upon the table. He talked in a very businesslike manner. Not as one who is opening a proposition, but rather as one who has already reached an agreement and is now merely giving the details a final summing-up. He told Carrol what was wanted of him, not persuasively, but as if a refusal would have astonished him too much for words. He counted off his points on the tips of his fingers, and he kept looking at his hands instead of at Carrol's face, for he knew that if he did the latter, shame might undo all that he had accomplished with talk, threats, money.

After all, it was settled very briefly; one hour later Claney went back to his office in the jail and sent for Gus Norman. The latter came at once and was met with this question: "Can you give me a man with an eye in his head and a tongue he can keep from wagging too much?"

"Open up," demanded Gus Norman. "Then I'll tell you."

"I will. Here's the way it stands. I'm not going to tackle Jess Dreer in Windville."

"That's where he is?"

"It is. And I know the hotel he's living in—I guess they ain't more than one hotel there, for that matter. But I don't want to tackle Dreer in a town where he's known and where they's mostly his friends. I want to get him off by himself. Then I'll gather him in."

"That takes time."

"And I got the time to put in on it. I understand he's fixed fine in Windville and won't be apt to leave for a long time. Windville is so far in the hills that it don't hear nothing about what goes on in other places. It ain't ever heard of Dreer, maybe. Anyway, he's showing himself open up there, and everybody's for him. That's what Carrol says. First I want to send up a man and make sure he's there, and then give Dreer a letter."

"To tell him you're coming?" asked Gus Norman dryly.

"It's a letter from Dan Carrol," said the sheriff.

Gus Norman gaped; and then the two grinned in silent enjoyment.

"My boy Joe is the one for you. He's just up and around. And I guess he ain't got any reason for loving the Valentines and them that stand in with the Valentines. I'll bring Joe to you. Besides, riding is his long suit."

And Joe Norman was brought.

He was a very short distance into his twenties; a dark, handsome boy. His eyebrows met in a straight, black line; but the eyes themselves were rather wide and weak. His chin, too, was of Grecian roundness and strength, but his mouth lacked decision. He was the sort of youth about whom one would not venture to predicate much that was good or much that was bad. He obviously needed ripening; ten years would tell the tale with Joe Norman.

He had taken one great step toward full manhood in the past month. He had stepped up and faced his first gun fight without flinching. He had felt the tear and burn of a bullet through his arm. And now that he was himself again, the experience had fully doubled his self-reliance. Into his hands the sheriff, after a moment of explanation, delivered the letter, and the next morning in the early dawn Joe started north.

There were two ways to Windville. One was a straight

cut through the mountains, a journey up hill and down dale—dipping into little valleys where there were miserable ranches—and rising again to rocky heights. It was a leg-breaking short cut. The other means of approaching the town in the mountains was by no means simple. It would have wrecked the staunchest buckboard that was ever built, but it did not embrace half as many precipitous drops and back-breaking climbs. It was fifty per cent longer in time and a hundred per cent less in effort. So Joe took the roundabout way.

He was a skillful judge of the strength of a horse, and he handled his mount so well that he reached Windville a short time after dark. He went straight to Windville's one hotel.

Not that this was any imputation against the size and wealth of the little city in the hills, but Jack Turner had gathered most of the business of the place into his own hands and he had built this rambling structure which contained blacksmith shop, general merchandise store; hay, grain and wood, saloon and hotel, all in shed after shed, shack after shack, story after story, a confused jumble of which the proprietor himself did not know half the details. It had grown up in the course of two or three generations as wildly and as freely as if it had sprung of its own strength and its own volition out of the rocky soil.

To find a man in this place was like finding the proverbial needle. Joe Norman went straight to the source of all information—the bar; and to guide his inquiries he had only one bit of information—Jess Dreer was a gambler.

It was an old situation that met him in the saloon. Two men were doing the spending. One stood at each end of the bar, each trying to set up more drinks than the other, and each drawing his own crowd of followers about him. Joe Norman instantly took a place in the exact middle—neutral ground, it might be called. And there he remained while the bartender served several rounds of drinks. He kept his own first drink untasted on the bar before him, and presently this sign that he wished to speak privately across the bar was noticed.

The saloonkeeper approached and lent a hasty ear, for he was perspiring with his labors.

"Is there a game running around here?" he asked.

"Sure," and the other nodded, and lifted his eyebrows as he made the reply. "Go straight back. First door to your left. You'll hear the noise where you start going down the hall."

The first impulse of Joe Norman was to follow this advice. But it occurred to him as singular indeed that Jess Dreer, no matter how bold, should be sitting in at so public a game. So he remained standing at the bar with his drink still untasted until the bartender bent close to him again, this time with a frown.

"Anything wrong?"

"Nope. But ain't there a game where I *won't* hear the noise?"

The bartender returned no answer. He scurried down the bar and presently he flashed a keen glance at the stranger.

"Harry!" he called, and to another man in a white apron he said: "Take my place for a minute, Harry. I see a friend."

He came from behind the bar. Joe Norman had already taken the hint and retired to an obscure corner.

"Now, who are you, and what do you want?" was the first query.

"I want a game, pardner."

"Sure you do, but why?"

"Because I got a friend sitting in on it."

"Who?"

"His name don't matter," said Norman cautiously.

"Well, he's a tall gent—three inches taller'n me. Broad shoulders, long pair of arms, long, lean face, steady sort of eye. Know him?"

The bartender continued to dry his hands on his apron.

"Hmm," he said. "And who'll I say is here?"

"No name. Just tell him that a friend has got a message."

"Gimme the message, then."

Joe Norman hesitated. It might be that this fellow knew nothing, but he had to take the chance. Looking the bartender squarely in the eye, he smiled and waited in silence.

It seemed that this smile meant many things. "Oh," murmured the other. "Oh, that's it, eh? Well, come along. Maybe you ain't right, but I'm no mind reader."

He led past half a dozen little flights of steps, through many a crooked hallway, and came at length to a door which was totally black. No edging of light showed around it, yet on this he rapped. After a moment it was opened a little, and the light burst out. Joe Norman saw now that the edges of the door were padded with felt, the better to shut out light and sound.

From within he saw nothing, heard nothing except the subtle whispering of card on card as someone dealt swiftly, and the fall was deadened by the cover of felt on the table. It was the most exciting sound Joe Norman had ever heard.

In the meantime the bartender was conferring with an unseen man at the door, and in a murmur. At length the door was closed, and he turned to Joe.

"Come here. He'll see you in the next room."

He led the way to a dingy little square room with no light except a smoky lamp in a corner and there he left the spy.

CHAPTER 35

The sound of the door closing was to Joe Norman curiously like the click of a trap which held him in. He had been rehearsing his part all during the long ride of that day, but now his mind misgave him. It might be that Jess Dreer had seen him in Salt Springs. It might be that even the bartender had recognized him. That might have accounted for the sidewise rat look that the latter cast at him from down the bar on the occasion of his second question.

At any rate, obeying a sudden impulse of panic, he hurried back to the door and tried the knob. It was locked!

The blood rushed back upon the heart of Joe at that. There was a tingling at the roots of his hair, a deadly coldness on his face as though a breath of night wind had struck him. They knew him, then?

He stepped lightly to the window. It was open, but there was no gallery across it. Below him was a sheer drop of how much he could not well estimate in the darkness. Thirty feet, perhaps. He was trapped beyond doubt. He felt something behind him now—something impalpably taking hold on him, and when he turned, he found that Jess Dreer had silently entered the room and stood at the other side of it, rolling a cigarette.

He had never seen Dreer before; he had been refused admittance to the prison. But how could he tell that Dreer had not seen him? The rolling of the cigarette might mean anything. Perhaps the outlaw wished to appear careless at the very moment when he was striving most to throw the other off his guard. But there was no mistaking the man. He fitted so closely with the description of the broad shoulders, the singularly long arms, the active fingers, that Joe Norman felt that he had seen a photograph of the man—that he was remembering the lean, long face.

"How are you?" the outlaw was saying. "You got a letter for me?"

"Yep," murmured Joe. He was wondering if it had seemed suspicious, having been found at the window in that manner.

"Lemme have it, will you?" and with the same gesture in which he lighted his match, he nodded toward the table.

On the table accordingly Joe put the letter. And it seemed to him that while one eye of the tall man dwelt on the burning match, the other was fixed on the visitor. Presently he inhaled the first deep breath and sauntered to the table. He paused with his hand on the letter.

"I dunno whether I know you?" he murmured.

"You don't. But maybe you'll find my name in the letter."

"You know what's inside?"

"Nope, but I think he put my name in at the bottom."

"How d'you know?"

"I asked him to."

The outlaw hesitated another moment and then ripped open the end of the envelope and shook out the contents. He raised the paper.

It was infinitely instructive to Joe to watch the reading of that letter. The tall man seemed totally absorbed in the contents, but he had raised the paper high, so as to catch the lamplight over his shoulder, and with his back to the light he was in a position to keep his visitor in the corner of his eye. By a certain tenseness about the face of the man, Joe knew that he was doing two things at once—reading on the paper and reading on the face of his messenger.

A month before the thing would have unnerved the

youngster. But during the month he had looked death in the face and now, setting his teeth, he waited calmly for the end.

And this was what Jess Dreer read:

DEAR JESS: I'm breaking the rule and sending you a letter. The reason why is that there's a big deal ahead. I know it is not your system to team it with anybody, but I thought maybe you'd change your plans for a bunch of my friends.

They want you. They want you bad.

Here's the idea. They got a can of money spotted. They got some experts with the soup and can openers. And they'll have the whole job staked out. But if anything goes wrong, they want to have a good fighting head along to take charge. That's why they want you. They'll let you in deep. One third of everything. And nine chances out of ten you won't have to lift a hand.

If I thought they was any call for you to get mixed up in a scrap, I wouldn't send these boys to you, but I think the thing is dead easy. Also, they won't be any widows and orphans made out of this job. It looks like such a good thing that I had to let you in.

Here's another thing. You can trust these gents the same as you would me. Just say the word, and they'll tip you off to what's coming. The chief thing is to get a gathering place staked out near Windville. The idea is for you to find the place. Then one of the gents will go on ahead, meet you, find out where the shack is, and go back and meet the boys, who'll be on the way. It's a neat little scheme, and your trail will be covered inches deep. As ever, your pal,

DAN.

P.S. The gent that brings you this is one of the bunch, of course. His name is Hank Loomis. You can go as far with him as you would with me.

D.C.

Over the contents of this letter he cast his glance again, then thrust a corner of the paper into the lamp chimney until the flame leaped, the paper caught, and went up in a yellow blaze. He dropped the filmy cinder to the floor and crushed it to a black stain with his foot. Then for the first time he gave his undivided attention to the messenger.

"You're Harry Loomis, are you?" he asked.

The word tripped on the tongue of Joe, but he blinked and caught himself in time.

"Hank Loomis," he said.

"Sure. I guess that was what the letter said. You know me?"

"You're Dreer, I guess."

"Sure. Glad to know you. Sit down?"

"Thanks."

"You must of known Dan quite a while, eh?"

"Tolerable long."

"Well, sir. I'm glad to know any old pal of Dan's. Him and me has been pretty thick, off and on. Lots of good stuff in Carrol, eh?"

"I'll tell a man!"

The blood was beginning to run warm and free in the veins of Joe Norman at last.

"First look at Dan you'd think he was a sour sort. But he ain't. No, sir, Danny has a sense of humor. Ever hear that story of his about the tenderfoot and the forty-foot rope?"

Joe Norman chuckled.

"Yep, that's a good story, and they ain't nobody can tell it like Carrol."

"That's right. They ain't. Well, old Dan and me has had our times together."

"I reckon you have, right enough!"

"I remember one night down to Lawson—but maybe Dan told you about the time him and me rode the old spotted bull?"

"Sure. I'd like to died laughing at that yarn."

"And the way that old bull jumped the fence, and I fell off?"

"Yes, sir, he thought you was a goner."

"Tell you how it was. We'd been drinking just before."

"I remember Dan saying you'd blotted up some redeye just previous."

"And I didn't no ways have no control over my legs."

"That's nacheral enough."

"But I'll tell you one queer thing, Hank."

"Go ahead."

Joe leaned forward, grinning. He had heard of taciturnity in this man, and such voluble and friendly talk astonished him.

"Here it is," continued Jess Dreer, smiling broadly in turn. "In my time, off and on, I've known some gents with pretty strong imaginations, but I never seen one to match you, Hank Loomis."

And as Joe stared at the tall man, he saw that the other's smile was set, mirthless, derisive.

"Because you got a pile of ability to remember things that never happened." He dropped his right hand a little and leaned in his chair so that he had a perfect chance for his revolver. But Joe Norman made no move to fight. The blow had fallen and stunned him. And he remembered again—for the hundredth time—that he was actually in

203

the presence of the slayer of Jud Boone. And how many others!

"Speaking personal," continued the big man, "I've known Dan Carrol for a long time, and I've never heard him tell a funny story. And it wasn't me that rode the bull. And Dan Carrol wasn't never in Lawson."

The last remnant of his smile was gone.

"And so—" he said and waited.

Only one thing did Joe Norman see, and that was the bulge and fall of the muscles at the base of the outlaw's jaw as he set his teeth. And he knew that when he faced the leveled gun of Charlie Valentine, he had not been so near death as he was now. He was cornered, hopeless. Out of his very hopelessness he found the nerve to do what he did.

He leaned back in his chair and laughed—laughed straight in the set face of Jess Dreer. And from between his wrinkling eyelids he saw the outlaw wonder.

"I'll tell you what, Dreer," he said, sobering, and with a sudden burst of confiding. "I've made a mess of this. I guess I done wrong. But I'll tell you how it was. When the chief wanted to come up here with the letter, I begged him to let me bring it. You see, I wanted to be the first to see you. I sure begged to come, and the old man let me take the letter. He wasn't none too sure he was right to let me go, and now I see that he was right in doubting. Then when you got to talking, I thought I could bluff you— well, I was a fool. I don't hardly know Dan Carrol, but he knows the rest of the gang and he knows I'm straight. Does that clear me?"

He laughed again. His very hysteria made the laughter more real.

"I sure got tripped up quick, Dreer!"

The big man rose to his feet. He was frowning, in a quandary, and he stared down at Joe Norman.

"Hank," he said slowly, "I sure got an idea that you're double-crossing me. Dan named you—and Dan's *got* to be straight! Well, I'm going to take the chance. Take the chance on you. But I tell you now, son, you been near a bad time. But you go back to Salt Springs. Tell Dan Carrol that I don't like this game. That it ain't in my line. He ought to know that. But tell him that I know the luck was agin' him the last time we was together. He'll know what I mean by that even if you don't. And now, if he thinks it would sort of square accounts for me to play this game, I'm his man. I'll do the job. But the profits goes to Danny and not to me. Will you make that clear?"

"Sure."

"Well, be on your way, then. I guess they ain't any too much time."

He held out his hand and gathered that of Joe Norman in the lean, powerful fingers.

"Son," he said quietly, "are you straight?"

"Why," gasped Joe, "sure I am."

The tall man let the hand fall.

"I guess you are," he said slowly. "Anyway, you showed a pile of nerve a minute back—because I meant business. I thought—no matter what I thought. So long, Hank!"

And Joe Norman heard the door close behind him as he turned away. Once more it made him think of a trap, but this time it was closing upon Jess Dreer. And he, Joe Norman, was pulling the levers that closed on the famous outlaw.

CHAPTER 36

In the dawn of the next day Joe Norman took horse and rode again for Salt Springs with a rested mustang under him; and in the first dark of the night he reached the town once more. A great many things may happen in the mind of a man between dawn and dark, and a very great many had happened to Joe Norman. Vague motions were passing through his small soul all that time, troubling, overwhelming him, almost.

For he began to lose the malignant hatred of the Valentines which had spurred him on at first. He was seeing himself in a different light. The whole thing sprang out of the smile of Mary Valentine at that dance. It had gone to his head. It had robbed him of his senses. Then the pang that had gripped him when she turned away from him the next time they met; the hasty word that burned his tongue the moment he had uttered it; then the meeting with Charlie Valentine. And out of that the affair went on into other hands.

Still it was the smile of Mary Valentine that was the starting point. It dazed the boy to think how much had come from flirting with that slip of a girl. It was because of that flirtation that he had fallen. And then, to avenge him, Jud Boone, the man-killer, had been called in to strike down Charlie. And to meet the power of Jud Boone, the Valentines had appealed—through Mary herself, perhaps?—to a still more dreaded name, Jess Dreer himself. So Jud Boone had died, but still that smile of Mary worked. It was poison running through many minds.

Jud Boone was dead, and now the cause was taken up anew. There was another goal—Jess Dreer himself, against whom all the power of the Normans, all the cun-

206 of the Normans, all the cun-

ning and strength of the law, was turned. And what was the cause? Because Mary had smiled!

One man shot, others brought to the verge of death, one killed in the midst of his prime as a fighter, a jail broken, a town cast into confusion, and twenty men ready to take the trail for the head of Dreer—all this out of the smile of a girl.

Two things connected themselves in the mind of the boy, at the end of all this remembering—Jess Dreer and Mary Valentine. They were the beginning and the end. He felt that there was also a kinship between them. She was more beautiful than other women. And Dreer was stronger than other men. And surely there had been no spite or malice in Mary. He was able to recognize that, at this distance. He saw that she had simply been playing a game that other people, without her will, turned into deadly earnest. Truly, it was not fair to accuse the girl. No more than it was possible to accuse Jess Dreer of sneaking crimes.

A dozen times he jerked back on the reins and brought his horse to a stand as he remembered those words: "Son, are you straight?"

And he had lied. Something told him that another man, the moment the first deceit was known, would have gone for his gun. But Jess Dreer had waited. He had put his trust in Carrol, and Carrol had sold him. Vaguely, Joe Norman wondered how any human being could sell such a man as Dreer. His right hand tingled still, in memory, where those bony fingers had closed over it. And he felt that the glance of the outlaw, plunging into his soul, had found good metal there, and something clean, and he had been trusted for his own sake as well as for that of Carrol.

His head would jerk up when that occurred to him.

Suddenly he was in Salt Springs. And he was sorry. He wished that what lay before him could be postponed. He wished that the trail still stretched far ahead of him, so that he could think, his thoughts keeping time to the sway of the mustang.

But now the horse was put up, and he was in the sheriff's office at the jail, with his father before him and Claney at one side. He was seeing them both in a new light, and a filmy figure was between them and him—the face of Dreer.

His father took one look at him and then growled: "Bad news!"

"It can't be bad news," said Claney. "He's just fagged. Sit down, Joe."

And Joe sat down. His mind was working dimly, but like lightning. He was seeing many things, but none of them clearly. Chiefly he felt that what had at first been a natural thing, the carrying on of a feud just as he had heard the family used to do in the old day in Kentucky, was now different. It was cheap, false, dirty—it was the betrayal of a fine man.

"Well," said the sheriff at last, "bad news or good news —out with it!"

"Bad news," said Joe slowly.

"Well—"

"I didn't find Dreer."

That was all he could think of. It gave him a moment for further thought.

"Then why the devil did you come back? Why ain't you up there looking for him?"

That from his father.

"I done what you told me," he said stubbornly. "And he wasn't there."

"Did you ever see such a boy? And why didn't you hit his trail and find him? Afraid?"

"They wasn't any trail. He ain't the kind that leaves a trail."

208

The two older men silently glared at him. Then they stared at one another.

Suddenly Claney leaned forward and stretched out his left arm on the desk. He began to count off his questions with the forefinger of his right hand, touching each of his left-hand fingers one by one and then curling them back so that at length a clenched fist was shaking under the face of the boy. That was his attitude of public questioning. That was the attitude under which more than one sneaking cattle thief had wilted.

"Where'd you go first?"

"The only place they was to go."

"That ain't answering me. Where'd you go?"

"To the hotel."

"And you asked for Jess Dreer?"

"I ain't fool enough for that."

His father put in: "The boy has some sense, Sheriff."

"Shut up," said Claney, "I'm doing this! Well, who did you see?"

"Looked over the bartenders and picked out the wisest-looking gent of the bunch. Then I stood off by myself at the bar and fooled with my drink till he seen I was waiting for something. Finally I got him over to one side—"

"And asked him where Dreer was?"

"Nope, I asked him where they was a game going on."

"Good!" chuckled the father.

"Shut up!" cried Claney savagely. "What did he say?"

"That if I went down the hall I'd find a game—I could hear the boys talking."

"What did you say to that?"

"That I wanted to find a game that wouldn't make so much noise. Then he loosened up and asked me what I wanted. I told him I wanted to find a gent that looked like Dreer, and I told him what Dreer looked like."

"And?"

"And then he looked me over for a minute and finally he made up his mind I was on the inside and he told me all about it. Dreer had been there playing a game pretty steady. But the day before he hit the trail."

"What trail?"

"I dunno, and the barkeep didn't know."

"Why not?"

"I dunno."

The sheriff gritted his teeth. "Then—we're done! The whole game's off, and Carrol is in five thousand!"

"Take him the letter," said Gus Norman, "and make him give back the coin."

"Couldn't be worked—but I'll try. Let's have the letter, Joe."

"Why—I—burned the letter, Sheriff."

"You what?" interrogated the sheriff angrily.

"Was I going to keep packing around a letter to an outlaw that'd be about enough to hang me, after the letter wasn't no good any more?"

The sheriff settled back in his chair.

"What'd you do to it?"

Gus Norman was about to explode, but the raised hand of Claney stopped him.

"I—burned it, of course."

And he fought the critical eye of the sheriff. Claney began to smile.

"Joe," he said, "you've done noble—but not noble enough. You been lying!"

"Me?"

"Don't stand up. Don't pretend to get mad. You changed color the minute I mentioned the letter, son, and I seen it. Talk turkey, now. What happened between you and Dreer?"

Gus Norman cursed and exclaimed. "He's been bought off! I'll—"

"You'll forgive him if he tells us the straight of it. Now talk, Joe. You're among friends. But if you double-cross us, we'll make it hot for you."

"It'll be the last day he spends under my roof," declared Gus Norman fiercely.

"Steady, Gus. Here, Joe. Have a drink. That'll help you."

The nerve of Joe Norman had remained steady up to this point. The offer of the drink—the tacit assumption of friendly superiority, crumpled his powers of resistance. And all in a minute the lies of the interview were torn to pieces and thrown away. The truth was blurted from his lips, and the trap from which he had tried to free Jess Dreer was set and cocked by his own hand.

CHAPTER 37

From her window, Mary Valentine watched the moon go up. She could have named every hill as the pale light picked it out, but her mind was too absent for that. Voices sounded in other parts of the house, but she heard them as from a great distance. All the world was blurred for her and had been blurred for many days. Sometimes she found herself wondering at the change that had come over her; sometimes she would waken in the middle of the night with an old hunted feeling. But there was nothing on which she could put her finger and say: This or that has happened. It simply seemed that she had drifted into a new life, misted with unhappiness.

No wonder then that the knock was twice repeated before she called, and the door opened to Morgan Valentine. He came slowly across the room to her.

"Sitting here in the dark?" he asked.

"It is dark. I was watching the sunset. I didn't notice how the time ran."

He waited a moment. Then: "They's a caller for you, Mary."

"I'm not feeling like callers, Uncle Morgan."

"Honey, I wish you'd make an exception."

"Well, if you wish it."

She rose. After all, it made little difference. Except that she had grown to have a singular preference for being alone.

"I do wish it. You're going to fly out at me for asking you to see him when I tell you his name."

"I won't fly out at you. I'll promise that."

"Oh, girl, sometimes I almost wish you would have the old tantrums. Well, it's Joe Norman."

"Joe Norman?"

"There you go!"

"I—I couldn't help it. Joe Norman!"

An intolerable disgust crept into her voice.

"He's a pile changed, honey. He asked me to see Charlie first. He shook hands with Charlie—told him he knew he'd been in the wrong—that he was sorry so many things had come out of it. Charlie shook hands right off and now they ain't any malice between 'em. Will you see him, Mary?"

"You want me to?"

"I'll tell you why. I sort of feel that if you shake hands with Joe Norman and call it quits we'll all get back to the old standing. Same as we used to be before all these things happened—all these things that begun with the shooting of Joe Norman."

She shook her head, but in the darkness he did not see.

"I'll go out and see him, then."

"Thank you, Mary."

They went out through the living room.

"Joe's in the parlor. He said he'd wait in there alone."

CHAPTER 38

Mary passed down the hall and paused a moment at the door. Joe Norman was the man who, indirectly, had exiled Jess Dreer. But finally she opened the door and stepped in with a calm face. Joe rose to greet her.

He was so changed that she almost cried out. The youthful curves were gone from his face. He seemed suddenly to have grown up. His eyes were dull and very deeply shadowed.

All her anger, all her loathing melted away. She went straight to him and took his hand.

"If I'd known it would be as easy as this," said Joe Norman, smiling faintly, "I'd of come before."

She brushed that remark away.

"But you're changed, Joe. What's happened—" She checked herself suddenly.

"I was thinking the same thing," murmured Joe. "You're changed, too, Mary. Thinner. Not so much color. But—it sort of makes your eyes look bigger. And you're quieter, too."

She was wondering why there was no sting in seeing him. "Do you know, Joe," she said suddenly, "we were

213

both too young. And what's happened has waked us up, changed us both. If there'd been any bad feeling, it's all gone now."

"I'm glad to know that," said the boy soberly. "I'm leaving Salt Springs and going off. I wanted to shake hands and know that it was square between us before I started."

"But where are you going, Joe?"

"I'm cutting loose. I don't know where I'll land."

"You've been in trouble, Joe."

"Pretty bad. You see—me and my folks—you'll hear about it, anyway, so you might as well hear it from me. We had a difference, and they sort of threw me out, Mary."

"I'm sorry, Joe. Very sorry."

"Thanks. But between you and me, I have an idea that it was the best thing that ever happened to me. I was different all the time, and just lately I've found it out."

He began to study the floor, hunting for something to say and finding nothing; and the girl was silent likewise.

"I suppose I'll be going. But we don't see you around much lately. I hear folks talking about it."

"I've settled down. I stay about the house. You'd think I were waiting for something to happen to see me. Goodby, Joe."

He took her hand, but at the door he turned again.

"Something sort of bothers me about what you said just now, Mary."

"You can talk straight out to me, Joe. We're old friends."

"I was wondering—if you really wasn't waiting for something or for somebody?"

She flushed at that.

"You ain't mad, Mary?"

"No—I guess not. What put the idea in your head?"

"Well, people say a good many things. I won't believe 'em, if you say they're wrong; I haven't believed 'em up to now. But what they say is that it was you that got Dreer away from the house that night. And that it was because of you that Dreer met—"

"We won't talk about it."

But he was studying her face, and the pain in it. All at once he dropped his hat and took her hands.

"Mary, it's true?"

"About—"

"About Dreer? You're sort of fond of him, Mary?"

"No, no! I hardly know him!"

"He's the kind you only have to see once to know. I seen him once, and I know him already better'n any man I ever met. Mary, it's true. You're fond of him, sort of?"

"You've heard too much talk, Joe. Forget all that."

Once more he turned toward the door. When he looked back again, she caught in his face an expression of profound pity. An instinctive fear rose in Mary Valentine; she slipped between him and the door.

"What's behind your questions? Tell me that before you go. Do you know something—about—him?"

She was making no attempt at concealment now. Her heart was in her white face, in the great eyes that met the eyes of the boy. And he winced before her.

"Joe!" she cried under her breath. "They've taken him! That's why Uncle Morgan and the rest have looked at me so queerly the last day or two. They've known, but they wouldn't tell me!"

"Mary, I swear it isn't that!"

"You're lying, Joe. I can see the whole truth behind your eyes. Oh, Joe, tell me what's happened! Tell me they haven't taken him!"

But the boy shrank from her; there was something like fear in his face. He said, wondering: "Mary, you *do* love him!"

"I do. I'm proud of it, Joe. I love the ground he walks on and the air he breathes. One shake of his head is more to me than all the talk I've ever heard from men or women. You see that I've humbled myself to you, Joe. I've hidden nothing. And now—be just as true to me. Tell me what you know!"

He shook his head, agonized.

"There's nothing that can be helped. It's as good as done already."

"What? For Heaven's sake, what?" She stopped, her lips parted.

"Joe," she whispered, "he's already dead! They've hunted him down—with numbers!"

"No, no!"

"I can stand it—so long as I know. Anything is better than imagining."

He could not speak.

"Only one thing. Tell me where it was?"

"If I'm wrong to tell you," said the boy, "God forgive me. I've done you wrong before, Mary."

"I'll forgive it all—everything that may happen—but tell me the truth, Joe!"

"Then—it ain't happened yet, Mary. But it'll happen before morning is well on. An hour after the sun comes up. That's the time they've set."

"Then why are you here? Why haven't you raised the town?"

"To save an outlaw?"

It crushed the words unspoken on her lips.

"Besides, they kept me at home under guard for fear I'd do something. When I got out, I came here. It was too late to follow 'em when they let me loose."

"When did they start?"

"Late this afternoon."

"And now it's night!"

"Yes. Too late to do anything, Mary."

"Where—"

"Near Windville."

She ground both hands against her face.

And then she heard him say: "It's too late. Even if it was day, it'd be too late, though then I might try to ride across the hills on the short cut. But by night—it'd be suicide, Mary!"

She had come to life suddenly.

"Oh, Joe, you know that short way? Would it take me there before morning?"

"Even then it'd be an hour too late—even if you killed your hoss, Mary."

"But if I could fight all night—and come within an hour of saving him? Joe, you'll show me the short cut?"

"I'd do more'n that. I'd ride with you, Mary. I got a — debt to Jess Dreer that needs paying terrible bad. But it ain't possible, I tell you."

She became calm, though her hands were shaking.

"I'm going into my room to change my clothes to an old suit of Charlie's. While I do that, you go out to the barn and get the boys to saddle Uncle Morgan's Gray Tom for me. You'll do that, Joe?"

"Will nothing change you, Mary?"

"I'm not going because I have hope, but simply because I got to do something. Joe, will you help me?"

"I will."

"God bless you!"

And she was gone through the door like a flash.

CHAPTER 39

Hope is contagious; even Joe Norman was touched by it as he hurried out to the stable. He gave the word from Mary Valentine, and it was obeyed with some hesitation, for no one on the ranch had ever heard of another person than Morgan Valentine himself riding the gray stallion. But they were accustomed to taking the word of Mary as a law second only to that of the master of the house. Or even before it, on occasion.

So they led out Gray Tom.

He was a fine fellow of fifteen three, muscled beautifully for speed, with long antelope legs.

"And enough bone in 'em to write poems about," as Joe Norman himself had said.

The saddle of Mary Valentine was cinched on the long back of the stallion, and then she came herself, running as freely and swiftly as a man in her boy's clothing. One word to Joe, one wave to the stableman, and they were into the saddles side by side and off at a rattling gallop.

The difference between the two mounts was at once apparent. Joe Norman rode a fine horse that would have rejoiced the heart of the most particular cattleman, a sturdy, stout-hearted, durable-legged animal with speed enough for any. But in the very beginning the cow horse was straining his utmost to keep up, and Gray Tom was running well within his strength, with a wide-stretching gallop. He carried his head high and free, while Norman's horse was stretched out straight as a string.

"You'll kill your hoss before you're halfway there!" shouted Joe. "Rein in, Mary. You'll kill Gray Tom!"

"Let him die," she answered through her teeth.

"Morgan Valentine'll never forgive you."

"I'll live without his forgiveness. Faster, Joe."

"My hoss won't stand it. He's busting himself wide open now."

She looked across at the laboring animal and at once saw the truth. If she were to keep with her guide, she would have to alter her speed, and reluctantly, with a sob breaking in her throat, she drew the rein of Gray Tom.

Even then they were cutting across the hills at a dizzy rate—and Windville so many and many a mile across the broken mountains!

They were striking straight for the tallest and blackest of the peaks now, and presently they dipped down a sheer bank and into the dry bed where a great river had once run. The shod hoofs of the horses beat up a terrific rattling, and the echo from the stones knocked against the banks and came back at them, before and behind.

It was hard going, too, with the danger always before them that one of the horses might pick up a sharp rock at any time and be rendered helpless, useless for that night's work. But Mary Valentine was setting the pace, and Joe reluctantly spurred up beside her.

It was dangerous going, but the river bed gave them a perfect grade by which they ate into the heart of the high country. And Mary cried out in her disappointment when the gravel road terminated in an abrupt mound, where a landslide had buried the old bed.

There was nothing for it but to hit up the slope which lay straight head of them; as they struck the softer soil above the bank, Mary reined in her horse and raised her hand.

"Do you hear, Joe?" she whispered.

"Nothing. Where?"

"Out of the river bed behind us."

"What?"

"Listen again!"

He bent his ear and now, indistinctly, he made out the far-off clattering of a horse that galloped across the pebbles.

"It's Morgan Valentine," he said gloomily. "They've told him about you taking Gray Tom, and he's following you. Mary, be reasonable. Give up and go back!"

"I'll die first," sobbed the girl. "Come on, Joe. Hurry!"

And she sent Gray Tom scurrying up the slope.

Joe Norman followed reluctantly, shaking his head. But in this uphill going the shorter-legged mustang did far better, by comparison, than he had done in the level. He was made for the sweat and grind of climbing, jumping, side-stepping rocks, vaulting over fallen trees. And obstacles that maddened the high-spirited Gray Tom were taken in the most casual manner by the cow pony.

It was only a brief climb to the first ridge, but when they came out on it, Joe Norman stretched out his hand and caught the reins in the hand of Mary.

"Look ahead!" he commanded.

The girl obeyed, and her heart sank.

Ridge after ridge lay before them, sharp-crested, with the rocks on the summits glittering in the moonlight and the forest everywhere black, somber. It was such a sight as everywhere sends the thoughts of men to the shelter of a home. And as she looked on it, despair fell on Mary Valentine.

"And that's not all," said Joe Norman. "They's a lot more of it than you can see from here. We're just on the edge of it. Them ranges are like rows of teeth. And the sides of some of 'em are as slippery as teeth. Mary, give it up. They ain't any use. You'll kill Gray Tom, and you'll kill my hoss. I don't care about that if we could gain anything in the long run. But we can't. We're beat before we start. We was beat before we left the house, and I knew it, but I thought I'd come out with you and let you take the first run, so's the night wind would calm you up some, and you could see it was impossible."

"Then you lied, Joe. You said it could be done by day."

"I dunno. Maybe it could be done by day. But by night it's pure suicide. Will you believe me, Mary? There's slides that take your breath even when you got the sun to help you. But the moon ain't any good for ticklish work. It just shows you a pile of things that really ain't there. And the real dangers it covers up. Will you believe me, Mary, and turn back?"

"Go back yourself, Joe. I'll go on. I've got to go on. But you go back, and I'll find a way."

She touched Gray Tom with her spurs as she spoke, and the big stallion sprang out to the full length of his stride. He landed far down the slope, crashed upon some loose rock, staggered, and then plunged out of sight in the thicket with the noise of a living landslide.

Joe Norman screamed: "Mary! You're gone mad! Mary!"

Only the noise of her wild descent roared back at him. He spurred his own mustang with a shout of horror and galloped after her. But more carefully, letting the half-wild horse have his head partly to himself, for he knew that the instinct of the brute was all that could save them from being dashed to pieces a thousand times in such a place; no cunning of hand or sharpness of eye could warn the rider in time.

It was a nightmare to Joe Norman. Somehow, they came out on the clearing at the bottom of the slope, and stretching across the open ground, he saw Gray Tom flash in the moonlight and then lunge once more into the dark of the forest toward the next ridge.

An exultation that was half the cold of fear ran through the veins of Joe Norman. He spurred his horse frantically, and striking the far slope at full speed, they followed the crash of Gray Tom, leading the way. Close to the top, he shouted again, and when he reached the ridge, he found that she had reined her horse for a moment and was waiting for him. Gray Tom was panting as if he had run twenty miles.

"You're killing him," he warned her. "But let him die, then. More to the left, Mary. You see that tall, bald rock? Holy Mount they call it? Strike toward that!"

"Thanks, Joe. But faster, Joe. You keep me back!"

"I keep you back to sense. But come on!"

But there was no keeping the girl back. Once more she spurred Gray Tom, and once more the stallion, frantic in this wild ride, leaped out through thin air, smashed into the thicket far below, and went thundering toward the bottom of the slope. A sort of frenzy seized on Joe. With spur and quirt he sent the mustang flying down after the girl, and the wild horse went snorting, dancing like a sparring pugilist through the maze of young trees and shrubs, and coming out at the bottom almost even with Gray Tom.

In the middle of the narrow valley floor Joe Norman drew rein with a low cry of warning. The girl checked her horse.

"Look up and back. Up to the top of the last ridge, just where we come over it!"

She obeyed, and distinctly outlined, black against the moonlit sky, she saw a horseman top the ridge and shoot down into the forest with a noise that came distinctly to them.

"That's not your uncle, Mary. Your uncle would never ride as crazily as that. Who is it?"

"I don't know. It might be Uncle Morgan. But there was something I recognized about the way he sat the saddle, sort of sidewise. But come on, Joe. Whoever he is, he can't catch us."

And they drove together at the next slope.

Fear was in them now, not so much of the dangerous trail which they were following as of the unknown man who rode so desperately after them. For if he had been a friend, surely he would have tried to hail them. From the top of that last ridge he could easily have reached them with his voice, but they had not heard a sound.

This slope was not so heartbreaking as the others, but, nevertheless, Mary Valentine held Gray Tom in. The harshness of his breathing was beginning to alarm her, and she knew that it is possible to break the heart of a horse in a very short time if he is allowed to run himself out. So she nursed the stallion up the slope. He was in better condition already when he reached the top, and as they swung in a canter down a more moderate fall of ground beyond, Mary swung close to Joe.

"I've remembered who that was like," she called. "The man who's following us is Sheriff Caswell!"

CHAPTER 40

It was a calamity of the first water. What was the use of riding to Jess Dreer if they brought his deadliest enemy in their wake? One hope remained, and that was to distance the sheriff and reach Jess far enough ahead to allow him to escape.

So they gave their minds grimly to their work.

They had not even time to talk, save a broken phrase here and there, but as the ride continued, she gathered the full details of the plan of the Norman clan against Dreer.

Gus Norman was to ride ahead of the rest and go

straight to Dreer. There he would interview the outlaw and take him to a shack which he knew in the hills near Windville. Mary learned the location of the place by heart from Joe, who had heard Gus go over its description a dozen times to a dozen different members of the gang. He would take Jess Dreer to this ruined old cabin as to a rendezvous.

Then he would leave the outlaw there and go to meet the others under pretense of calling in the members of the crew who were to take part in the fake robbery.

The moment Gus had joined the others, they would swing down around the cabin and open a plunging fire from the rocks above. If, as was apt to be the case, they did not kill Dreer at the first discharge, they would, nevertheless, have him in an utterly helpless position. At worst, they could easily set the cabin on fire and kill the outlaw as he attempted to flee from the cover. To make his escape entirely impossible, the first discharge would be chiefly directed against the roan mare, Angelina. On foot, Dreer's chances of a dash for liberty would be less than zero.

Mary did not hear this story in one fluent narrative, but an interrupted series of explanations, exclamations, and phrases here and there gave her ample groundwork on which to build the complete picture of the plot.

Sometimes, as her hatred of the whole clan of Normans swelled in her, she felt like snatching a revolver from the holsters and firing it into the breast of the man beside her. Sometimes a great wonder grew in her that out of the very list of Dreer's enemies had been furnished the man who gave life to this wan ghost of a last hope.

Now the labor of the ride cut off the very possibility of thought from her mind.

They had struck what Joe assured her was the longest and most severe of the hillsides that they would encounter on the entire ride. It led up to a dangerous slope beyond, generally called The Slide, on account of the precipitous angle of the drop of ground. And now Joe Norman, who had been a weight upon her spirits in the beginning, was rapidly reviving.

He began to throw out hopes. Never, even in daylight, had he ever heard of such a distance through the hills being covered in such a short space of time. To be sure, the hardest part of the ride lay before them, and they would have to take it with horses completely fagged, but, nevertheless, there was the glimmering of the first dawn of hope. It might be done. Half the night was spent, but the other half, before that fatal time of an hour past dawn, they might reach the shack and give the warning to Jess Dreer.

He told her this while the horses sweated and grunted up the long rise. Once, on a shoulder of the slope, they paused by mutual consent to give the animals a breathing space.

Then, far and dim below, they heard the horse of the pursuer coming up the slope.

At this, they hurried on, the mustang now showing a condition fully as good as that of Gray Tom; but when they came out on the brow on the crest, Joe Norman stopped the girl with a yell of alarm.

The face of the hill was dished away. It had literally disappeared, and the head of Gray Tom was hanging over an abyss.

"A landslide!" groaned Joe Norman.

By the moonlight they could make it out plainly now. First there was a straight fall of cliff for a dizzy distance. Below this an apron of debris was spread, covered with what seemed to be stubble in the distance, but what they knew to be the splintered hulks of trees.

Even as they stood, their horses side by side, looking at one another in utter despair, the ground quivered beneath them. They were barely able to spur onto firmer ground when the entire table where they had stood before gave way, shuddered, yawned wide, and a thundering avalanche rushed down the slope.

The noise of the fall died away. A thick silence fell. Then the echo from the far hillside picked up the noise and sent it rumbling and rushing back at them, as if the landslide had roused some monster in the valley and made it roar defiance. When that echo died away, they could hear another sound distinctly from the hillside behind them—the noise of the pursuer following up the slope. He would be upon them in a moment.

"Quick, Joe!" pleaded the girl. "What can we do?"

"They's only one way out," said Joe Norman sullenly, "and that's to go back. We've had our work for nothing."

"I tell you, there has to be a way!"

"None in the world. Straight yonder—there's the direction for us. But we'll never get there."

She swung her horse around with a cry of grief and impatience and rode him along the ridge, desperately close to the edge of the landslide. Her shout brought Norman beside her. She was pointing down through the moonlight.

"Don't you think if we put our horses back on their haunches, they'd go down that sliding all the way to the bottom?"

He looked over, and shuddered as he craned his head to look, for she was much nearer the edge on Gray Tom than he had dared to ride.

At this place the landslide had not ripped away the soil to the sheer face of the rock. There was no right-angle face of stone, but a skirting of the raw dirt came up to the edge of the ridge and swept away down to the floor of the gulley at a dizzy angle. Halfway down, it veered out toward a more generous angle.

"Mary," he said, lifting his head, "you got a pile of courage even to think of it. I'll tell you what. It'd be just the same as jumping a hoss over a cliff. Except that a cliff would kill him a little quicker."

"But if we had luck—"

"No kind of luck could save us, Mary. Plain suicide. Suppose a hoss could keep upright sliding down, he wouldn't be able to pick his way. All he could do would be to sit back on his haunches and slide. And if he struck a big rock or a tree stump—or anything to knock him over —why, he'd keep right on rolling over and over till he hit the bottom with a smash. He'd be dead long before that, and his rider would just be a red smear trailing out behind him."

The moonlight somehow helped to paint the picture vividly. She saw herself on Gray Tom shooting down the slope—the rock lifting suddenly out of the moon haze— the crash, the toppling of the horse upon his side—and then death.

Then she heard the noise of the pursuer coming up the slope, terribly near now. Fear of something behind, unknown, balanced the fear of what lay before her.

"Joe," she cried, "good-by. I'm going."

"No, no! Mary!"

He flung himself from the mustang and strove to reach the head of Gray Tom, but she had swung the stallion straight out to the edge of the ridge, and as Joe sprang forward, he saw the ground tremble, quake, and sink down.

He whirled about; he was barely in time to spring back to solid ground, and when he looked again, Gray Tom, with a snort of terror, was plunging down the slope.

One thing favored Mary, and that was the very fall of the ground, for it launched her smoothly and slowly on the downward journey. The chief trouble was that the rush of earth and stones around him maddened Gray Tom. He tried to straighten and spring away from that senseless confusion, but the girl flung herself far back in the saddle, and throwing all her weight on the reins, managed to pry him back on his haunches—far back. He was almost sitting down. Then the impetus of the drop caught them, and they shot down.

The ridge was whipped away from behind them; she looked far ahead. The distance to the floor of the gulch seemed treble as far as it had been from the top of the ridge above her. Nor was the ground half as smooth as it had appeared, viewed at the close angle. There were patches of muddy clay; there were streaks of gravel which, when they struck them, sent a raging avalanche pouring before them.

But the danger was not in the speed of the slide. It lay in the projections which jagged up and back at them like shark teeth. The end of a tree stump jumped at them from the night. A ragged edge caught her shoulder and ripped the sleeve away to the wrist, and when this was past, she saw a certain doom before them in the form of a big rock. There was no dodging it, and it was far too bulky to sway away from. Chance entered there and saved them.

The slide had swerved on either side of the boulder, and Gray Tom, in turn, was swerved along the path of least resistance and whipped by the rock.

Now they struck the apron of more level going. It spread out flatter. Gray Tom had lurched to his feet and was going at a mad gallop, floundering through loose soil, rushing on so that the air sung in the ears of Mary Valentine, and then, how, she did not know, the floor of the gulch was flat before her and Gray Tom had drawn down to a rocking canter.

He was trembling like an aspen through all his bulk, but he was unhurt. Her own blood had turned to ice, but looking back to the sickening height, she saw a tiny figure gesticulating. Then exultation swept over Mary. Her blood ran warm again. If there had been a chance before, there was a double chance now.

She put the spurs to Gray Tom and rushed for the next hillside.

CHAPTER 41

At the top she turned for a last look at the slide, and pausing an instant at the crest, she saw a tiny, dark figure slip over the edge and go downward with bulletlike speed.

Her heart rose. Was it Joe Norman? Had he taken courage by her example? The moment the thought came into her brain, she knew that it was impossible. After all, it was not in Joe's nature to rise to great emergencies. He had done his utmost in guiding her so far through the night on that dangerous course, and now he would turn back with the adventure half accomplished. In all his life he would never rise to a greater thing than that.

It was Sheriff Caswell who had taken the slide; now his horse was a dim streak crossing the floor of the gulch. Sheriff Caswell! He was one of those bulldog men who make great risks seem small and who turn the impossible into the commonplace.

She turned Gray Tom straight ahead and began to ride like mad. Strangely enough, the fear for Jess Dreer had grown small in her mind. The one thing which she most dreaded was the man who relentlessly followed on her trail, and to get clear of him, she rode the stallion without care, without caution. She flung him at heartbreaking slopes. She rushed him down precipitous hillsides; but always, looking back from crest to crest, she could see the dark figure following. But growing smaller, to be sure. Then, at length, the pursuer had disappeared.

For the first time in several miles she thought of Gray Tom, and the moment she looked to him she saw that he was in a serious condition. His breath came with alarming harshness; his neck and shoulders were lathered, and he staggered under the burden of his rider. Yet he kept gallantly to his work up the slope, and when she reined him, he came up on the bit and fought her to get ahead.

Only a moment of this, then his hindquarters sank. He stopped. She thought for an instant that he had stepped in a hole, until the great shuddering of his body told her what had happened. Then she sprang from the saddle, but it was far too late. Gray Tom had crumpled helplessly to the earth.

She caught his head in her arms, and as if he thought that this was a signal for him to stand up, he pricked his ears, tossed his head, and lurched forward. It was the last effort, and it broke his heart. When he struck the ground again, he was dead.

Beside him the girl knelt, and seeing his eyes dim in the moonlight, she closed the lids as though he had been a man. And truly Gray Tom had died a man's death.

She was helpless now, but in spite of her helplessness a great assurance was filling her mind. One death had been paid for Jess Dreer, and surely there must be some reward for that great effort. In her first frenzy she even dreamed that she might complete the journey in time on foot, and she ran stumbling to the next hilltop.

There she paused with a cry of joy, for in the low, wide valley below her she saw the dark, huddled outlines of a ranch house and its outlying buildings.

Back to the body of Gray Tom again, running now as she had never run before. She untied the girths and after a fierce struggle was able to draw them through under the body of the horse. Then, drawing the stirrups over her shoulders and pulling the saddle high on her back, she began climbing again at a shuffling run.

A thirty-five-pound saddle is the clumsiest burden ever invented. Even a man would have groaned under it before the walk was over, but Mary Valentine was staggering with exhaustion before she reached the door of the house.

In answer to her knock and her shouting, footsteps at length ran toward her from within, and the door opened on a man in his shirt, a lantern in his hand, his feet not yet worked down in his boots. He was one of those black-haired fellows whose beards grow up to their eyes. Another time she would have been terrified by that face; now she minded it no more than if he had been a painted thing.

She told him swiftly, briefly, how her horse had dropped. She must have another. She had money to pay any price he asked. But speed was the thing she needed. The man was maddeningly slow.

"Selling a hoss by night," he declared, "is like marrying a girl whose face you ain't never seen."

"Don't you see," she cried, "that I don't care if I'm cheated? But I want the best thing on four legs that you can give me."

"The best thing I got comes high, lady. I wouldn't take a penny under three hundred for my Jerry; and I wouldn't be hungry to sell him at that."

She assured him that she would add another hundred to the price if he would throw the saddle on the horse quickly and let her be off, and with this assurance the rancher came to life. Five minutes later he came out of the corral with a long, low-built brown horse with Mary's saddle on its back. She thrust the money into his hand, and without waiting for him to count it, she was off again at full speed.

Her new mount had not the reach of Gray Tom, had not the same elastic spring in his gait, but before she had gone up the first slope, she was delighted with her purchase. Jerry was raised among these hills and trained to the work in them. He seemed to have eyes in his feet, and he wove among the shrubbery and trees and over the loose rocks with hardly ever a pause or a stumble.

The hill ended in a broad plateau, the first level going in many a mile, and she leaned over and gave Jerry his head. He did surprisingly well in spite of his short legs, and with every jump the heart of Mary rose. It was not dawn yet. There was not even a glimmer of light in the east; surely Windville could not be so far away.

At the edge of the broad clearing she heard a neigh behind her, which Jerry answered as he ran, and looking back, she saw again the same stalwart figure pursuing her, the same sidewise seat in the saddle. Sheriff Caswell!

It was easy to tell what had happened. He had come upon Gray Tom; he had followed down into the valley and arrived at the house of the rancher on her very heels. There he had changed his horse for one of the farmer's, and now he was measuring strides with her again, but on an equal basis, as fresh as the Jerry that stretched out under her.

During the next half mile she made a trail of speed, but her follower kept the pace and even gained. It told Mary Valentine, more plainly than words, that she must do something more than stretch the legs of her horse if she wished to shake off this bulldog of the trail. And she made up her mind with the cold quickness of a desperate man.

She swung Jerry from the trail on which he was running at that moment, and pulling him into a thicket of brush, she drew from its case the light rifle which she always carried when she rode. With the butt snuggled into the hollow of her shoulder and her left hand at the balance, she waited, hearing the sheriff come crashing after her. She wondered, as she sat the saddle in the patch of heavy shadow, at the steadiness of her nerves. There was not a quiver of fingers or arms.

Now the head of the sheriff's horse shot snakelike from among the trees, and a second later the whole group was in view. She snapped the muzzle of her rifle up, steadied it, caught her bead, and let the rifle swing easily, following the speed of the moving horse. When she fired, the animal sprang straight up, came down with a lurch and stagger, and then sank to the earth; the sheriff was already clear of the stirrups. She saw him run a step or two toward her, his revolver in hand, but then he paused abruptly.

She had twitched Jerry around and sent him flying up the trail again. No enemy behind now; and since the sheriff was out of the way, her mind fell back on the great duel in which she was engaged. She had a horse under her, fresh, strong, willing; she had against her the inevitable rising of the sun and the rough tract of hills and valley. One stumble might ruin her chances in the race.

Yet she dared not ride with caution. A gathering chill in the air, a depression of mind, a general relaxation of nerve force, and an aching pair of eyes warned her that the dawn was coming. Looking up from a hollow, there was only the blackness of the forest above her. But, topping a rise of ground, she saw that the trees on the rolling horizon were jagged as teeth reaching up. They were outlined by a light from behind. It was dawn!

It brought her heart up behind her teeth, knocking. Into her mind surged pictures of Jess Dreer by the fire in her home; of Jess at her window; and of the outlaw behind the bars in the Salt Springs jail, nonchalant in spite of his manacles, smiling his assurance at her. It came to her that he had never spoken to her of such things as now went hot and thick through her blood. He had remained aloof, yet she had read in his mind the unspoken things.

She had raised Jerry to a murderous pace. Would he stand it?

The stout mustang ran with his head well down, like a cattle horse running a dodging cow. For a horse cannot dodge well when his head is high in the air. He spread out along the ground as he gathered speed, but never once did he miss footing. Once a rotted log crushed under his heels; once a pebble rolled and staggered him; but not once was Jerry at fault. Toiling up the steep slopes, or zigzagging heavily down the precipitous mountainsides, he never once flinched from the labor.

She could have blessed that honest brute heart, and she began, with the light to aid her, to help him with all her power of hand and eye. She kept well forward in the saddle to throw the weight an inch or so more toward Jerry's withers. Keeping as near as possible to the direction which Joe Norman had plotted for her, she yet was able to cut off vital angles here and there, and often swerved from the straight line to give Jerry the advantage of better ground for running.

And still the light increased with terrible rapidity. She topped a rise of ground. To the right a point of flame startled her like a rising forest fire, but when she looked again, she saw a regular semicircle of red. And still nothing but ragged ranges ahead of her. When would they split apart and reveal Windville? And from Windville, how far to the lonely cabin?

In a sudden burst of grief she clasped her hands against her breast, and the tears broke from her eyes.

CHAPTER 42

From the broken door of the ruinous shack Gus Norman looked up to the hills. Behind them his men were gathering, drifting slowly toward the hollow between the hills and the double-eared peak which rose like a mule's head. It was a black mountain now, with the rising light of the day behind it. The sun was well up; in a few minutes, now, he could ride to that hollow and find his men waiting, all the proven twenty who had started on the ride. Now that he was in the place, he was more satisfied with it than ever. The shack lay in a roughly cut bowl, with a rim of higher ground all around that would give perfect protection to his riflemen in point-blank range of their target. Even if Dreer sought protection in the hut, having avoided the first volley, he would be a lost man. Through those rotten walls a rifle bullet would range from side to side. They could honeycomb the shack in five minutes of concentrated fire, half of them aiming breast-high and half shooting at the level of the floor, in case he tried to lie down.

No wonder, then, that Gus was smiling when he turned back into the hut. Dreer had kindled a fire and was warming his hands over it. He kept his face religiously toward Gus Norman. Early in the night Gus Norman had noted this. Indeed, he had had flashes of hope that events would turn out so that he could take this celebrity single-handed and gain the glory all for himself. One moment of carelessness, and his gun would flash and speak.

But that moment never came. If Dreer had to turn his head, it was only for the split part of a second before he had his eyes on the other once more. And Gus Norman began to respect his companion as much as he hated him. Just as a dog, say, might respect a wolf.

"The time's almost here," he said, turning from the hills. "The boys will be waiting for me up yonder, pretty soon."

"Rainier," answered Dreer, "the thing I don't understand is why you didn't have 'em meet here in the cabin."

"Because I don't like to have 'em meet until I'm with 'em. Each one of them boys, Dreer, knows that he's to ride to the hollow yonder, and that he's going to meet me there, but about three of 'em don't know the others in the crowd. That's my system. I play a lone hand. I let in the other boys, one by one, on part of the game, but I keep everything dark except just the part each one is going to play."

"Not a bad idea. I suppose Hank is one of the new men?"

"Yep, he's new, right enough."

"And raw, Rainier. I'm surprised that you use a boy like that."

"I'll tell you what, Dreer. I was a fool to send him to you with that letter. I might of knowed that he'd try to talk too much or something like that. But he'd been on my hands for a long time without doing nothing. He wanted to earn his salt. So I told him to go along and fetch that letter to you."

"He told me it was that way. But he looked like a rat in a trap. Couldn't meet my eye."

"You scared him, Dreer. Same as you scare most of 'em. Tell you what, when I told a couple of the boys that I was aiming to get you in on my next job, they acted like a cyclone had hit 'em. Acted as though you ate men alive."

"And why the devil do you want me, Rainier?"

"Because you're a good man to have, Dreer. You can

keep a cool head. We'll strike up a partnership before we're through."

"Not in a thousand years. I've told you that before. I'm in on this one job, and the only reason I'm in on it is because my pal, Dan Carrol, has begged me to go through for him. After this I'm out."

"Wait till you count the easy money, Dreer. I've heard others talk like you until we've got the can opened and the stuff in our pockets. Then they change."

He turned toward the door again.

"I wonder if it ain't time to go now?"

"You seem sort of anxious to see them boys," remarked the outlaw suspiciously.

"Fact is," replied Gus Norman, "that they's a couple of 'em I ain't laid eyes on for a long time. I'm kind of home-sick for 'em."

He went to the wall and took down a saddle from the peg.

"Well, I'm off, Dreer. Back inside of half an hour."

"Take your time. But what's that?"

A heavy matting of grass covered most of the valley, muffling the sound of all who approached, but near the cabin there was a gravel coating to the ground. On this gravel, now, came the loud clatter of a galloping horse, and rushed on the cabin. Both men faced the door, but neither of them had time to reach it, when a foaming horse lunged into view and from the saddle leaped a slender youth, who staggered when his feet struck the ground. He recovered himself, turned toward the cabin, and Dreer saw the face of Mary Valentine.

"Oh, Jess," she cried hysterically. "I'm in time. But watch him!"

There had been one convulsive movement on the part of Gus Norman, but now he apparently saw that it would be impossible for him to reach his horse and escape. He stood with a sullen face in the corner.

"What's the matter, Rainier?"

"Rainier?" said the girl. She entered the cabin and stood with her feet braced, her legs trembling with weariness. "He's no more Rainier than I am. Rainier is a mere robber. That man is a sneaking murderer, Jess. That's Gus Norman."

"My, my," said Jess Dreer softly, but his face was black. "I been thinking you was a little wrong, Gus Norman, but I never come within miles of guessing. Not within miles!"

"You got me two to one," said Gus Norman, fixing his eyes on the girl. "You got me cornered; I'll talk turkey."

"Not two to one," said Jess Dreer. "Not by no means. One of us is a girl, Gus Norman. I'll send her out of the cabin, and you and me can finish up with a little chat man to man. Eh?"

Norman's mouth worked convulsively behind his beard. For one instant his wolfish face grew so savage that it seemed he was about to draw, but he controlled himself.

"No use," he said doggedly. "I won't fight you, Dreer. I ain't a trained man-killer, and you know it. Nope, I ain't got you, yet, but you ain't got me. I'll tell you why. The minute they's a gun fired, Dreer, them hills will come alive. They'll be twenty men come hopping for this cabin. You're a hard man, Dreer, but d' you think you could get twenty fighting men?"

He leered at him as he spoke.

"No, son. We split fifty-fifty. You can go out with me, and I'll call the boys off. That's square."

"Except that you lie," broke in Mary Valentine. "Don't you see it in his little animal eyes, Jess? The truth is that his gang of Normans and Sheriff Claney are all cached up yonder, between the ears of that mountain. They're waiting until they get his signal that you're here, and they aren't expected to be there, waiting, until an hour after sunrise. That was the plan."

Jess Dreer watched Norman silently, and under that stare the older man backed up slowly until his shoulders struck the wall.

"Just step out to my saddle and get me the coil of rope you find on it, will you, Mary."

She obeyed; and a minute later Norman was trussed beyond hope of movement.

"I'd ought to kill you, Norman," said Jess, "but I leave butchering for the slaughterhouses."

He turned to the girl at last. Until now he had given her not a word of welcome, but now, as his glance went slowly, leisurely over her, words became too light for use.

Her hair had fallen loose under the brim of her hat; from one white arm the sleeve had been torn; and now she was shrinking into the shadow, as if ashamed of her man's dress.

"Mary," he said at last, "what have you done for me?"

"It was the short cut that brought me here; I thought it was too late when I got the news, but now—I'm here, Jess, and you're safe! I've been thinking on the way—I've been seeing you—dead! You see? You seem more of ghost than real right now."

He raised his hand to stop her, growing thoughtful. And his lean face puckered until one might have thought that he was becoming angry.

"You rode through the mountains from the ranch? You did it at night?"

"There was the moon—almost as bright as day, Jess."

He shook his head.

"I didn't know they was any women like you, Mary. I didn't know they was even any men."

"But stay away, Jess. Stay away! I'm afraid of you! Don't come stalking at me like that!"

"I was going to shake hands," said Jess Dreer, "to show the world in general, and mostly to show you, that Jess Dreer has a pal at last. And heavens, girl, but I've led a lonesome life."

A smile began to tremble on her lips—surely she had never been so lovely as she was now in the shadow, in those ragged clothes—but the hand which she extended toward him was arrested halfway.

"Jess!" she screamed, looking past him. "Caswell!"

He whirled as the first word left her lips; whirled toward Caswell, who stood, gun in hand, at the door; and the marvel of it was that he was able to get his gun from the holster and fire before Caswell could send home his shot. He fired, and the sheriff wavered as though he had been struck with a fist; then his own gun spoke, and there was a clangor of steel. The revolver flew out of the hand of Jess Dreer, struck the wall, and dropped with a clatter on the floor, while Jess Dreer stood staring stupidly down at his disarmed hand.

Mary, with a wail of terror, caught out her own weapon, but the slow voice of Dreer stopped her.

"Put away that gun, Mary. You see, Caswell ain't like that thing in the corner. He's a man, and he won't fight a woman. So just put up your gun. I reckon this little play is all over."

CHAPTER 43

She hesitated, and then obeyed.

"It isn't possible," she moaned. "He *can't* be here!"

Sheriff Caswell stepped through the door, his left arm dangling oddly by his side.

"To tell you true," he said quietly, "a couple of times during the ride it didn't look noways possible to me, either. Once when we come to the slide, and then when you shot my hoss." He shook his head. "That wasn't hardly fair play, but then I never see a woman that wouldn't shave pretty close to the shady side of things. This is how I'm here: I went back to the ranch after you drilled my hoss and got another, and my second hoss was some piece of deviltry and leather. They wasn't no wear out to that hoss, but I wore him out, anyways. He dropped a while back, and I come on by foot and staged this little surprise party just when I'd give up my last hope. Jess, I'll trouble you to go over there and cut my friend Norman loose. I see you been entertaining him a plenty."

Without a word Dreer obeyed. At the touch of his knife the rope fell apart, and Gus Norman rose. He showed no exultation because of the presence of the sheriff. In fact, he hated the man who had seen him tied and helpless.

"Looks like you're making ropes popular for clothes, Jess," went on the sheriff. "First it's Claney; now it's Norman. If you don't mind, I'll give you the same sort of a rig —unless you'll give me your parole, pardner?"

But Dreer smiled.

"Of course, I'm a goner. I've always felt, Caswell, that if you ever got your teeth into me the game would be up. And now I suppose it is. But I'll keep trying."

The sheriff sighed.

"All right, Jess. Then it's the rope; which I hate to use 'em on a man-sized man. Norman, will you oblige me by slipping a couple of nooses around Dreer's arms and legs?"

The other spoke for the first time.

"Pardner," he said viciously, "they's one thing that would put him out of trouble. Why not try it and save the rope?"

He touched his revolver significantly.

"You do what I say," said the sheriff. "I don't need no suggestions."

So Gus Norman went ahead sullenly with the work of tying Dreer. Presently the sheriff spoke again.

"You needn't sink them nooses into the flesh, Norman."

"Thanks," and Dreer nodded.

"And now, if you'll take the lady's guns, I'll be real obliged, Norman. Thanks." He added, to Mary: "You might get careless. I've seen it happen."

He sat down cross-legged on the floor; a great spot of red was growing and spreading around his left shoulder.

"Now, Norman, just cut away my shirt and make a bandage for this shoulder of mine. Then ride into Windville and send out a buckboard, so we can all go in together."

"You mean you're going to trust Dreer to another jail?"

He added softly: "He's worth just as much dead as he is alive, Sheriff."

"Listen," murmured Caswell. "You're getting me real peeved, Norman. In the first place, I don't like the way you say it; second place, I don't like the thing you say. Dreer is going to stay alive till the judge hands him the rope. Now, do what I say. You can be back here in two hours. I'll take care of 'em in the meanwhile."

And Gus Norman, with a black face, obeyed, and drew

the bandages which they improvised hastily around the sheriff's shoulders.

A moment later he was on his horse and clattering away.

"So here we are," murmured Jess Dreer. "Mary, could you do me a terrible big favor?"

She had been sitting with her head bowed in her hands, trembling. "Yes," she murmured.

"Wonder if you'd be any hand at rolling a cigarette?"

"I've done them for the boys often. Yes."

"Pocket of this shirt is where the makings are."

She took out the papers and tobacco. "And one thing more. Smile for me, Mary."

It was a white caricature of a smile with which she obeyed him. She said nothing while she rolled the cigarette, placed it between his lips, and lighted it. He thanked her with a nod.

"Are you in a pile of pain, Sheriff?"

"Not me, Jess. I'm comfortable, well enough. Besides, it's only a couple of hours to wait."

"Less'n that. Norman ain't going to town. He's got his gang and Claney cached away up in the hills yonder. He'll be back with 'em inside an hour and a half, or less."

"But how can they move me without a buckboard? I can't sit a saddle with this."

"It ain't you they're worrying about. They're thinking about me. Steady, Mary!"

"Yes," she whispered, and set her teeth.

The sheriff looked from one to the other with a frown; then he shook his head.

"May I ask one thing?"

"A thousand, Caswell, and welcome."

"Where was you and the girl figuring to head together?"

"I dunno," said Jess Dreer, as though the thought had

just come into his head. "What was we figuring on, Mary?"

She could not speak; but a pitiful ghost of a smile came on her face and went out again as she looked at him.

"They ain't any use of feeling cut up, Sheriff. It was simply the end of my luck. The old gun went back on me."

"Went back on you? Jess, that was the neatest snap shot I ever seen. There I was standing with the gun in my hand, and yet you beat me to the shot."

"Maybe it looked that. But as a matter of fact she hung in the holster. And when I got the gun on you at last, I had to hurry the shot. A hundredth part of a second more —I'm sorry to say it, Caswell—and you'd of been dead as a thousand years ago."

The sheriff moistened his pale lips.

"I kind of half believe you, Jess. But then, wasn't it luck for you that my shot hit your own gun instead of hitting you?"

"It wouldn't of hit me. My gun was two inches away from my side. That snap shot of yours was traveling wide, Caswell, when it hit my gun. No, I figure the luck was with you."

The sheriff cautiously raised the back of his hand that held the gun and wiped the perspiration from his forehead. He shifted his position a little to one side, so that he could look at a more favorable angle on the girl, but as he did so, forgetfully he threw his weight on his left arm. There was no muscular reaction, of course, but the bones of the arm shoved up against the injured shoulder and strained heavily against the bandage. The sheriff, white with pain, settled suddenly back in the shadow.

"That hurt you, Caswell?"

"Not a bit, Jess. Just a twinge. That's all."

But a moment later he knew that he had belied the situation. The strain had loosened the bandage at the same

244

time that it opened the raw wound, and when the pain subsided a little, he was aware of something hot running down his side in a steady trickle. He tried to raise his shoulder so that the bandage would press again on the wound and cut off the bleeding. It was no use.

With a touch of coldness he realized that an hour at least must run before Norman returned, and in the meantime, what might not that steady flow do to him? It would render him helpless as a woman.

As the smile occurred to him, he looked at the girl. Aye, more helpless than this girl, certainly, who had ridden with the daring of more than most men that night. Dreer himself was securely bound. But what of the girl? How could he disarm her in the same manner?

"Jess," he said, "they's one thing I want to ask."

"Fire away, Sheriff," replied the outlaw, maintaining his unvarying good nature.

"I could of had Norman tie the girl, you know."

"Sure, I know it."

"And if it come to a pinch, it'd sort of run agin' nature for me to fight a woman, Jess."

"I know that. You're white enough, Caswell."

"Well, then, all I ask is that you won't let the girl help you no way to escape."

"I'll promise I won't take no help from her."

"Don't!" cried Mary Valentine suddenly. "Don't say it, Jess. I tell you, something is happening. And he knows it! He knows it!"

The sheriff grinned feebly at her.

"I know it, Mary Valentine. But he's promised."

"You tricked it out of him!"

"You got something to learn, lady," answered the sheriff. "No matter how you get it, Dreer's word is good as gold. I'm going fast, but mind you, Jess, not a finger of help from the girl!"

"What the devil is the matter?" cried the outlaw. "What's got into you, Caswell? You look like a ghost!"

"Look!"

He swayed over and showed a thin pool of crimson beside him. His smile was ghastly.

"I busted her open ag'in."

Jess Dreer groaned. Then: "Caswell, you fool, would you die like this?"

"I dunno, Jess. Yep, I'd put death under taking you. I've got you, son, and I'll die sooner than let you go loose."

"Let's dicker, Caswell. Mary, here, will bandage you up so's you'll be safe. They ain't any danger if that bleeding can be stopped. You're safe, and you let Mary cut my ropes."

The sheriff sighed, and then shook his head.

"Here I stay," he said, "living or dead. And there you stay, Dreer, until they come for you."

CHAPTER 44

A silence fell between them; and the bright, desperate, hopeful eyes of Mary Valentine went from one to the other. She had risen to her feet.

The head of the sheriff sagged; he jerked it straight again with a mighty effort.

"Your oath, Dreer!" he said hoarsely.

"Yes. I intend to stay by it. I'll take no help from her. But if you won't make an exchange, then Mary'll fix you up, anyway. Mary, tie up his shoulder again. Caswell, you're going under!"

246

The sheriff turned his shadowed eyes upon the girl with a last appeal.

"Will you do that?" he asked.

"And let Jess die?" said the girl. "Trade you for him?"

"There's no question of a trade," broke in Dreer. "I'm a goner, anyway. There's no chance for me to get loose without the use of my hands or my feet, and without your help. There's no question of an exchange. It's only a matter of saving the sheriff."

"If he drops," said the girl, very white of face, "then you can try to get away. As long as he has his senses and that gun, you haven't a ghost of hope. I won't raise a hand for him, Jess."

"Caswell, won't you talk to her?"

"I've never begged for bread or money," said the dauntless sheriff. "And I won't start now begging for my life."

"Then I command you, Mary. D'you hear me? I command you to give Caswell a hand."

"I won't do it, Jess. That's flat."

"Ain't you got a drop of mercy in your body, girl?"

"Not for your enemies, Jess. Not a drop!"

"I'll tell you a thing I never thought to talk about. It was Caswell that gave me the watch spring that gave me the chance to break away from the jail. He saved my life once. I got a life that I owe to him. He wouldn't let the dogs take me. He took his own chance. And now he's got me in a fair-and-square fight, the first time any man on earth ever did. Mary, for Heaven's sake be a woman. Go help him!"

"You can break my heart, Jess, but you can't budge me with your talk. You're more to me than he is!"

"It's a question of what's right, not one man agin' another. Girl, I tell you he's always played fair on the trail. He's never once used a dirty trick agin' me!"

"No," she said faintly. "I won't raise a hand."

Jess Dreer groaned, for the sheriff, the gun falling from his hand, lurched suddenly sidewise and lay on the floor. There was a hoarse cry of satisfaction from Mary. She ran to Jess, whipping out and opening her pocketknife as she came.

He stopped her with a shout.

"Keep off! If you touch the ropes, Mary, I swear I won't stir after my hands are free. I won't stir. He has my word, Mary, and my word stays good, whether he lives or dies!"

"You're mad, Jess. It's your chance. Our chance together. Oh, Jess, is your word worth more to you than I am?"

She was on her knees, imploring him, wet-eyed. And the face of Jess Dreer turned gray with pain.

"Aye," he said slowly, at length. "Worth more to me than all the men in the world and all the women. I've got myself the name of a murderer and a robber, girl. What have I got left except my own honor?"

"Who knows it? Who gives you credit for it? Who in the wide world would believe what you're doing now?"

"Me and God know it," said the outlaw quietly.

She changed her tactics swiftly.

"Are you going to give up like a woman, Jess? Aren't you going to make one try for your life? Aren't you going to fight? Aren't you going to use your own strength, even if you won't let me help?"

"Tear off the old bandage and put a new one on Caswell and I shall."

"What if he comes back to life? What if he comes out of his faint?"

"We'll risk it."

She obeyed him, then, with frantic haste, first casting one glance through the door, and seeing no sign of horsemen sweeping down the long hillsides. Seconds were worth hours now. The old bandage was ripped away under her knife. She tore off her own outer shirt; and, after tearing it to strips and knotting them together, she managed to make the bandage strong and firm, and the welling of the flow ceased. The sheriff still breathed, though faintly.

"Jess, now yourself!"

But he was already at work. He had planned it swiftly while she worked over the sheriff. Had there been a single cutting instrument in the cabin, so much as a blunt-edged mud scraper at the door, he could have in time frayed the ropes that held him. But there was nothing he could use. His own knife was in his pocket—but how could he reach it without the use of Mary's hands?

If there was no steel to cut the ropes, there was at least the fire. But how to reach it? He had no use of his hands to get out the coals, even if the few sticks in the flimsy old stove had not already burned away to ashes.

He reached his decision at last. Squirming across the floor, he planted his shoulders, swung up his legs, and with one strong thrust of his feet brought down the old stove in a clattering ruin.

A faint smoke went up from the fragments.

He scattered the iron parts, still using his bound feet, for his hands were tied together before him and the elbows were made fast against his sides. The iron was knocked away, but now there was not a trace of a coal. He swayed to his knees and searched, with Mary leaning beside him, desperately questioning him as to his purpose, and getting no answer. And then he found it—two small, swiftly darkening bits of wood coal. He blew on them, and the red returned.

Yet this alone was not enough. He must have fuel. With terrible labor he worked across to the sheriff, tore open his coat, and drew out a packet of letters and loose papers with his teeth. Then, with this prize in his mouth, back to the coals. Over them he piled the papers, and then began to blow.

But it seemed that the contact with the cold paper had completely taken the life from the coals. He blew, but there was no answering upward trickle of smoke. He blew again, and now a faint, pungent odor came to his nostrils. He blessed it with a cry, and in a moment the paper blackened, curled back and a tongue of flame went up. Over the papers, now, he scraped with his feet the remnant of the wood. The loose ends, in turn, took the blaze and crackled.

That done, he got again to his knees and held his bound hands over the point of the flame. If the ropes had held them farther apart, it would have been a simple matter to burn the ropes away, but the wrists were hardly an inch apart, and to ignite the cords he had to sear his own flesh.

And there was Mary Valentine, on her knees beside him; her teeth were set when his teeth set; her head went back in agony when he groaned, and a horrible, sickening odor of burned flesh rose to them. And then—the cords caught fire! Slowly—very slowly. It was maddening to see them blacken, char, before they caught the yellow flame. But at length they were afire. He strained his wrists. One cord parted with a faint snap.

Mary Valentine cried out hysterically with joy.

Then a voice called from the corner of the cabin.

"Dreer! Jess Dreer!"

They turned. The sheriff had regained his senses. He sat with his back braced crookedly against the wall, an expression of half-drunken determination and agony on his face, and the revolver in his hand.

"I've seen you, Dreer, and I can't stop you. But the law says—alive or dead—and dead you shall be!"

He raised the gun, grinned with effort as he deliberately sighted it, and then crumpled again on the floor.

The last of the cords parted, and Jess Dreer shook away the smoking fragments.

"But they're coming, Jess!" cried the girl at the door. "They're coming fast. Look!"

Far off, streaming down the hillside, he saw the cavalcade. But they came leisurely; what call was there for hurry?

"First, Caswell."

He took the sheriff under his arms—he could feel the slow heartbeat as he did it—and bore him through the door. Then he swung into the saddle at the same time that the spreading fire in the shack ran up the wall with a great crackling. The smoke and the flame had been a signal to the posse. It came now on the dead run. He could tell even at a distance of a mile and a half.

"Is your horse good for anything?"

"A little. He was played out, but he's tough as leather."

"Then ride on first; I'll drop behind a little and keep 'em off if they should press us."

"Not in a thousand years, Jess. Besides, the cowards won't dare to press Jess Dreer on an open trail. I know them!"

He answered her with a smile.

"How far do you go on this trail, lady?"

"How far do you think, Jess Dreer?"

"To the end of the world, I reckon."

"We won't argue the point," said Mary.

And they cut up the slope at a sharp gallop and dipped over the rim, side by side.